8/8/19

hosts
and loves
and via email
up-to-date by signing up for
juliesbennett.com

Maureen Child writes for the Mills & Boon Desire line and can't imagine a better job. A seven-time finalist for a prestigious Romance Writers of America RITA® Award, Maureen is the author of more than one hundred romance novels. Her books regularly appear on bestseller lists and have won several awards, including a Prism Award, a National Readers' Choice Award, a Colorado Romance Writers Award of Excellence and a Golden Quill Award. She is a native Californian but has recently moved to the mountains of Utah.

Also by Jules Bennett

Twin Secrets
Claimed by the Rancher
Taming the Texan
A Texan for Christmas
Most Eligible Texan

Also by Maureen Child

The Baby Inheritance
Maid Under the Mistletoe
The Tycoon's Secret Child
A Texas-Sized Secret
Little Secrets: His Unexpected Heir
Rich Rancher's Redemption
Billionaire's Bargain
Tempt Me in Vegas
Bombshell for the Boss
Wild Ride Rancher

Discover more at millsandboon.co.uk

MARRIED IN NAME ONLY

JULES BENNETT

RED HOT RANCHER

MAUREEN CHILD

MILLS & BOON

First Published in Great Britain 2019
by Mills & Boon, an imprint of HarperCollinsPublishers,
1 London Bridge Street, London, SE1 9GF

Married in Name Only © 2019 Harlequin Books S.A.
Red Hot Rancher © 2019 Maureen Child

Special thanks and acknowledgement are given to Jules Bennett
for her contribution to the *Texas Cattleman's Club: Houston* series.

ISBN: 978-0-263-27185-0

0719

MIX
Paper from
responsible sources
FSC® C007454

This book is produced from independently certified FSC™
paper to ensure responsible forest management.

For more information visit: www.harpercollins.co.uk/green

Printed and bound in Spain
by CPI, Barcelona

MARRIED
IN NAME ONLY

JULES BENNETT

Legacy means passing down a gift and there's no greater gift than love. This is for you, Lori. Your love and light will shine on forever.

One

"I didn't know who else to turn to."

That statement alone added to the already sickening feeling in the pit of Paisley Morgan's stomach. As if life hadn't knocked her down over and over, now she stood on the other side of Lucas Ford's desk as he continued to glare at her like she had nerve walking in here.

Well, she did have nerve. After dumping him years ago and never speaking to him since. But that was all in the past. Wasn't it?

He leaned back in his leather desk chair and remained silent, and she couldn't help but second-guess just how much her bold move twelve years ago had affected him.

Had he not moved on? Found someone else to drive insanely wild with desire just from one piercing blue stare? Had he ever thought of her? Because there hadn't been a day she hadn't questioned her decision to let him go.

Paisley had bigger issues to worry about than their past and what Lucas may or may not be feeling seeing her show up unannounced. Like the fact that her biological father could be Sterling Perry—the man loathed by nearly the entire city of Houston for his scheming, stealing and money laundering. Not to mention he was arrested for conspiracy to commit fraud.

"What makes you think Sterling is your father, and why should I help you?"

Paisley gripped her clutch in one hand and the letter from her late mother in the other. "I have reason to believe he's my dad and I need you to investigate to see what you can find out."

Lucas stared at her another minute, giving her a visual lick as he came to his feet. He was still just as ruggedly sexy as she remembered, but those shoulders had gotten broader, the creases at the corners of his eyes deeper and the strong jaw firmer.

Lucas Ford could always make her breath catch as a young woman and it was no different now, even though years had passed since she'd seen him. Her body responded just the same. There were some memories that were too alive to be pushed into the past. Those vivid moments were always part of her everyday life, no matter how she'd tried to move on.

"What's this reason you have?" he asked.

Paisley swallowed and glanced down to the letter in her hand. She didn't bother unfolding the paper as she tossed it down onto his desk. She bit the inside of her cheek to keep her emotions in check. Now was not the time to fall apart. Remaining strong in front of Lucas was imperative, especially considering he hadn't seen her in over a decade. Vulnerability and tears wouldn't get her what she wanted; what she needed.

And Lucas was her stepping-stone to finding out the real truth since the obvious choice of her birth certificate had been left blank on the father line.

If there had been any other way than to contact Lucas…

He reached for the letter, opened it up and shoved one hand in his pocket as he read. She knew every word written in her mother's flawless, delicate writing. It was the content that had Paisley so unsettled and questioning everything she'd ever known and what kind of future she'd ultimately have.

Lucas's eyes darted back to her. "You believe this? Your mother wasn't the most—"

"I'm well aware of my mother's faults," she defended. "That's not why I'm here."

Lucas muttered a curse beneath his breath. "I didn't mean that. Despite what went down between us, I was sorry to hear about your mother."

Paisley nodded her acceptance of his apology as another wave of emotions threatened to clog her throat. She'd mentally pushed through the difficult past few months. The flood that had torn through Houston had ultimately claimed her mother's life and left devastation and destruction in its wake. It had also left an unidentified body on the construction site of one of Sterling Perry's properties—the elite Texas Cattleman's Club. Even after all the time had passed, there was still a mystery surrounding the identity of the deceased. There was no ID on the person and no distinguished markings. The entire ordeal was a mess.

An even bigger mess since the person they thought had died, Vincent Hamm, had actually texted his boss and stated he quit and was taking off for the Virgin Islands. So, clearly a man soaking up the rays wasn't the unidentifiable body found on Sterling's construction site.

Sterling already had issues going on with the whole scheme he had concocted, which had left a good portion of the region's banking system in an uproar and many families had lost everything they had… Paisley's mother included. When she'd passed, Paisley had had to use her own savings to pay for her mother's burial since there had been no life insurance.

As if dealing with the financial hit of Sterling Perry's debacle wasn't enough, Paisley feared for the future of her bridal shop now that she had no cushion to fall back on. But Paisley truly believed she could salvage her future, her finances. If the all-powerful billionaire was indeed her father, maybe she had a chance.

"I need to know if Sterling is my dad," she went on. "I know Mom wasn't the most dependable or honest, but I also don't know why she'd lie about something like this or why she'd write a letter and never actually give it to me. I found it tucked into a book she'd been reading."

Lucas glanced back down to the paper in his hands.

"Sterling doesn't deserve to know the truth if you're his daughter."

"Maybe he doesn't know anything," she replied.

Paisley took in a deep breath and went for the whole truth. "Listen, I know I'm the last person you wanted to see come into your office."

"Actually, Sterling would be the last person, but since he's incarcerated, that's a nonissue."

"As I was saying," she continued, hating how vulnerable she felt standing before the only man she'd ever loved. "I'm not your favorite person. I get that. If you need to lash out and deal with the past first, fine, but you're the best in this business and I need your help."

A corner of his mouth kicked up. "Been keeping up with me, Tart?"

A shiver slid all through her at the nickname that stemmed from her favorite candy. He'd been the only one to call her that, but she'd never forgotten. Clearly, neither had he. That instant reminder from the past of the bond they shared gave her a sliver of hope that maybe he wouldn't just throw her out of here without hearing her out or at least giving her the chance to defend herself.

He remained silent as he just stood there with a look she couldn't quite describe. Part of her recognized the desire, but there was a layer of something else and she couldn't tell if it was disdain or frustration.

The way Lucas used to look at her would have her clothes falling off in record time. They'd never argued, they'd had their future all mapped out…until one day she'd realized she had to let him go.

"Are you going to help me or not?" she demanded because getting caught up in nostalgia was not going to help her sanity or her business.

"My assistant can take down all the information and the deposit for my services." Lucas tossed the letter back onto his desk. "I'll be in touch."

Anger bubbled within her. He was not going to dismiss her that easily. True, they'd ended on abrupt terms, but that didn't just erase all they'd shared to that point. She wouldn't let him just brush her aside when this was all she had left.

"First of all, I'm not dealing with your assistant, I'm dealing with you." He was about to see just how serious she was about getting his help. "Second, I don't exactly have all of the funds right now. But I promise you will get every dollar you are owed. I'm not leaving until you agree to take this case."

Lucas took in a deep breath and circled his desk. With slow, methodical moves, he came to stand directly in front of her, bringing with him a waft of aftershave that smelled expensive and downright sexy.

Expensive and sexy? That summed up Lucas Ford in two simple words. He'd always been in a totally different league, but she'd been naive enough to believe the difference wouldn't matter.

She'd been so utterly wrong and they'd both been crushed in the end.

"You need me." His bold statement was as honest and real as anything they'd ever said. "You're stuck without my help. Is that what you're saying?"

Paisley gritted her teeth and nodded. He had her in

a difficult position and he damn well knew it, but she'd meant it when she said she wasn't leaving without his help. She had nothing left to lose, but she had everything to gain.

A smile spread across his tanned face and made those bright blue eyes shine with amusement and something akin to deviousness. "There might be a fee you can afford."

Lucas didn't know what game he was playing, but once he'd started talking, he couldn't stop himself. Paisley waltzed in here looking too damn sweet and innocent than should be allowed—and he knew she was neither. She couldn't be, not with the way she'd pulled a Dear John breakup with him twelve years ago. That had obliterated any "sweetness," and he'd stolen her innocence one stormy night in the garden shed on his father's estate.

They'd been each other's firsts so of course she'd stuck with him. He refused to admit it was because he was foolish enough to actually think they'd marry and live happily ever after.

Now she came to him with another type of letter, this one dropping a veiled hint that the devil himself was her biological father.

Oh, she didn't come out and name Sterling, but the clues she dropped with words like "billionaire" and "well-known Houston businessman" and the real red flag of "a man nobody wants to mess with."

Sterling Perry had ruined so many lives over the years and the trickling effect would last for some time to come. In fact, Sterling was the whole reason Lucas had entered into private investigator work to begin with. Once Sterling had ruined Lucas's father, wiping out the businessman's reputation when he spread lies about stolen money and Sterling claimed to have proof to back up his claims. All of it turned out to be bogus, but the damage had been done. It had ruined Lucas's father.

Lucas had vowed to work to seek justice for those who couldn't obtain it themselves.

Most recently, Sterling's crooked investments had bankers scrambling to secure their reputations and businesses. So many small businesses were affected, like Paisley's wedding shop.

But now he'd been arrested for conspiracy to commit fraud and Lucas hoped like hell the man never saw the light of day again…though something more damning would have to be found for Sterling to be put away for the amount of time he deserved.

Lucas never liked Sterling, never even wanted to mention the man's name, and now Paisley was asking him to research the guy? Was there a ring of truth to this cryptic letter?

As much as Paisley had hurt him, Lucas still couldn't imagine a monster like Sterling having a child like Paisley. The last thing he wanted to do was get wrapped up in either of their lives…and if those two lives were entangled? Damn it. He turned cases down on the daily simply because he didn't want them for one reason or another. He could quit working now and never have to worry about making a living again. Money had never been the issue and that wasn't the reason he hesitated now.

Something pulled at him. No, not something. Paisley. Even after all these years, she had some damn hold over his conscience. He knew she worked hard for her business and she struggled now, both emotionally and financially.

Plus, he knew that emptiness at the loss of a parent. How could he just ignore her when she needed someone and clearly, he was it?

But he wasn't a fool, and he was going into this with more experience than he'd done before and his generosity would most certainly come at a price.

"Listen," she started before he could get to his offer. "I know I hurt you years ago—"

"You left a damn note." A note he'd held on to for too long until he'd finally tossed it into his fireplace and watched it burn while he'd downed copious amounts of his favorite bourbon. "After all we'd shared, I deserved better. Or maybe the serious relationship was only one-sided."

"You know that's not the case," she defended with a layer of hurt in her tone. "I had to let you go, Lucas. Your father…"

Intrigued, and maybe a little pissed at the fact she was even here, Lucas crossed his arms over his chest. "My father, what?"

Paisley licked her lips and tucked her hair behind her ears. A slight nervous habit she'd clearly never outgrown. An instant later, she squared her shoulders and tipped her chin.

"Your father told me I was holding you back," she stated. "You were all set to head off to Harvard with a full scholarship and, well, he was right. I would've held you back. You would have put all your goals on hold to stay with me."

Gritting his teeth, Lucas thought back to the night he'd found her letter on the seat of his truck. Upon reading it the first time he'd thought it was a joke, but then he'd read it a second and third time, knowing full well his Paisley had gotten scared and hadn't trusted what they had…she hadn't trusted him.

Ultimately, that had been what hurt the most. She hadn't had enough faith in him and the fact he would've conquered anything to be with her. Forever.

But he hadn't known the bit about his father until just now. That was a new pain. The betrayal from his own father who witnessed how distraught Lucas had been and kept urging him to move on with his life and put adolescent relationships in the past.

Pushing aside the raw memories, Lucas dropped his arms and shrugged. "That's a nice story. Maybe it's true, maybe it's not. Doesn't matter at this point."

Paisley opened her mouth as pain flashed in her hazel eyes. Then she merely nodded as if she couldn't even come up with a plausible defense, which just proved his point that she didn't have one. Seeing her again did bring back a rush of memories, but even more maddening was the fact that her standing before him had his body stirring.

Damn it. He could block out the hurt, he could even block out how foolish he'd been to think they were a forever thing, but he couldn't block out the way she'd felt lying against him or how her warm breath washed over his torso as she eased down his body.

Lucas muttered a curse and circled back around to take a seat at his desk. If he didn't get these lustful thoughts under control, this impromptu meeting would turn embarrassing real fast. He prided himself on being the best, taking on elite clients, and one proverbial blast from his past threatened to turn him back into a horny teen.

"Coming here was a mistake," she murmured as she took a step forward and reached for the letter on his desk.

Lucas snaked his hand out to cover hers, waiting until her gaze met his. The instant she looked at him, Lucas knew he had her. She was in a bind and he could help…with a price. He didn't want to be a dick about this, but he also had his own wants and needs. No reason they couldn't help each other, right?

Besides, he'd given up on fairy-tale thinking long ago. He knew *love* was just a four-letter word people tossed around to benefit their own needs.

"The only mistake would be you walking out again, Tart."

Her lips thinned. "If we're done with the past, then stop calling me that."

She was still so damn sexy when her cheeks tinged pink when she got angry. Every part of him wanted to give her hand a yank until she stumbled down onto his desk where he could give her a proper reunion.

But business came first. She'd taught him that valuable lesson.

"I'll help you," he told her, keeping his hand on hers. He slowly rose to his feet and leaned across the desk. "I'll discreetly dig into this story about Sterling being your father and I'll save your bridal shop because I know you're on the brink of financial ruin."

Paisley's lids lowered, out of shame or frustration he didn't know. "And you want something in return. What is it?" she asked, focusing back on him.

Lucas released her now and tucked that wayward strand of honey-blond hair behind her ear. "Marry me."

Two

Oh, he was the most infuriating, arrogant man she'd ever met. Of all the things he could've asked for…

Was he mocking her and the life they'd had all planned out?

Or did he honestly believe marrying him would solve all of her problems? As if Lucas Ford had some magic wand that came with a marriage certificate and he'd wave it around like her sexy fairy godfather and she'd see stars and hearts.

Okay, that all sounded fabulous, but even he wasn't that powerful. And if he could manage all that, there was no way in hell she'd marry him. Her life was a mess and she wasn't in the mood to play games.

That was why yesterday she had simply snatched the letter from his desk and marched out of his fancy office without a word. She'd told herself she'd figure this all out on her own…somehow.

First, her bridal boutique, Lilac Loft. Paisley slid two ball gown wedding dresses down the rack to make room for the new beaded A-line that had been a special order. Each wedding was special and each bride was treated like she was the only customer. Paisley prided herself on giving each wedding the time and attention it needed. She'd had one part-time employee, but Paisley had to let her go when the whole financial debacle happened, thanks to Sterling.

Talk about feeling terrible. Paisley had hated letting Margaret go. The young girl had been so sweet, but the extra expense was just pushing Paisley to a position she wasn't comfortable with.

Paisley slid her hand down the clear bag that protected the beaded gown and couldn't help but let her daydreams get the best of her—an occupational hazard.

One day she'd have her own fabulous gown from her own store. She'd walk down the aisle lined with her favorite flowers—lilac—to the man of her dreams waiting at the end. A man that was not blackmailing her into marriage simply because they shared a past.

What was his angle, anyway? Did he just want to prove that he could get her? Did he just want her in his bed?

Paisley turned and pulled another plastic-wrapped, embellished gown from the shipment box. Each dress that passed through her store had the ability to make any woman feel like royalty, or a freakin' warrior if that's what she chose. Wedding gowns were the pinnacle of each ceremony. And while the focus should be on the happy couple, everyone knew all eyes were on the bride and what she wore. That second she stepped to the beginning of the aisle was like her own little red carpet moment.

Paisley had dealt with brides who wanted all the bling and poof, while other brides preferred short and simple. Some wanted a veil while others preferred a simple flower or even a sparkling headband. Paisley loved her job and that each customer brought unique opinions and ideas for their special day.

Unable to resist, Paisley hung the second gown up and pulled the zipper down. She parted the plastic and slid her fingertip over the intricate beadwork. Each time she mentally planned her wedding, she volleyed back and forth between wanting an intimate wedding with a little simple, body-hugging strapless dress or a lavish cathedral wedding in an elaborate gown with a train that trailed the aisle behind her, à la Princess Diana.

Regardless of the dress and the venue, the man and the marriage itself were all that mattered. One day she would marry, she'd have kids and live happily ever after. She didn't think that was a fantasy at all. She made her living off believing such realities and truly felt with her whole heart that there was someone out there for everyone.

Her someone wasn't Lucas Ford. She'd once thought he was, but if that were the case, they would've ended up together before now. She didn't think fate threw her the curve of taking her mother away only to give her back the one man she truly loved.

"That's a beautiful dress."

Paisley startled and spun around, her hand to her heart. The devil himself stood before her, only there were no horns and a pitchfork. Only a black Stetson and a shiny belt buckle for this one.

"I'm not open yet," she informed Lucas.

With that black suit and black shirt, he looked absolutely perfect amid these crisp white gowns. Like the mysterious cowboy coming to sweep away his bride. If only her life were that simple and utterly romantic. Her heart fluttered at the idea.

"Door was unlocked," he replied as he leaned a shoulder against the back door leading to the storage room.

Paisley tucked the dress, and her fantasy, away and turned her full attention to her unwanted guest.

"My sign says Closed," she retorted. "But I assume you don't follow rules. So, what do you want?"

"You left my office without an answer to my proposal."

Paisley snorted and resisted the urge to roll her eyes—barely. "Any other man would have taken my silence and dramatic exit as answer enough."

"Other men don't know you like I do, Tart."

"Would you stop with that?" she demanded.

"Why?" he asked, pushing off the door and stalking toward her. "You don't like remembering us?"

"There is no us." No matter how much she'd wanted them to last. Back then her dreams had included Lucas. Now she had new goals and none of them involved an old boyfriend.

"Listen. If you'd get your pride out of the equation, you'd see that marrying me is the smartest move for you."

He took another step toward her until he stood way, way too close. That expensive, masculine cologne wafted around her, pulling her tighter into his web of charm and seduction.

Hell, at this point she didn't need all of those past memories tugging her into submission. The man Lucas had grown into was doing a fine job of that on his own.

"You'll owe me nothing for finding the truth about your father," he started, those bright blue eyes holding her in place. "I'll make sure your business doesn't fall victim to Sterling, as many others have, and you'll never have to worry about money again."

"And I only have to sell my soul to obtain all of that?" she asked.

Lucas's eyes raked over her, then landed on her mouth. "It's not your soul I'm after."

Despite Paisley's best attempt at trying to ignore his suggestive remark, a shiver crept through her. Her entire body tingled and her common sense and her hormones were waging their own battle and she knew—she just knew—which would come out on top.

"We're not the same people we once were," she reminded him. "We're not even close."

"We could be closer."

He smirked and reached for her, but she skirted around him.

"Would you stop with the charm and one-liners that you think will get me to drop my panties?"

"You wear panties? I recall a time you didn't."

Paisley gritted her teeth and reminded herself violence was not the answer. Regaining control of this conversation was the only way to show him she was not so vulnerable that she'd marry him. She didn't need someone to ride to her rescue, damn it. She just needed someone to find out the truth about her father and, unfortunately, Lucas was the best in the field.

Paisley headed toward the front of her store. Standing amid stunning wedding gowns while staring down a tempting proposal was not helping her sanity. And she was tempted...but that was just the memories reminding her how perfect they'd been together at one time. No matter what happened between them, their chemistry could never be denied or forgotten.

She'd tried to forget. Life would have been so much easier if she could've erased the feel of his touch, the comfort of falling asleep in his arms.

"I'm not marrying you," she stated, hoping one of these times he'd believe her...and she'd convince herself not to fall for his charm. "If Sterling is my father, I won't need your money. Sterling will want to take care of what's his and I deserve for him to give back after what he did to my mother. I just need to stay on my feet now that everything's been pulled away."

Paisley moved to the entrance and arranged the blush-pink throw pillows on the white sofa. They were perfect, but she needed to do something that didn't involve looking or touching Lucas.

"You'd rather take that bastard's money than let me help?"

If she didn't know better, she'd say he sounded almost hurt. Paisley steeled herself against any emotions. That was not what this was about and they'd gotten too far off track.

"All I need from you is to find the truth," she reiterated, spinning back around after beating her pillows. "Do you want to take the case or not?"

Lucas rocked back on his heels and shoved his hands in his pockets as if he hadn't a care in the world. Must be nice to not worry about the possibility of losing your business or potentially finding out your father was a murderer. Not to mention trying to mourn the loss of your mother. There was only so much heartache a person could take without breaking, and Paisley refused to break in front of Lucas.

"Do you really think Sterling will recognize you as one of his own and just welcome you into the fold?"

Well…yeah. She did, but what if he didn't? What if he didn't care? He already had plenty of children and it wasn't like he needed her for anything. Paisley was just…irrelevant.

"Regardless of how he reacts, I want the truth." Paisley turned and crossed to the front door. She flicked the closed sign to Open and tugged on the antique doorknob. "I'm not for sale, so unless you're here to plan a wedding to someone else, we're done."

The antique etching on the knob dug into her palm, but she kept her grip tight. Her nerves were shot and she hated how Lucas thought he could manipulate her into some absurd binding commitment.

She stared straight ahead at the wall of mannequins,

each draped with an elegant gown. She would not let him win this round. If she had to work to find the truth herself, so be it.

His feet scuffed across the hardwood floor as he drew closer. Lucas stopped just beside her and leaned in. That warm breath of his washed over her collarbone, her neck, sending shivers up her arms she couldn't afford to relish.

"When you come to your senses, you know where to find me."

She closed her eyes as he walked by, and attempted to hold her breath so she didn't have to inhale that sexy scent of his. But, even after he was gone, his presence lingered. A powerful man like Lucas knew how to make an impact without saying a word.

But she'd gone to him initially, so she had no one to blame but herself for awakening the beast.

Still, taking the risk had been necessary because there was no one to tell her the truth and Paisley deserved to know who her father was. It wasn't like she could just march into the jail and demand Sterling tell her what he knew…if he even knew anything to begin with.

Lucas was the best P.I. He would and she believed could find the truth so the benefit of the outcome would far outweigh the pain of marrying the only man she'd ever loved and lost.

Blowing out a sigh, Paisley moved through her bridal boutique and headed for her white antique desk toward the back. She often did consultations here, but today she needed to check her emails and make sure her incoming orders were on time. Timing was everything in this business with jittery brides and deadlines.

Paisley took a seat at her desk and pulled up her messages on her laptop. The most recent one stopped her heart.

No. This could not be happening.

She read through the email once again, praying she'd read it wrong. Her hands shook as she tried to clasp them in her lap. Tears burned her eyes, and her breath caught in her throat.

The thirty-five-thousand-dollar gown she'd ordered for a bride was now no longer needed. The wedding had been called off and the mother of the bride was refusing to pay the remainder of the fee she'd agreed to pay. She was sure Paisley would understand and could return the gown.

Sure, in theory that sounded great, but in the real world a gown with that price tag couldn't be returned like a pair of shoes.

Paisley didn't know if she wanted to just sit there and cry or throw a tantrum. Her eyes darted to the minibar she kept for brides and their guests. Mimosas for morning guests and rosé for the afternoon and evening crowd. Paisley had never indulged while at work, but today was proving to be worthy of a good buzz.

Once she got home, she'd open the bottle of Reisling she'd been saving for a special occasion; after all, she'd given up on something special actually happening.

Slouching back in her seat, Paisley wondered how she'd ever recover from not only the Sterling debacle, but now the major setback with the gown that she would be stuck with. A gown that cost more than her car. A blow like this could absolutely destroy her business and her livelihood.

Dread curled low in her belly. There was a temporary answer to her problems. She just didn't want to admit it even to herself.

But at this point, she didn't have much of a choice. She was going to have to marry Lucas Ford.

Three

Sterling Perry sank on the edge of his cot and rested his elbows on his knees. This was no way for a man of his standing to live. He was Sterling Perry, damn it. When he spoke, people snapped to attention and obeyed his every command.

Whoever the hell had framed him would regret the day they ever crossed him. This was no accident. Someone outside these prison walls knew the truth and they'd yet to come forward. He wasn't a damn murderer.

But here he sat, still in this blasted cell, all because he'd made a few minor mistakes and then a body had been found at one of his construction sites once the floodwaters receded. The body hadn't even been identified, so how the hell did they even have a motive to pin all of this on him?

Sterling had been locked up too damn long, having been denied bail. According to the powers that be, they considered him a flight risk.

Bullshit. He wasn't going anywhere, except maybe to see his son, Roarke. One would think a crusading attorney son would come to his father's defense, but not Roarke.

What the hell did a man have to do to earn a little respect?

According to his attorney, there was another chance to petition for bail coming up. Sterling needed out of this place and he needed to get back to the Texas Cattleman's Club because he sure as hell had every intention of becoming the president of the newest chapter.

Sterling came to his feet and blew out a sigh. He wouldn't be in here forever and the time he'd spent so far had only got his gut churning and mind rolling. Roarke had never approved of Sterling's business dealings, so it shouldn't come as a surprise that he hadn't come to his father's aide.

But was he even Roarke's father? Because Sterling had some serious doubts about his late wife's fidelity.

Maybe there was a way to get that rumor out there without sounding like a jaded husband. Shouldn't Roarke know the truth? There was that period where Sterling's wife had been sneaky, distant. He'd always suspected an affair.

He wouldn't be surprised one bit if Roarke was a love child.

Sterling couldn't help the smile that spread across his face. Soon. Very soon people would know just how powerful and mighty Sterling Perry truly was. If they thought he was a shark before, they'd better watch out. Even these bars couldn't hold him back.

The murderer needed to be found, and Sterling needed to secure his position at the club and find the truth about Roarke. There was too much to do and he had run out of patience.

Lucas didn't even try to hide the smile as he waited for the penthouse elevator to slide open the next morning. The security guard for his building had already notified Lucas of the petite blonde heading his way…and according to Nyle, she didn't look too happy.

All the more reason for him to celebrate. If Paisley was here and in a bad mood, that could only mean one thing. Wedding bells would be ringing soon.

Lucas hooked his thumbs on his belt loops and whistled. "Here Comes the Bride" seemed appropriate, but there was no need to completely piss her off so he went with an old country song instead.

The door whooshed open and Paisley stepped into his penthouse. That narrowed gaze and set jaw said more than any words could. Yes, definitely not the time for "Here Comes the Bride."

"Beautiful morning for a visit," he called out to her.

Paisley shot him a glare and Lucas bit the inside of his cheek to keep from laughing. He hadn't been out at all, but the sunshine beamed through his wall of windows.

"Stop looking so damn smug," she stated, marching

farther into his penthouse. "This is not going to go the way you think."

As she brushed past him as if she had every right to barge into his home, Lucas chuckled. Oh, he had every intention of getting exactly what he wanted—Paisley in his bed and her having his child. That didn't seem like a high price to pay for all he would be doing for her.

Lucas spun on his heel and followed those swaying hips into the living area.

"First of all," she started, spinning around with her finger pointed right at him like a dagger, "we will get married, but make no mistake, this isn't some happy-ever-after. Don't think that I love you or I have some fantasy that this will be some fairy tale."

Love and fairy tale? No, none of that had entered his mind. What did love have to do with marriage? Thankfully, she knew exactly what this was and wasn't.

Well, there was one thing she didn't know, but he'd save the heir talk for a bit later. He had her here now and he needed to keep her since he was making headway.

"Any other stipulations?" he asked her.

Lucas felt it best to just let her think she called the shots. So long as he got what he wanted out of the deal, he didn't care what she thought.

He wanted a child of his own and justice against Sterling Perry. And Paisley could give him both.

"I want a prenup and everything we agree on in writing," she added. "There will be no surprises at the end of our marriage and my business will not suffer."

Lucas couldn't help but admire her for putting their past, and her emotions, aside to keep her dream alive.

He had his own dreams, but they were quite different from hers.

"What brought you here now?" he asked, crossing his arms over his chest and leveling her gaze.

"There was a…minor setback at the boutique." She fidgeted with the strap of her bag resting on her forearm. "I just realized that I can't do it alone and as much as I hate being here, I'm not going to let my business fall simply because my pride got in the way."

Another notch up on the scale of admiration. Maybe she had changed from the girl who had been too afraid to face their difficulties head-on.

Regardless, they were different people now and nothing about their past played a role in this situation. He wasn't the same naive boy he was back then, young and in love—or what he thought was love. Lucas had a lucrative business and while he might not believe in love in the terms of marriage, he did believe in love of family and he wanted one of his own. He wanted to have that security of passing a legacy down to his children.

Lucas dropped his hands to his sides and closed the space between them. As he grew closer, Paisley tipped her head back to stare up at him and that perfect mix of colors in her eyes never failed to punch him in the gut with lust.

Lust he could handle; in fact, he welcomed it. Having Paisely again wouldn't be a hardship.

"Just so I have everything clear for my attorney to draw up the proper papers, you want me to make sure your business is set to continue to prosper, you need me to find out the truth about your father and you want all of this to have an expiration date."

She pursed her lips as her eyes darted away. That slight slip of her resolve had him swelling with the knowledge that she might come off as headstrong, but she still had that underlying vulnerability he remembered.

And that was the damn crux of the situation. He wanted to be the one to save her. Even after the ridiculous way things ended and all the time that had passed, he couldn't deny the ego trip at the fact she'd come to him for help. Which only meant she'd been thinking of him.

At some point, he'd want answers about the past. Not that it would make any difference, nor did he want to relive everything, but he did wonder. And that bit about his dad going to her? Lucas wasn't so sure that was the whole truth.

"Are you even going to ask what I want out of this?" Lucas couldn't stop himself. He reached out and trailed his fingertip down her creamy cheek and along her jawline. "Or are you just going to trust me?"

She licked her lips as she continued to stare. "I…um. I assume you'll tell me."

Easing his thumb over her moist bottom lip, he smiled. "I want you in my bed. For as long as we're married, we will be man and wife in every way. There's no way I can live with you and not touch you, not want you. Not have you all to myself."

Paisley's eyes widened as she gasped. "You know

I'm not staying forever. Why would you want to pretend this is real?"

Lucas was done playing games. He framed her face with both hands and covered her mouth. The bag she had on her arm bumped his abdomen, then fell with a thud to the floor.

Paisley let out a little squeak as he all but consumed her. She opened for him, just as she always had. Some things never changed. She'd never hesitated with her response to him and now was no different. She gripped his biceps as if she needed to hold on or hold him in place—either way was fine with him.

Damn. She tasted just as sweet as he remembered. Lucas threaded his fingers through her hair and tipped her head back. Paisley arched against him as he nipped at her lips and slowly pulled away.

"Was that you pretending?" he asked, his voice surprisingly stronger than he actually felt. "Because I just want to make sure I don't get confused about what's real or pretend."

Paisley took a step back, then another, until she bumped into the curved staircase. Her shaky hand went to her lips and she closed her eyes.

Lucas was having a bit of a problem keeping himself in check. He wanted nothing more than to strip her bare and take her right here in his living room. But that was how they'd been when they were younger. They'd been all over each other. Young love had carried them so far, but ultimately, not far enough.

Still, having her in his home stirred something primal in him and he was positive he didn't want her leaving. Call him selfish, but he wanted Paisley and he wanted her right here.

"Chemistry doesn't mean anything," she retorted.

If there had been any conviction in her tone, he might believe her. If she hadn't arched that sweet, curvy body against his, he might think she didn't want more. But he knew better. She'd come to him, pride aside.

She could have chosen anyone else to help her, but she wanted him. Despite everything that happened in their past, they still had a bond and he knew she trusted him with her case.

Lucas reached for her, sliding his hand across her cheek and up into her hair. "You want to end the marriage, I get that. Do you have an expiration date?"

Those hazel eyes never wavered from his. "If Sterling turns out to be my father and recognizes me, then I want out. I don't want someone to take care of me forever. I want to stand on my own. But I'm not stupid enough to ignore the fact that I need help, because I won't let my business suffer. It's all I have left."

So, it all came down to money. Most things in life did, he realized. Plus, he understood the need to protect something you'd built. Wasn't that the reason he wanted a child to pass his business down to? All she wanted was to keep her shop running and live comfortably— which she could right here in his penthouse.

"Fine." Lucas leaned down, brushed his lips over hers once more before stepping back. "You will be in my bed every night. Nonnegotiable. We'll marry in Vegas, have our honeymoon and I'll get to the bottom of the letter about your father."

"Vegas?" she asked, quirking a brow. "That doesn't sound like you."

"It's fast, simple." Lucas smiled. "Unless you wanted to prepare and plan. A cathedral wedding would be fine, and actually not bad for my reputation. We could invite the press and—"

"Vegas it is." She narrowed her eyes. "One more stipulation. You're buying the gown of my choosing."

Lucas could care less about the gown—more what was beneath. He'd have something sexy and sheer ordered for her for their wedding night and have it waiting in their suite.

He'd also have his jeweler get a stunning rock sent over as soon as possible. Their marriage might not be traditional, but Lucas wasn't going to have his wife walking around with anything less than the best.

"Done," he finally agreed.

Paisley stared at him another minute, cautiously keeping her emotions guarded, which he didn't like. The Paisley he used to know had always been an open book, and she kept slipping into that state, but he could also see the independent woman she'd worked so hard to become. She was strong, she was resilient…and she was his.

Finally.

She'd have his ring on her finger and her body in his bed. This might not be the way he'd imagined they'd end up together, but they were going to be together nonetheless. They'd both get what they wanted.

Lucas had been naive years ago to think love would carry them through all their happy days and into old age. Then life smacked him in the face with a dose of reality and he finally saw that love didn't exist. Money, power, careers—those things lasted and could be controlled. Love was nothing but a made-up emotion for people who lived in a fantasy world.

Love wasn't for him…and never would be.

Four

They still hadn't discovered it was me. Sterling Perry was exactly where he needed to be. Oh, he hadn't murdered anyone, but the fact that he was taking the fall for my mistake thrilled me more than I should allow.

The man was a dirty bastard and deserved to rot in prison...or hell. Either were appropriate for the selfish, greedy man. He ruined my life, ruined so many others. The town and TCC were better off without him.

So long as he stayed in prison and the body wasn't identified, I'd be home free. I'd already lost so much, I deserved happiness and that was exactly what I'd be going after...no matter who I had to step on or over to get there.

Ryder Currin was another who'd ruined my life, but he'd pay, too. He deserved no less than the treatment

Sterling was getting. They'd both pay, maybe in different ways, but they'd pay.

People would remember me for great things, not the murder that I was forced to commit. I'd had no choice! My hands had been tied and then I'd panicked. But then my plans had fallen into place. I will ultimately come out on top. You wait and see.

My future will be secure and everyone will know my name.

I promise you that. Wait and see.

"What the hell is that?"

Paisley glanced down at her one-of-a-kind lace jumpsuit. The plunging neckline, the open back, the slit up the front of the legs to her thigh…they were all sexy, flamboyant and one hundred percent not part of the wedding "gown" of her dreams.

Which was why she'd purchased the tacky ensemble—with Lucas's credit card, of course. The nude swatches of material were strategically placed beneath the lace, but the rest was bare skin.

Oh, the look on his face was priceless and worth every bit of nerves she had curling in her belly.

Mustering up all the confidence and attitude, Paisley held her hands out wide and gave a dramatic turn. "You like? I figured since we're in Vegas, I might as well have some fun. But I wanted to be sexy for my fiancé."

His eyes raked over her and that visual sampling he gave had her trembling. This wasn't supposed to arouse her. She wanted to torment him. Damn him and those baby blues she never could ignore.

"Every damn person can see through that," he growled.

Lucas grabbed her arm and ushered her to the nearest nook at the Hunka-Hunka Burnin' Love Chapel. Despite the name, this was the classiest chapel on the strip and Lucas had paid to have the absolute best. He also paid for them to have the place to themselves, save for the man marrying them and a couple witnesses.

"This isn't like you," he stated, backing her into a corner.

Paisley placed her hands on his firm chest and stared up at him. "Marrying for anything less than love isn't like me, either, yet here we are. I think I look damn good, thank you for noticing."

Lucas placed a hand on either side of her face, caging her in even more. With her own hands trapped between their bodies, Paisley tried her hardest not to curl her fingers into him in an instinctive attempt to feel more.

His rich, masculine scent enveloped her just the same as if he fully wrapped his arms around her body. The man exuded power without saying a word and Paisley knew if she didn't keep her mind sharp and her heart guarded, she'd find herself falling for him once again.

And she wasn't so sure she'd ever fallen out of love to begin with. Leaving him certainly hadn't been her idea, but her hands had been tied and as much as the move had hurt, she'd known Lucas had needed to get away from her to achieve his goals.

Wasn't that the old saying? If you love something set it free? Well, she'd done exactly that and look how all of that turned out. She was in Vegas in the tackiest outfit she could find, ready to sell her soul.

Lucas leaned in closer, and his warm breath tickled the side of her neck at the same time he trailed his fingertip down the low V of her dress between her breasts. Shivers raced through her and there was no way she could ignore the trembling. Her body was clearly betraying her when all she wanted was to stay in charge. So much for that.

"My little conservative minx." He trailed his lips over her neck, traveling from one side to the other. "You think I'm upset about this? You're mine, Tart. Let anyone look, but I'll be the one touching you, pleasuring you."

Paisley closed her eyes, unable to stop the visual images from rolling through her mind. Lucas continued feathering that fingertip across her heated skin, and she cursed herself for playing games. She should've shown up in something with a high neck and full sleeves. But no, she'd wanted tacky, yet sexy as hell just to be spiteful.

"If we're done playing games, let's go make this legal."

Before Paisley could take a breath, Lucas covered her mouth with his. His body pressed hers against the wall, and she barely had time to register the glorious contact before her body arched to his and he slid his hands up her bare arms. He curled his fingers around her shoulders and urged her even closer.

The power from his touch, his strength, had her knees going weak, but the way he kissed her…there were no words. There was something passionate, hot, yet gentle about him.

Lucas slid his lips gently across hers before easing back.

"Just wanted to practice the whole kiss-the-bride part," he said with a smirk. "You ready to become Mrs. Lucas Ford?"

Ready? Now that she was here, Paisley worried she'd gotten in over her head. But despite everything, she trusted him to find the truth.

Paisley smiled wide and patted his cheek, ignoring her thumping heart from that heated kiss. "I'll keep my own name, but thanks for the offer."

The woman was going to be the death of him. If she didn't kill him with that smart mouth, that damn svelte body wrapped in lace would surely do the trick. The only parts of her flesh he couldn't see were the areas a skimpy bikini would cover.

Paisley had the ability to order any wedding gown in the world and she'd chosen the most ridiculous, sexiest jumpsuit. Damn it if he wasn't even more aroused and intrigued at her snarky act. At least this wouldn't be a boring marriage.

He was counting on her being just as fiery in bed.

"You may now kiss your bride."

At the officiant's word, Lucas circled her waist with his hands and pulled her hips to his, instantly capturing her lips. Much like moments ago in the hallway, Paisley melted against him. She had always been a passionate woman and now he was going to get to experience that all over again.

Paisley broke the kiss and flattened her hands on his chest. "I think that covers it," she stated with a breathless sigh. "I'll take a nice bottle of prosecco in my suite, please."

Lucas dug his fingertips into the dip in her waist. "We've barely begun," he murmured. "And it's not your suite. It's ours."

Paisley pulled away and smiled over gritted teeth. "I'm ready to get to *our* suite and relax."

Lucas shot a wink to the officiant. "The honeymoon can't start too early."

Paisley twisted out of his grasp and turned to go back down the short, narrow aisle. Lucas nodded to the witnesses and turned to follow his bride. Never in his wildest dreams—and he'd had some wild ones—did he ever think he'd marry Paisley or have the woman standing in practically nothing as he slid a band of diamonds onto her finger.

Speaking of, Paisley hadn't reacted one bit when he'd put that ten-carat flawless diamond on her finger when they'd taken off from Houston. In fact, she'd stared out the window and barely said a word to him.

Maybe he shouldn't have gone for something so traditional. Someone like Paisley would want an emerald or a ruby. He should—

No. Hell, no. What was he thinking? He wasn't getting her something else. Between the engagement ring and now the wedding band, she had enough on that finger to help support her shop. This wasn't for love or until death did they part. Paisley already had an expiration date on their marriage.

Of course, if she produced an heir, there was no way he'd divorce her. He didn't just want her in his bed, he wanted her to give him a child. Paisley had always wanted children, or she used to when they were together before. They'd often dreamed of one day having their own family.

Lucas slipped his arm around her waist and guided her out to the waiting car. As soon as he settled in beside her and the driver closed the door, Paisley turned to face him.

"I sent a copy of my mother's letter to your email," she started. "When we get back to the room, we can start digging into that and you can share what you've discovered so far. I can answer questions about my mom's past, but—"

Lucas leaned over and covered her mouth with his. He shifted so that he pressed her against the back of the leather seat as the driver took them down the Strip. Lights from the hotels flashed through the windows, but nothing else mattered except the fact that his new bride instantly wanted to get down to business.

Well, he did, too, but a completely different kind.

Paisley shoved against his chest and turned her head away. "Can you focus?"

Lucas curved his hand around her upper thigh and gave a slight squeeze. "Oh, I'm plenty focused."

Those hazel eyes with flecks of emerald landed on him. "You promised to help find the truth and I want to be part of that process."

He stroked the inside of her thigh with his thumb. "You're my wife now. You'll be part of everything."

Her brows shot up. "I thought you'd try to exclude me."

"I see no reason in leaving you out when this is your life I'm dealing with."

Clearly his response shocked her. She shook her head and glanced out the window as the car turned into the front of their hotel.

"I'll never understand you," she murmured.

Lucas didn't bother hiding his smile. He was banking on her being kept off guard. He wanted her wondering what he'd do next. Pretty much like she had always done to him, and today with that damn lace number was no exception.

That was just one of the things he'd always loved about her—her ability to keep him on his toes. The way she'd challenged him and always had him guessing what she'd do next had made for a great relationship...until the ultimate moment when she'd caught him off guard and destroyed his heart.

"How much did this scrap of lace cost me?" he asked.

The car came to a stop and Paisley turned to him with a smile on her face. "I don't recall, but it was worth every penny. Wouldn't you agree?"

Her door opened before he could answer and the driver extended his hand to assist Paisley. Lucas went out into the night after her and nodded his thanks to their chauffer.

As he and his bride waltzed through the spacious five-story lobby, she got some looks. Not because of the nearly sheer getup—this was Vegas, after all—but because she was so damn stunning that she could've been wearing a sack and she still would've drawn attention.

As they approached the elevators, Lucas settled his hand on the small of her bare back and swiped his card that would take them to the VIP floors. They weren't staying in a traditional honeymoon suite, but the nicest high-roller penthouse available. The three-thousand-square-foot room complete with their own waitstaff was ready and waiting for them.

Lucas would immediately dismiss the staff and have them on standby should he and Paisley need more food and wine. Other than that, he fully planned on keeping his wife all to himself tonight.

No way in hell were they going to worry about Sterling Perry or her mother or some damn letter.

Lucas had just one concern: How the hell did he get that lace jumpsuit off?

Five

Paisley's hands shook as she stared at the enormous bathroom in their suite. Her entire apartment could fit in here and there would still be extra space.

The heated marble floors, the open shower big enough for a party, the wall of mirrors and the chandelier with so many twinkling lights…there was just so much to take in and she didn't even want to know what this place cost per night.

She also knew Lucas wasn't ready to dive into the letter or the truth. He was ready to dive into her pants. Paisley wasn't even going to pretend she wasn't looking forward to feeling his body against her again. She was human; she had basic needs.

But there was nothing basic about what she and Lucas had once shared. He'd always been an attentive lover, but they'd been so young. Clearly they'd both changed over the years.

Paisley took a step back and glanced at herself in the floor-length mirror. She certainly didn't have the same body she'd once had. Gravity and doughnuts had made a few alterations.

Might as well get out of this ridiculous outfit. She'd been in such a spiteful mood when she'd gone wedding dress shopping for herself. Of course she had her favorites. There was one magnificent gown she'd had her eye on for the past few months.

Like any woman, especially one owning a bridal boutique, Paisley had her own vision of her big day. But there was no way in hell she was wasting any of that fairy-tale stuff on Lucas. Because one day she would marry for love. She'd get that gown of her dreams, the sparkling accessories, her mother's simple diamond necklace, maybe even plan a destination wedding or a grand cathedral ceremony. Or maybe she'd go with a classy garden wedding.

None of those daydreams mattered now. All that mattered was trying to get through her current marriage with her heart still intact and finding the truth about her father.

She honestly didn't know if she wanted Sterling to be her biological dad or not. He'd destroyed her finances, not to mention that of others, and he was just an evil, spiteful man. He currently sat in a jail cell, after being denied bail, because he was accused of fraud and not too long ago a body had been found on one of his work sites.

The thought sent a shudder through her. No, that was not the type of man she wanted for a father.

On the other hand, knowing who and where she came from would at least give her a sense of belonging. She certainly felt a yawning void since her mother's passing. There was an emptiness in her life she hadn't expected, and a large part of her seemed to just be going through the daily motions. The sense of being lost and floating along seemed to grow worse. Her heart ached and she was so utterly confused she truly had no clue what to do next.

Marrying Lucas didn't help.

He'd had her suitcase brought up to the suite before the ceremony. Paisley had changed at the chapel so she could surprise her husband. Mission accomplished.

Paisley had brought her robe into the bathroom a few minutes ago and hung it on the back of the hook next to the garden tub. She had no clue what to expect when she stepped out, but she was thankful he was giving her a few minutes of space.

The tap on the door pulled her from her thoughts. There went that alone time.

"You plan on hiding much longer?" Lucas called through the double doors.

Paisley sighed as she straightened and reached around her neck for the hidden closure. "Almost done."

The doors opened just as her top fell to her waist. Lucas's vibrant eyes zeroed in on her bare breasts as he remained in the doorway. Paisley didn't bother covering herself. He might as well see that she wasn't a stick-thin twenty-year-old like she used to be.

From the clenched jaw and tight lips, he wasn't disappointed in her curves. That fact not only boosted her confidence, but sent a shiver of arousal through her. She hadn't cared what he thought about her until just this minute. Which was silly because she was happy with her body and wouldn't change for any man.

"I knew that getup looked like you were wearing nothing beneath," he stated. "But you sure as hell were bare."

Paisley smiled. Feeling extra saucy, she slid her thumbs into the material gathered at her waist and shoved it on down to pool at her feet. Carefully, she stepped out of the garment, leaving her standing before him in only her spiked, strappy heels.

He'd already shed his jacket and tie and loosened the top button on his black shirt. His hair was rumpled from his Stetson, his sleeves were rolled up onto muscular forearms, and judging by the way he looked at her, it would be a miracle if they didn't set this place on fire just from the electricity charging between them.

Chemistry...they still had it. Quite possibly even stronger than their first time around.

Regardless of the circumstances surrounding their marriage, there was no denying their attraction and there was no use fighting it. Paisley wondered if she needed time to grasp their new, temporary reality, but all she needed was that boost of courage that only came from one of Lucas's sexy stares.

"Had I known what you weren't wearing, we would've taken the long way here from the chapel." Lucas stalked toward her, unbuttoning his shirt and discarding it across the floor. "Do you even know how sexy you are? More than I remember."

Did that mean he'd thought about her over the years? Paisley wasn't about to admit she'd done her fair share of fantasizing. She was stronger now, more independent…or trying like hell to be. The blows she'd been delivered lately had forced her to admit vulnerability. She hated needing anybody, but there was also no need in being stupid about her situation. She needed Lucas now, in more than one way. He'd always been her weakness.

Before he could touch her, Paisley put her hands on his bare chest and looked up at him. "This can't be more than, well…this."

His brows drew in. "What?"

"Sex. This marriage isn't more than you helping me and sex. I can't get hurt, Lucas."

His fingertips trailed over her hips, into the dip of her waist and over the sides of her breasts. All the while he kept his gaze locked firmly on hers.

"You think I'd hurt you?"

He took one step, closing the last bit of distance between them. With a quick, expert move, Lucas reached for her hands, pulled them down to her sides and gently behind her back. With one firm grip, he secured her wrists and towered over her.

With his free hand, he covered her neck and stroked his thumb along the sensitive spot behind her ear, and then he ran a fingertip over her lips.

"I'd never hurt you," he murmured. "But I'm keeping myself guarded as well since you were the one who broke my heart with a letter and a vanishing act."

He gave her no chance to defend herself as his hand disappeared, quickly replaced by his mouth.

Paisley had no choice but to arch against him in this current situation. He had complete and utter control and the very female, aching, needy part of her wanted him to do whatever he planned. She trusted him completely with her body. It was her heart that she had to keep protected.

At least they were both in agreement that their hearts had no place in this marriage. Now, if she could just remember that as they went through the rest of their days as husband and wife while playing house.

Paisley opened to him, welcoming the passion. There was something so familiar, yet so strangely new with having Lucas consume her. That young adult body had turned into manly muscle and the sometimes timid touch was now all demanding. A man who knew what he wanted, and who he wanted, was so damn sexy.

There was no question that Lucas had every intention of remaining dominant and maybe, just in the case of the bedroom, she'd let go of the reins for now. She found his strength and power arousing and refreshing from guys she'd dated in the past.

Paisley looped her arms around his neck, threading her fingers through his thick hair. Was it naive of her to want to get lost in him for just a bit? This was no typical wedding night, but that didn't mean she wouldn't thoroughly enjoy herself and the man she now called her husband.

Lucas lifted her and walked to the vanity. The cool marble against her heated skin had Paisley shivering, but that shock was nothing compared to the man standing between her spread legs looking like he wanted to devour her.

With his heavy-lidded eyes homing in on her, Lucas took one step back to rid himself of all his clothes. He stood completely bare before her, a sight she never thought she'd see again, let alone in this instance. Lucas Ford was her husband and she had a very real feeling that someone was not going to come out the other side unscathed.

"Stay with me, Tart."

His husky words pulled her back. She didn't want to be anywhere else. She didn't want to worry about tomorrow or even next month. She only wanted this moment with Lucas...the way it should've been so many years ago.

She reached for him. "I'm right here."

Lucas lifted her legs by gripping the back of her thighs and eased her to the edge of the counter. Paisley clung to his shoulders in anticipation.

"Protection?" she asked.

Those baby blues traveled from between their bodies up to her face. "I want to feel my wife. Are you worried? I've always used something, except with you."

When they'd been younger and so lost in each other they'd forgotten a couple of times. She wagered a mental battle with herself, but ultimately knew what she wanted.

"You're the only man I've ever been with that way."

Lucas's eyes darkened as he pulled her hips closer and finally joined their bodies. Paisley closed her eyes, wanting to hold on to every single sensation and freeze this moment.

So much for guarding her emotions.

"Look at me," he demanded.

The second she locked her gaze with his, Lucas began to move. The tips of his fingers dug into her hips and she tipped her pelvis just so, enough to create the most pleasurable experience for both of them.

There was something so intimate about staring at Lucas, something she couldn't put her finger on. But she didn't want to look away. The man held her captivated as he continued to pump his hips. He reached between them and touched her at the spot she ached most.

Paisley cried out as a wave of pleasure crashed into her. Her head dropped back as she squeezed her eyes shut. A second later, Lucas's hands framed her face and tipped her head back up to meet his demanding kiss.

Her body continued to spiral out of control as he claimed more and more from her. There was nothing outside these walls. No secrets, no worries. Everything that mattered was right here, raw and abandoned. Real emotions they couldn't hide.

The moment Paisley's shivers ceased, she pulled from the kiss and glanced up to Lucas. He looked down at her, hunger in his eyes and the muscles in his jaw clenched.

Paisley smiled as she leaned back on her elbows and locked her ankles behind his back. The act of relinquishing total control had Lucas flattening a hand on her abdomen as he pumped harder, faster.

When he trembled, Paisley became utterly captivated

as his climax consumed him. She kept her eyes locked onto his and Lucas didn't look away, which only turned her on even more.

The man was demanding, cocky, arrogant…even during sex.

Why did that all have to be so damn arousing? She'd already been pleasured, yet she wasn't quite ready to give up this warmth, this passion.

Once he calmed, Lucas reached down and cupped both of her breasts. Paisley waited, wondering what he'd say or do next. When the silence became too much, she finally eased all the way up and dropped her legs to rub against the sides of his.

"If you only wanted sex from this marriage, I'd say we're off to a hell of a start," she told him, trying to maintain her nonchalant image.

Lucas leaned down and captured her lips for a short, hot kiss that had her toes curling. Then he eased back and gave her that naughty grin she'd never forgotten.

"Sex is a given," he retorted. "But I want a child. Our child."

Six

Maybe now wasn't the best time to make that announcement. Lucas should've carried her into the grand bedroom with a wall of one-way windows overlooking the Strip. He should've taken his time with her, laid her out on the bed and showed her exactly what they'd missed from their years apart.

But better she knew what she was getting into. Better she knew why he married her…or at least part of the reason. Paisley didn't need to be informed of the whole revenge scheme he'd thought of if Sterling turned out to be her biological father.

"A baby?" she repeated, her tone leaving no question as to her irritation. "You married me thinking I'd be… What? Your ticket to fatherhood? Isn't this something you should've mentioned before we said 'I do'?"

She pushed off the counter and edged around him to the silky red robe she'd hung near the tub big enough for a party. He watched as she jerked the lapels closed and knotted the belt at her waist.

Figuring he should put on something, Lucas grabbed his black boxer briefs and stepped into them.

"I knew you wanted something from me," she muttered as she pulled her hair from the robe, sending the tousled strands down over her shoulders. "I should've been more selective on who I asked help from. This is…"

She shook her head and raked her hands through her hair. Lucas crossed his arms over his chest.

"I didn't mean I wanted you to give me a child now," he told her. "I do want a child, someone I can pass my company down to. Neither of us is looking for love, but there's no reason we can't get what we want."

Her mouth dropped open as her brows shot up. "Do you hear yourself? I asked you to find the truth about my father. You're asking me to give you a human being. One of those will bind us together for life. Is that what you want with me?"

"I don't believe in love, so finding someone to share my heart isn't an option. Children are family and that's a whole other aspect of feelings and one I am open to." He took a step toward her, but stopped when she put her hands up. "We always discussed children. Remember?"

"I remember," she stated, dropping her hands to her sides. "I also remember that we were in love at the time and had unrealistic expectations on life and our future. This isn't some young lover's dream, Lucas. You can't

just bring a baby into the world because you want someone to take your business. That's…that's…archaic."

Lucas wasn't about to get into an argument on his
wedding night—regardless of the fact this wasn't a typical wedding or marriage. The last thing he wanted was
too much conflict at this early stage.

"We can discuss this later." He reached down and
gathered his clothes, then scooped up her lace jumpsuit. "For the rest of this weekend, can't we just enjoy
the honeymoon?"

The way she stood there with that messy, sexy hair,
those killer heels and that silky robe made Lucas want
to throw her over his shoulder and march right into the
bedroom for round two.

Hmm…was that archaic as well?

If she knew he was using her as a way to seek revenge on Sterling, she'd sure as hell never agree to a
child. The ground he treaded on was shaky at best and
each step he took could be fatal to his plan.

"You get this weekend," she told him. "And then
we're getting to the bottom of Sterling and my mother
and whatever history they had."

Surprised she gave in, Lucas nodded. "I'll make Sterling my top priority."

Because if Sterling was indeed Paisley's father,
Lucas had every intention of letting his new father-in-
law know just who was in charge and who ultimately
would come out on top.

Lucas stared up at the neon sign attached to the dingy
bar Paisley's mother used to work at decades ago. Just

because the place still existed didn't mean anyone would remember Lynette Morgan.

But he had to start somewhere other than a cryptic letter so here he was. He often put his best men on the grunt work of the jobs they took on, but this case was too personal. Besides, Lucas liked getting back to the basics of his business.

The second Lucas tugged open the heavy door, loud country music from a live band spilled out. Couples danced on the scarred wood floor and the long bar that stretched from front to back was actually pretty crowded. Obviously there was a reason this place had stayed in business so long. He'd found the dive places were usually the hidden gems when it came to bars and restaurants.

Lucas eased his way toward the bar and zeroed in on the older bartender at the end. From the looks of the younger staff, that would be the only person in this place who might remember anything at all.

As he eased through a crowd of women who should be cut off their spirits, Lucas slid a photo from his pocket and rounded the edge of the bar. When the bartender glanced his way, Lucas waved a hand.

"What can I get ya?" the man yelled over the band.

Lucas flipped the picture up. "You recognize this woman?"

The bartender narrowed his gaze and leaned forward, then nodded. "Lynette. I remember her. Hated to hear of her passing. Damn shame."

Yes, it was. Lucas wished like hell Paisley hadn't lost her mother. To make matters worse, a complete bastard might turn out to be her father. Even so, Lucas couldn't let guilt and tragedy stop him from seeking revenge. Sterling had destroyed Lucas's father and it was time for him to pay.

"When she worked here, did she have any guys that hung around or anyone she mentioned dating?"

He hated yelling over this crowd, but he and Paisley had gotten home from Vegas a couple hours ago and he wanted to get this ball rolling. He figured a Monday night wouldn't be too crowded, but apparently this was half off wing night.

He'd chosen to come straight here for one because he wanted to dive straight in, but he also needed space to think. The damn woman was driving him out of his mind with want, lust, need. He didn't recall needing anyone the way he'd found himself craving her the past few days, not even when they were together the first time.

They'd spent their honeymoon in the suite, completely naked, save for the few times she'd thrown on his shirt when they'd had carpet picnics. They'd even made love on his private jet on their way home.

So, yeah. The chemistry was stronger than ever.

"There was an older man that came around," the bartender stated, pulling Lucas back into the moment. "Wealthy. Don't know his name, but he always wore a suit and tossed out hundred dollar bills for tips. Always thought the guy was arrogant."

Buster's Bar was certainly not the type of establishment you'd toss around wads of cash. That type of cockiness sounded like Sterling Perry, but this definitely wasn't enough proof to confront the guy.

"Would you know his name if you heard it?" Lucas prompted.

"I never heard Lynette say," the old guy replied. "But she sure was smitten with whoever it was."

Lucas nodded and shoved the photo back into his pocket. He pulled out another and held it up.

"Do you recognize this man?"

The man's eyes narrowed and he thought for a moment. "It's been a long time, but I don't think I've seen him before."

Lucas gritted his teeth against the frustration and offered a smile. "Thanks for your time."

"Can I get you a beer?"

Lucas offered a smile. "Next time," he promised. He figured he'd bring Paisley back sometime. There might be more questions once he dug a little deeper.

He weaved his way back through the crowd and out into the night. Just being away from his wife for an hour had him itching to get home. Yes, he'd needed a few minutes to himself, but now he realized he wanted to be with her. Their time in Vegas had been intense, but too short. Lucas wanted to schedule another getaway for them soon. First, though, he'd have to find the truth about Sterling.

Maybe this wasn't a traditional marriage, maybe Paisley wanted an end date, but he was taking full advantage of being married to the one woman he'd always wanted. She'd gotten away once, but he had no intention of letting her go again. His reasons were just a tad different this time.

Before, when he'd been young and too trusting, Lucas had been expecting them to live forever after on love and happiness. Now they could live on determination and passion. Hey, that was more than most relationships, right?

He wasn't under some delusion that he'd ever marry for love. Such a notion was for fairy tales and fiction novels. He did want a child and he hadn't lied when he told Paisley he wanted her to be the mother. There'd been no other woman that had filled that bill so the whole fatherhood thing was something he'd thought had been off in the future. But then she'd walked through his office door and the opportunity had landed in his lap.

By the time he got home, Lucas was more than eager to see Paisley. The topic of the baby hadn't been brought up again, but he knew full well she wasn't done. It was something they needed to discuss and he'd much rather talk about a child than the revenge she knew nothing about.

For now, there was no reason for her to think anything other than the fact he was helping her business and they should start a family.

When he stepped off the private elevator, he froze.

What the hell?

Lucas dropped his keys onto the accent table to his right without even looking away from the newly decorated living area. This was...not his style. The throw pillows were everywhere. Some had polka dots, some

had stripes. There was a tray on the oversize square ot-
toman that held candles and flowers.

A few new pictures hung on the walls…pictures with
quotes that he didn't want to take the time to read. They
wouldn't be staying.

"Oh, hey! You're home."

Lucas glanced toward the open kitchen and nearly
swallowed his tongue. Paisley paraded through wearing
an apron and heels—only an apron and heels—holding
a glass of what he presumed to be his favorite bourbon.

"I hope you don't mind I brought a few of my things
over." She strutted toward him and held out the tumbler. "I just thought since I'm staying here, you'd want
me to be happy and feel at home."

The moment he took the drink, she turned away,
giving him the most impressive view of her bare ass
and those legs.

"Dinner will be ready in ten minutes if you want to
change," she called over her shoulder.

Lucas tipped back the amber liquid and welcomed
the burn. How long had he been gone? And how the
hell did she find the time to do all of this?

He followed her to the kitchen and watched in awe as
she pulled something from the oven that smelled better
than anything he'd ever created here.

"I hope you like chicken Cordon Bleu." She set the
pan on the stove and closed the oven door then reached
up to turn off the heat. "There's also an apricot and feta
salad to start."

Lucas crossed his arms over his chest and leaned
against the counter next to her. "Are you going to just

pretend like you didn't completely redecorate and that you're not cooking dinner completely naked?"

She shot him a half grin that didn't help his growing arousal. Damn, she was playing a game. She was playing *him*.

"First of all, I'm not completely naked." She had the nerve to pat his cheek before she turned back to dinner. "Second, with your archaic way of thinking, I just assumed you'd want me naked in the kitchen. Was I wrong? I'm just trying to be a good wife."

She stopped looking through the cabinets to stare at him, blinking like she was utterly innocent.

Lucas slammed the cabinet door she'd been holding open. In one swift move, he gripped her waist and hoisted her up onto the island behind them. With a squeal, Paisley held on to his shoulders.

"*Innocent* is never a word I would use to describe you." He stepped between her legs and stared directly into her eyes. "Are you done being a smart-ass?"

Paisley shrugged. "Probably not."

"What the hell am I going to do with all of those ruffled pillows on my sofa?"

Paisley laughed. "Admire how much they spruce up the place?"

"They look ridiculous," he grumbled.

Paisley toyed with the button on his shirt. "The honeymoon must really be over if I'm barely wearing anything and you're worried about pillows."

More like he was trying to hold on to the shred of control and not rip her apron off. How could he want her every second of the day? She seemed to have the same feelings, so why was he questioning this?

"Where were you anyway?" she asked, sliding one button undone, then another, and on down she went. "We barely got in the door and you took off."

"Because when we're alone all I want to do is get you on your back," he growled, jerking his shirt off and flinging it to the floor. "I had work to do."

She stilled. "About Sterling?"

Lucas took a step back. "Yeah. I went to the bar your mom worked at during the time she got pregnant with you."

"It's still there?" she asked. "I never go to that side of town, so I never thought about it. Was it all run-down?"

"It's not the best part of town, so it matches the rest of the old buildings," he agreed. "But the bartender re-membered your mom."

Paisley hopped off the counter, eyes wide. "What did he say?"

"He knew there was a wealthy man who always hung around, but he didn't know a name."

Paisley pursed her lips and glanced to the floor, her wheels obviously turning. Lucas, on the other hand, had short-circuited the moment she'd waltzed through looking like his every fantasy come to life.

Paisley turned her attention back to him. "I thought everyone knew who Sterling was."

Lucas stepped forward, reaching around to undo the ties at her neck and waist. "Maybe he does know Ster-ling, but this was a long time ago and he may not have known him then. People change."

The apron fell to the floor between them. Her eyes widened.

"Aren't you hungry?" she asked.

His body stirred. "Starving."

Lucas crushed his mouth to hers, palmed her backside and lifted her against his body as he carried her from the kitchen. Paisley wrapped her legs around him, one of her heels digging into his ass, but he didn't care. He wanted this woman with the snarky mannerisms and quick wit. He wanted her in his bed and he wasn't about to wait another second.

As he stepped into his master suite, her heels clattered to the floor. She threaded her fingers through his hair and groaned.

Those little noises had always gotten him. When they'd been younger, and he'd had considerably less control, those sweet sounds would nearly have him embarrassing himself before they'd even started.

Paisley pulled her lips from his. "Wait," she panted. "I don't want to be just another woman you bring in here. I mean, I know this isn't love or a real marriage, but I just—"

Lucas put his fingertip over her lips. "Clearly I've been with other women since you, but I swear, I've never brought a woman into my bedroom. Ever."

He would stay over at a lover's place, but this was his domain and it never seemed right to have someone invade his space.

Paisley seemed to relax as her lids lowered and she licked her bottom lip.

Every single thing that woman did drove him out of

his mind. She'd always held a different spot in his life than any other woman, but he had no clue since she walked back in just how much he'd missed her.

They'd been so damn young before—so clueless.

His eyes were wide-open this time…and his heart completely closed.

They'd been married for three days and they'd barely kept their hands off each other. That was the marriage he wanted with her, the marriage he *needed* with her.

Lucas made quick work of removing his clothes. The topic of birth control hadn't come up since that first time. He knew she was on something and he'd never deceive her with getting pregnant. He wanted that to be a joint decision…but he would sway her to seeing things his way.

Her hazel eyes raked over him. The way she always seemed to sample him with her eyes made him wonder just how she was going to feel once she discovered his true reason for marrying her.

Guilt had no place in the bedroom or his plan.

Right now all that mattered was that his wife was naked and standing inches from him. He circled her waist with his hands and lifted her onto the bed. With a slight bounce, she laughed and stared up at him with wide eyes.

Lucas rested a knee next to her hip and raked a hand up her thigh, over her flat stomach and on up to circle one pert breast.

Her immediate response to his touch was definitely one area that hadn't changed. Their connection had always been electrifying and unlike anything he'd ever had with anyone else.

Lucas reached back down, keeping his eyes locked on hers, and gripped the back of her thigh. He settled himself between her legs and thrust into her, earning himself a long, slow moan from his sexy wife.

How the hell was he going to go back to work? He wanted to keep her in his bed and forget all his responsibilities.

When she opened her eyes and stared up at him, Lucas leaned down and covered her mouth. He couldn't look into her eyes, not now. He was confused; he was falling back into their old patterns and forgetting that she'd broken him before. If she started developing feelings, they'd both end up hurt because that was not what all of this was about.

Revenge. That was the key component of his focus.

And the warmth of Paisley. He had to stay in this frame of mind because she took him to a place that he wanted to stay…if only that wasn't some unrealistic fantasy.

Lucas shifted his body fully over hers, dropping her leg and flattening his palms on either side of her head as he lifted slightly. Thankfully her eyes were shut. She arched and tipped her head as she locked her ankles around his back.

Yes. This was what he wanted. Physical connections were something he could most definitely handle, but the emotional ones had no place here.

Paisley curled her fingers around his shoulders, her fingertips digging into his skin. She let out another sultry moan and tightened all around him. Lucas gritted his teeth, following her as his body shuddered and he slipped into a euphoria only Paisley could give him.

He cradled her face with his hands, tucked his head against the crook of her neck and waited until their bodies settled. Then he rolled to his side, taking her with him, and wondered what the hell he was going to do when she wanted to call this quits.

Because he never wanted to let her go again.

Seven

"We need proof," Lucas stated as he loaded the dishwasher.

Paisley propped her feet up on the kitchen chair he'd vacated moments ago. She sipped her wine and admired the fine specimen that was her husband. Shirtless, cotton pants hanging low on his narrow hips, hair messed from their lovemaking.

Damn if this wasn't the sexiest thing she'd ever seen. A half-naked man cleaning the kitchen. Yeah, put images like this in a calendar and label it Domestic Men and watch them fly off the shelves. She'd hang one in every room.

"Paisley?"

She blinked and set her glass on the table. "I'm listening."

His brows drew in. "You're staring and I'm starting to feel like a piece of meat."

"Well, this marriage was your idea and from the way you parade around, I'm pretty sure you like me staring at your meat."

His eyes raked over her as she sat there in his shirt. They'd come back into the kitchen and eaten their cold dinner. Not that she was complaining. He'd come home with some pertinent information regarding her mother. At least they had a starting point, and she desperately clung to the hope that Lucas had provided.

"How can we get proof?" she asked, circling back to the main reason she'd gone to him in the first place. "I can't just ask the man if he's my father. I doubt he would even know how many love children he has running around."

Lucas slammed a plate into the dishwasher a little harder than she thought necessary. "Sterling has always been a bastard. Wouldn't surprise me a bit if he had more kids he ditched or women he lied to."

Why was he so irritated? Did it matter to Lucas if Sterling Perry was her father or not? Had Sterling done something to Lucas as well? Lucas was powerful in his own way, but Sterling was smarmy and vindictive.

"It's not like we can just go to the prison and ask," she muttered, thinking out loud.

"You're not going near that prison or that jerk," Lucas demanded. He started the dishwasher, then leaned against the counter and crossed his arms. "He's exactly where he belongs and I'll find the proof you need. That's why you came to me."

The conviction in his tone left no room for doubt. She knew Lucas was the best at his job and she knew he'd stop at nothing to find the truth for her. He was that kind of guy. His reputation didn't surprise her. The man was known for seeking justice and putting his clients' needs at the top of his list. She had to assume he'd do the same for his wife.

But still, Paisley wished there was something she could do. She could always call Melinda. She was not only a friend, she also happened to be one of Sterling's daughters. Perhaps Paisley could casually ask if Melinda remembered Lynette. If Paisley could put her mom and Sterling together around the time of the pregnancy, then that would help in getting the proof they needed.

At some point, she'd have to go to Sterling, but she wasn't about to tell Lucas that. He wouldn't like her take-charge attitude, but she also didn't plan on sitting back and playing the dutiful little wife like he expected.

If she called Melinda and probed…

No. She couldn't do that. The woman's father was in jail. How insensitive would that be to start asking a bunch of questions?

But Paisley could call and offer her sympathies for all their family was going through. That conversation could always lead somewhere promising, right?

"Your silence worries me." Lucas closed the distance between them and stood before her. He tipped her chin up, so she stared at his chest then dragged her gaze to his eyes. "I remember you getting crazy ideas and they came right after you looked like you were staring off into space."

Paisley smiled. "I don't know what you're talking about."

"Leave this to me," he commanded. "You weren't able to figure this out on your own before and I know what I'm doing."

"You're suggesting I don't?" She rose to her feet and pushed his hand aside. "I don't need to be kept in the dark, and you said you'd work with me on this. That doesn't mean shoving me to the side so you can feed me only information you think I need to know."

His lips twitched. "You're sexy when you're angry."

Yeah, well, he was sexy all the time, but there was no sense in feeding his ego any more than necessary.

"Don't sidetrack me with sex." As if he hadn't been doing just that for the past three days. "I'm serious. I need to know the truth. Between the unknown father, my business and losing my mom…"

Emotions clogged her throat. Breaking down now would not help her get anywhere and the last person she wanted to look weak in front of was Lucas.

He immediately wrapped his arms around her and ran his hands up and down her back. "Your mom wouldn't want you to get so worked up," he assured her. "I'm not just going to leave you to deal with everything on your own."

He eased her back, swiping his thumbs across her damp cheeks. "Despite what you think, I married you for more than sex."

When he didn't elaborate, she worried. He wanted a child—a topic they'd not discussed any more. But she wondered if there was more. Surely he didn't believe she'd just agree to something so…permanent.

There was definitely something else up with Lucas and until she knew what, she desperately needed to keep her heart guarded. Unfortunately, that was easier said than done because being with him again reminded her of how perfect they'd been in the past.

As if Paisley didn't have enough issues, what with a felon potentially being her father, being blackmailed into a marriage she was actually enjoying, losing her mother, losing all of her savings and her shop hanging on by a thread, now the horrid woman who stiffed her out of the expensive wedding dress was not replying to her messages.

This gave a whole new meaning to *runaway bride*.

Paisley gripped her steering wheel and turned in to the new, partially renovated Texas Cattleman's Club location. She'd called Melinda yesterday after her talk with Lucas. Melinda had been so glad to hear from her, Paisley almost felt guilty about offering to take her mentor to lunch. But these were dire times and she wasn't going to stop pressing until she had the truth…no matter what that turned out to be.

Meeting at the clubhouse was a little bit intentional on Paisley's part. She knew Sterling's construction company was in charge of the renovations and, despite being in prison, he was vying for the top spot of president of TCC. Of course he had competition from Ryder Currin, the man who'd brought the club to Houston to begin with.

The whole ordeal was a mess, but being in the new café was a way to keep some focus on Sterling and have Melinda in the mind-set to discuss her father. Thankfully, Melinda was a TCC member or Paisley wouldn't be allowed in, seeing as how she wasn't a member.

As soon as Paisley stepped into the café, she scanned the rustic yet classy space. Here old-world charm met the Wild West. This café was definitely going to be a hot spot.

Paisley smiled as she found Melinda seated in the back. A little jumble of nerves formed in Paisley's belly. She didn't want to be completely self-centered with this meeting. She truly did love Melinda and wanted to catch up.

Her old mentor came to her feet and pulled Paisley into a hug.

"I was so happy you called," Melinda stated. "It's been too long."

Paisley eased back and reached for her chair. "It has. You know how it goes, though. Time just goes too fast. I've been so busy with the shop."

Melinda sat back down and offered a beaming smile. "How is your shop doing? Every time I drive by I daydream about those stunning dresses in your window. I choose a favorite and then you switch them out and I have a new favorite."

"Why do you think I swap them out so often? I can't decide which one I love more. But it's been difficult lately," Paisley said honestly. "I lost quite a bit of money and my savings, not to mention my mother lost everything she had when Sterling's… Well, you know the story."

Melinda winced and her smile vanished. "Oh, no, Paisley. I'm so, so sorry." Her friend shook her head and sighed. "I'm embarrassed, actually."

The waitress interrupted to get their drink orders, so they went ahead and ordered their food as well.

"You have nothing to be embarrassed for," Paisley said once they were alone again. "I can't imagine what you're going through having your father in jail. I'm the one who's sorry for you."

Melinda nodded and took in a deep breath. "It's been rough, but we'll get through."

Paisley knew her friend was made of tougher stuff than most. There was no doubt Melinda would be just fine, but Paisley had to probe…just a little. Melinda didn't dabble in the family business—she was so much more. She was a philanthropist and headed multiple charities. Those she worked on for struggling ranchers really put her in good graces with the Texas Cattleman's Club.

But Melinda was close with her father and maybe she knew more than she'd ever want to admit. But Paisley was desperate. If Sterling turned out to be her father, this marriage to Lucas could come to an end…before she got any more attached to her husband.

"Our situations aren't the same, but I understand the void," Paisley told her friend. "Since losing my mom, I've had a hard time figuring out my new normal. There are days I think I'm okay, but then something small and unexpected will remind me of what I lost."

Melinda reached across the table and gave Paisley's hand a reassuring squeeze. "I cannot even imagine. I never met your mother, but she had to have been re- markable."

"She was," Paisley said with a smile. "Lynette Mor- gan was one tough woman. She will be missed by so many."

Paisley purposely dropped her mother's name, hop- ing for a spark of recognition in Melinda's eyes.

Nothing. There was absolutely no flash of anything other than sympathy and sadness. Damn it.

"Let's discuss something else," Paisley suggested. "I didn't call you to hash out all of the bad that's hap- pened."

Melinda nodded and pulled her hand back. "First, I do want you to know that I'm terribly sorry about what my father did and how it affected you. Well, you and the entire city of Houston. That was another reason I was glad you called. I really didn't know you were harmed by his actions, but I don't have many friends lately, con- sidering my last name. I think he's innocent, but he's still in jail, so maybe clearing his name is proving to be too difficult."

Paisley hated all of this for her friend. Melinda was nothing like Sterling Perry. Melinda was amazing, kind, generous. Sterling was… Well, Paisley wasn't wast- ing her mental space on him right now. She wanted to enjoy this lunch, even if she didn't get the answers she was hoping for.

Paisley reached for her water glass, and Melinda gasped.

"What is that rock?"

The woman immediately grabbed Paisley's finger and examined the rings from all angles, then shifted her focus back to Paisley.

"Congratulations." Melinda beamed. "Who's the lucky guy?"

Paisley swallowed. The rings on her finger still seemed so foreign and quite a bit over-the-top. Despite owning a bridal boutique, Paisley typically leaned toward the conservative side.

These rings Lucas had presented her with were anything but.

"Lucas Ford," Paisley stated. "We dated a long time ago and recently…reconnected."

Reconnected? Paisley inwardly groaned. She made it sound like they'd bumped buggies at the grocery and struck up a conversation about old times, when in fact, she'd turned to him for help and he'd blackmailed her and now she couldn't keep her clothes on around him.

But best to stick to the basics here, considering the real story was a mess and one that made her sound like a helpless female.

"I'm so happy for you," Melinda announced. "I hadn't heard about a wedding. Did you do something small?"

Of course a bridal shop owner would likely make the gossip fodder, but not this wedding. There was no press, no invitations or bridal showers. Paisley had been robbed of all of that, but every step of this was of her own making. She'd had to decide between her dream wedding to a man she loved or a quick ceremony with a man she could never love again.

"Actually, we flew to Vegas." There was no way to un-tacky their nuptials. "We didn't want to wait and since we're both nearly alone in the family department, we just didn't see a need for something large."

Thankfully the waitress brought their drinks and food and cut off any more wedding talk. The last thing Paisley wanted was to be asked about the gown or have to try to romanticize the day. She could just imagine Melinda's face were she to know about the tawdry lace jumpsuit.

"I'm just thrilled you found happiness," her friend said. "Hey, I'm having a cocktail party next week. I'd love for you to come."

A party sounded fun and she should try to incorporate more good times in her life considering she'd been in a whirlwind nightmare.

"I'd love that," Paisley stated. "Should I bring Lucas or leave him home?"

"Oh, bring him if you like. I'd love to see the newlyweds together."

"We'll be there," Paisley declared.

She made sure to keep the conversation steered toward Melinda because not only did Paisley not want to talk about the wedding, she also didn't want to talk about the husband. There may be no hiding the fact that she was indeed falling for him all over again.

Eight

It was about damn time.

Sterling stepped into his country estate and breathed in the familiar scent of his home. Much better than that hellhole he'd been locked in.

Granted he was under house arrest, even after he'd paid millions to be released on bond. But he'd take house arrest over a cell any day. At least from home he had more power; he could control the strings of people around him and the outcome of his future.

First of all, he needed to get back in the saddle, so to speak, and make sure he was named president of TCC's Houston location. There was no way he'd lose to Ryder Currin. The man had had an affair with Sterling's wife, Tamara, years ago and Sterling was damn near positive Roarke was their love child. Sterling always claimed Roarke as his son, but never believed he truly was.

Roarke never agreed with how his father did business and Sterling wouldn't be a bit surprised if Roarke was the one feeding the lies to the media and the police about the whole financial debacle people were pinning on Sterling. Not to mention the damn murder.

He sure as hell never killed anyone.

Sterling just needed to get some rumors going about Roarke being Ryder's son. Sterling needed the upper hand to sabotage Ryder's bid for TCC President. There was only one person who could spread lies and gossip like wildfire and kerosene to help discredit Roarke.

Lavinia Cardwell.

Which was why his first order of business had been to invite his long-standing family friend over for a visit. Nothing like a catch-up session to kill two birds with one stone.

The first thing Sterling did while waiting on his guest to arrive was take a real shower with his thick towels and oversized walk-in shower with a rain head. There wasn't enough soap to wash off the grime from these past few weeks.

He'd just dressed and felt halfway normal when the doorbell chimed through the house. He'd made sure his staff was gone for the day, but he'd told his gate guard to let Lavinia up.

Sterling bound down the stairs, rehearsing exactly what he wanted to feed to the gossipmonger.

The moment he opened the door, Lavinia threw her

arms around him in a friendly hug and squeezed tight before easing back.

"It's so good to see you here," she said on a sigh of relief. "It's about time you got out."

Sterling couldn't agree more.

"It's good to see a friendly face," he replied, gesturing her inside. "Let's have a seat in the living room. Care for a drink?"

Lavinia stepped into the front room and shook her head. "No, thank you. But you have all you want. You've earned it."

He went to the bar in the corner and poured a shot of whiskey. "I sure as hell have. An innocent man shouldn't spend one second behind bars, let alone weeks."

Lavinia crossed her long legs and rested her arm on the sofa cushion. "I cannot even imagine how difficult that was. But I have to ask, do you know who set you up?"

Here we go. Time to plant the seeds.

"Do you think it was Angela?" she asked. "You two had been publicly fighting."

Sterling tipped back the shot and welcomed the burn. He set the glass on the bar and weighed his words carefully. Anything he said during their visit would be taken out into the public.

"No, I don't." He made his way to the sofa across from her and took a seat. "Angela and I may have quarreled over Ryder and her seeing each other, but she wouldn't do that to me. I wouldn't put it past Roarke, though."

Lavinia's brows rose. "Your son? I never would've thought of that."

Which was precisely why he was bringing it up now.

"Can I tell you something?" he asked, leaning forward for more of a dramatic effect.

"Of course. I'm here for you, Sterling."

"I think Roarke is Ryder's son." He let the words settle between them before he went on. "Tamara had an affair with Ryder Currin when he was just a stable hand. The timing fits for Roarke to be their love child, but I never said anything."

Lavinia gasped, her hand to her mouth. "You think Roarke set you up because he wanted you out of the way for his dad to be the club president?"

Sterling leaned back against the leather cushion and nodded. "I can't confirm this, but why else would he not stand by me when I needed my children the most? All of my kids have rallied around me, even Angela, and we've had our differences lately. Still, she believes in my innocence."

Lavinia pursed her lips. "This is all just so much to take in, but I see your point. I believe you were framed, but proving by whom will be difficult."

"I won't rest until the person behind all of this is found and punished," he vowed. "No matter who that turns out to be."

Even if that turned out to be the man he'd always considered a son.

Nine

Lucas attempted to go through the boxes Paisley had given him from her mother's house, but all he found were old, useless receipts, some baby pictures of Paisley and a few past due notices on bills that were dated a few weeks before her death.

Nothing. The search so far had turned up absolutely nothing.

Everything Lucas had attempted had resulted in a dead end. But he wasn't done exploring avenues. He still had a few calls out, one being to the hospital where Paisley had been born. It was another long shot, but perhaps there was a nurse who remembered…hell, he didn't know. A wealthy man visiting a barmaid? Not the best description, but Lynette's photo might help.

Every aspect had to be touched on, no matter if it

already seemed like a dead end. Exploring every part of people's pasts was what distinguished Lucas from other investigators.

Lucas prided himself on seeking justice and the truth. When he was a teen and Sterling Perry had taken advantage of his father, Lucas had vowed never to allow himself to be that vulnerable, that open to letting someone dupe him. He also knew one day he'd get revenge on Sterling…especially now that Lucas's late father wasn't around to do so himself.

And the timing of his plan revolved around Paisley. If she turned out to be Sterling's daughter, that would roll perfectly into getting close to the man and destroying him…all while not getting emotionally involved with his wife.

Lucas checked the time on his phone, noting there was no message from Paisley. She'd gotten up early and had gone to the boutique, but her shop had closed three hours ago. He absolutely hated that he cared, that he wanted to know where she was.

He hated even more that he let it bother him that she didn't consider this a real relationship. If she did, she'd be considerate enough to let him know where she was.

Damn it. Lucas stalked to his bar nestled in the corner of his penthouse. The wall of one-way windows gave him a picturesque view of their charming city, but right now, he didn't care. He was too pissed at himself for sliding into the role of doting husband a little too easily. He shouldn't care where she was; they had no real ties or expectations other than sex and him digging into Sterling. That was all they'd agreed upon.

Yet here he was brooding like a loser.

Sex could seriously cloud the vision. But even great sex with Paisley couldn't prevent him from destroying Sterling.

For completely selfish reasons, Lucas wanted him to be Paisley's father. That connection would certainly make the revenge that much sweeter since Sterling wasn't a fan of Lucas, either.

But for reasons he didn't want to delve into, Lucas almost hoped Sterling wasn't Paisley's father. She deserved so much better than an arrogant asshole whose every move was methodically thought out to what would benefit him most.

Lucas slammed back the bourbon and clanked his glass onto the mahogany bar top. He really should sip and enjoy the bourbon, but he was too on edge. His description of his potential father-in-law's actions could be applied to his own greed lately.

Wasn't that how he landed a pewter band on his finger?

Selfishness and greed. He'd never been lumped with those terms before, but he was sure as hell owning them now.

The elevator chimed, indicating a key card had been used to access it.

Lucas poured another two fingers and curled his hand around the stemless glass. No way did he want to appear like he'd been waiting. She was free to come and go as she wanted, right?

Hell, he didn't know the rules to this type of marriage. He'd given her one—that she would be in his bed like a real wife and she'd more than obliged.

He was still holding his tumbler when the elevator door slid open and Paisley appeared. The topknot she'd left with this morning had come down and her hair tumbled around her shoulders.

She looked sexy as hell in that short, button-up navy dress with matching belt and a pair of nude heels that made her legs appear as if they went on for miles.

Lucas clenched his teeth as she set her stuff down on the table near the elevator. She hadn't even looked his way, as if she didn't care if he was here or not.

Another niggle of irritation slid through him.

He was just about to say something—what, he wasn't sure—when Paisley rested her hands on the table where she'd dropped her purse. With her back to him, her head tipped down between her shoulders...shoulders that were shaking.

Ignoring the drink he'd poured, Lucas crossed the penthouse, his shoes clicking across the hardwoods. Just before he reached her, she jumped and spun around, her hand to her heart.

"I didn't see you here," she told him. "You startled me."

Clearly, she'd been in another world if she hadn't known he was in the same room. The smudged mascara beneath her eyes was like a punch to the gut. He never wanted to see tears on her, never wanted her to suffer for any reason. Despite their past and their messy present, that was one thing he couldn't handle.

"What happened?" he asked, swiping her damp cheeks. "Are you hurt?"

She shook her head. "No, just angry."

Angry tears. That was something he could work with, though he wished he didn't have to deal with tears at all.

"What happened?" he asked, ushering her into the living area.

"Just this bride who stiffed me for a bill that I can't possibly cover." She raked her hands down her face and sniffed. "It's ridiculous, really. I should've demanded payment in full before ordering such an extravagant gown, but she put down 20 percent and we had a contract for the rest. But the wedding got called off and she says the dress is just too painful to think about. She's refusing to pay the remainder."

Lucas listened as he eased her to the sofa beside him. He took one of her hands in his and squeezed it for silent reassurance.

"That was all via email, mind you," she went on. "Each call I've tried to make has gone unanswered, my messages ignored. I spent this evening after I closed calling the bridesmaids that came in with her and ordered their dresses, but none of them was any help... other than the fact they had actually paid in full for theirs. Apparently the groom chose one of the bridesmaids, so they're all arguing."

And here he'd been getting irritated because she wasn't home when all she'd been doing was trying to save her business. He certainly couldn't fault her for that and he'd be a complete ass if he tried. Just because this marriage was based on revenge and blackmail didn't mean he was heartless. Lucas cared for her once, and he cared for her now, but in a completely different way.

Now he had his eyes open and his heart shut. He was well aware of what this was and what it wasn't.

Still, he'd vowed to help her with her business and he wasn't going to sit by and just let her be taken advantage of.

"Give me all of the information you have," he told her.

Paisley jerked her focus to him, her brows drawn in. "Why?"

"Because I track people down for a living. What do you mean why?"

"This isn't your battle to fight," she explained, pulling her hand from his. "I'm not asking for your help. I just told you all of that because you asked why I was crying. I tend to cry when I'm mad."

"I remember," he murmured, recalling a moment someone had stolen her purse when they'd gone to the movie theater. She'd burst into tears because her favorite lip gloss had been inside. "But I'm offering to help because that's what I told you I would do. I'm not going to let your business take this financial hit. When that woman ordered the dress, I'm sure you had her sign a contract, so she's liable. If you want, you could sue her. Just the threat might scare her into paying."

Paisley swiped beneath her eyes and came to her feet. "The financial hit you're helping me with is the blow I took from the Ponzi scheme, not only from jilted brides."

She paced to the wall of windows and crossed her arms as she glanced out onto the city. Lucas remained on the sofa, watching her from across the room. Something churned in his gut, something he didn't want to put a finger on, didn't want to recognize.

The emotions he'd had for Paisley in the past hadn't completely died. A bond that strong couldn't, no matter how abrupt and shocking the ending had been.

That didn't mean he'd let himself get wrapped all around her again. Paisley didn't deserve some of the things that had happened to her, though. He wasn't about to just sit back and watch her livelihood destruct. That was one thing they still had in common—their drive to be the best at their careers.

She'd always wanted a bridal boutique. She'd always fantasized about their wedding when they'd been dating. He used to buy her hordes of bridal magazines back in the day and she would pore over them for hours.

"I just want her to pay," she finally stated, turning back to face him. "I'll give you her name and the contract she signed when she ordered the dress. Threaten legal action if necessary. I just want my thirty-five thousand dollars."

Lucas jerked. "For a dress? What the hell is it made of? Gold blocks?"

Paisley smoothed her hair over one shoulder and rolled her eyes. "Actually, it was hand sewn and the beading is from Italy. The designer is quite popular among celebrities and only a select clientele can even think about purchasing a Bella gown."

"Is that why you went with scraps of lace?"

Paisley's eyes narrowed. "Don't think it didn't cross my mind to stick you with a giant bill for a Bella gown. She's my favorite designer, but I opted to be spiteful in another way."

Lucas came to his feet and slowly crossed to her. Those eyes remained locked on him and the way she looked at him, like she used to seconds before she ripped his clothes off, had his body already stirring to life.

"By driving me out of my mind?" he asked as he closed in on her.

"Exactly." She tipped her chin and smiled. "Don't act like you didn't love seeing me. I know you, Lucas. Things might be different now, but you're still a man with basic wants and desires."

He snaked an arm around her waist and pulled her body to his. "There's nothing basic about my wants and desires for you, Tart. Never has been. You know exactly what buttons to push to make me ache for you even when you're not here."

Her brow quirked as her gaze darted to his lips.

"I missed you tonight." Damn it. He hadn't meant to let that slip.

"You mean I didn't check in?" she asked. "Are we back to those archaic rules of yours?"

"That's not what I meant." When she gave him another eye roll, he corrected himself. "Okay, fine. Maybe that's what I meant, but is it wrong that I want to know what's going on with my wife?"

She shuddered in his arms, and he wasn't sure if it was from anger over his words or if she was turned on.

"Is that the type of marriage we have?" she asked, still staring at him, her eyes searching for answers. "We check in with each other and discuss dinner or grocery lists and schedules? Because that's not the impression I had."

Lucas clenched his jaw and reached up to toy with the ends of her hair. He stared at the strands between his fingertips and weighed his next words. Every time she brought up their marriage she made him sound like a lovesick husband from the '50s. And damn it, she was right.

Not the lovesick part. But they did need some sort of boundaries before moving forward.

"Maybe we need to discuss what each of us expects," he stated, pushing her hair back over her shoulder and trailing his hand down the column of her neck. "Besides me saving your business and finding out about Sterling."

"Oh, so the baby is off the list now?"

Her mocking tone had him biting the inside of his cheek as he stared into her gaze. "No, actually it's not. But I thought we could keep this a little more…"

"Simple?"

Lucas nodded and circled her waist with both hands. He couldn't be this close and not touch her. He wanted to unfasten each of those little buttons and expose whatever sexy lingerie she wore beneath the dress, because he knew Paisley. She loved lace and satin.

"How about if I make dinner three nights a week and have it ready when you get home?" he suggested.

Paisley's brows rose. "Are you joking?"

"I don't want to make your life with me miserable."

She shook her head. "I'm just surprised you offered to cook. What about the other four nights?"

Lucas shrugged. "We'll order out or I'll take you wherever you want."

Her gaze narrowed and she pursed her lips. "Do you think all of this is going to make me give in to being your baby mama?"

Lucas couldn't help but laugh at her. "No, I didn't think things would be that simple."

Hell, he sounded ridiculous now, but seeing her so upset, well…damn it. He'd wanted to help. Was that absurd for her to believe?

"I don't have to be the enemy here," he defended.

Paisley stared at him for a moment before surprising him by wrapping her arms around him and burying her face in his neck.

"I don't know what you are, but right now I need you," she murmured before easing back slightly. "I don't have many people I can count on and I don't know what your angle is quite yet, but I have to trust you. For now, anyway."

He didn't like that niggle of guilt. He sure as hell didn't like that she doubted him and how much she could trust him. His revenge wasn't on her, but Sterling. Yes, he was using her to get to the old bastard, but he didn't want her hurt.

Lucas couldn't help but worry that no matter the outcome, a part of Paisley would be crushed. She wanted to have a father, especially since her mother was gone, but did she truly want one who was so deceptive and slimy?

"What do you say you get me that information on the bride and I'll call for takeout?" Lucas suggested.

Paisley tipped her head. "I can't believe you're not trying to get me out of my clothes."

Lucas laughed and started working on that top button. "I never said anything to the contrary. In fact, I say we have a naked picnic."

"At some point I really need to resist you," she grumbled.

Lucas moved down to the next button. "But not now."

"No." She took a deep breath, her breasts straining against the next button. "Not now."

He finished the trail of buttons and parted the material. When Lucas took a step back, he thought about forgoing dinner and the bride and just getting to his wife.

She stood before him in a nude lace bra and panty set and those heels, and she wasn't even trying to be sexy, she simply was. The woman was absolutely breathtaking after a bad day and a crying jag.

Would he ever get to the point he didn't want her?

"If you keep looking at me like that, we won't get dinner." She sauntered around him and headed toward the hallway. "And I do believe it's your night to cook."

Yeah. She was definitely going to be the death of him.

But what a way to go.

Ten

Paisley just finished a consultation with a bride renewing her vows when her cell rang. She glanced at the screen, surprised to see Lucas's name. He typically only texted or he would just pop in.

She swiped the screen and answered.

"Sterling is out on bail," Lucas declared.

The bomb he dropped had her knees weakening, her heart beating fast, her head spinning.

Paisley eased down into her desk chair and pulled in a deep breath. "When did he get out?"

"Apparently last night on several millions in bail," Lucas stated. "I wanted to tell you as soon as I found out."

She glanced to the antique clock on her desk, more for decoration than functionality. She calculated how much time she had left until her boutique closed, and how soon she could make it to Sterling's estate when she left.

"Don't even think about it," Lucas warned.

"You don't know what I'm thinking," she countered, gripping her phone tighter.

"Tart, I know you and you're trying to figure out how to go talk to him without me knowing."

She didn't care if Lucas knew or not. Right now all she thought about was time and how soon she could talk to the man who may very well be her father.

"Well, why wouldn't I want to go there?" she exclaimed. "He obviously knew my mother. Maybe she told him the truth all those years ago. He's the only one who could have all the answers."

Lucas exhaled loudly and Paisley could practically see him rubbing his head trying to maintain his patience. She'd hired him to find the truth, though she wasn't exactly paying.

Regardless, there was no reason she couldn't continue working her angles. Maybe Sterling didn't know anything, but she had to ask. Seeing him face-to-face would be the only way to tell if he was lying about his knowledge of her mother. This was too important to do over the phone and she didn't want to wait.

"Let me handle this," he finally told her. "I'm not trying to keep you out, but I do have a method and a plan. I promise, when the time comes to confront him, I will drive you there myself."

Paisley wanted to argue, she wanted to hang up, close her shop and head straight to Sterling Perry's house. But the other part of her knew Lucas was right. He did this for a living, plus she'd gone to him for his help, so going against it would only be counterproductive. She fully believed he had her best interests at heart. If he wanted to keep things from her, he never would've told her about Sterling's release.

Paisley just wished the process would speed up so she could know once and for all.

"I won't go," she conceded. "But I don't like this."

"Duly noted," he replied with a low chuckle. "I'm going to be late tonight, but I'm having your favorite Thai food delivered at seven. I figured that would give you enough time to get home, unwind, have a glass of wine or whatever."

Well, damn. Hard to be upset with the man when he was sticking to his plan of being in charge of dinner each night. Why did he have to do these little things that made her fall more and more for him?

"That wasn't necessary," she told him. "But I'm not about to turn down my favorite dinner."

"I didn't figure you would," he chuckled. "There's also a little surprise waiting at home for you."

At home.

The two words seemed to symbolize so much—like the possibility that they were creating a real life together and not some temporary arrangement that stemmed from blackmail.

"I love surprises," she told him. "But you don't have to do that."

"I know I don't," he stated. "Don't get your hopes up, though. The surprise is nothing major."

Maybe not to him, but the fact he'd thought of her

enough to even have a surprise said so much. Paisley's heart swelled at the idea that he wanted to give her something for no reason. But she couldn't let her mind travel to the place her heart already resided. Some part of her had to remain logical and firmly planted in reality. All of this was temporary. No matter how much she was falling for him, no matter how much she wished they could start something real, he only wanted her for a child and she needed him to find out the truth.

They weren't the same people they once were, so the love and trust they'd need to start a solid foundation just wasn't there yet.

Yet. As if he was going to fall madly in love with her and want a real future together.

"I need to run," he told her, interrupting her thoughts. "I might be late, so you don't need to wait up."

He disconnected the call, and Paisley set her cell down as she leaned back in her seat, processing the whole Sterling update. What would he say when she confronted him? Would he deny her or welcome her into the fold of the family?

Granted, that was if she ended up being his daughter. Paisley wanted so desperately to feel like she belonged somewhere. Oh, she'd never admit as much, because she was trying to be the independent woman she claimed. But right now, she was getting hit from all sides and, well, she was a bit needy. There was no room for pride when everything had been taken away.

Everyone had a vulnerable point in their life and she had to admit, she'd reached hers.

She wasn't going to stay down long, though. She

would climb back up out of this nightmare of losing her mother, not knowing her father, marrying a man who didn't love her and nearly losing her business. She'd ultimately find love and have a family like she always dreamed. Unfortunately, she just had to take the long way to get there.

With renewed hope that something in her favor would happen soon, Paisley went to work at her computer for the vow renewal bride. There was much to be done to keep other people's dreams fulfilled until she could get to her own.

With every corner he turned leading to another dead end, Lucas opted to head to the new TCC clubhouse. He'd been there for the grand party in the ballroom several weeks ago, but hadn't been since.

The renovations were nearly complete in the old historical Houston building, though there were definitely areas that weren't done. The ballroom, the café, several of the upstairs units, those were all finished. The outdoor area and several of the offices still had a way to go. But they shouldn't take too much longer.

Then the race would be on to see who the new president was. The Perry/Currin feud would never end at this rate. The decades-old rivalry kept carrying over from generation to generation, and there always seemed to be some new drama to bicker about.

They made the Capulets and the Montagues look like preschool playmates. Lucas almost wished Paisley wasn't related to anyone in that mess.

He figured coming to the clubhouse now that Sterling was out might give him some insight. Or at the very least, there would be gossip. Everything he could gather on Sterling could potentially be used. From what Lucas had heard, the man's own son hadn't bothered to help. Roarke was a crusading attorney and hadn't once offered assistance to Sterling.

That said quite a bit about Sterling's character. Though, in Roarke's defense, he hadn't been all that close to his father. The two clashed more often than not and had been known to have public arguments. But still, wouldn't a son come to the aid of his father in a situation this dire?

Just before Lucas had come to the clubhouse, he'd gotten a call from the hospital where Paisley was born. There was a night nurse who was still on the same unit, but she couldn't answer any questions. Privacy laws were the main reason, but she also just didn't remember.

He had to at least try, though he'd figured that angle would be another dead end.

There had to be some trace to Paisley's biological father, but Lucas had yet to find it. She deserved to know if that letter from her mother meant anything or if Lynette had just been guessing herself.

Maybe they could be bold enough to show Sterling the letter and demand a DNA test. Lucas wasn't sure Sterling would be so quick to cooperate, considering he had a mess in his life already without adding a long-lost child.

Not that Lucas would say this to Paisley, but her mother had been notably seen with many men over the years. She'd dated quite a bit. Being a barmaid back in the day, well, perhaps she'd taken more than one wealthy man home for the night.

Lucas sure as hell wasn't judging what anyone did in their free time. He was just trying to zero in on who Lynette associated herself with back then. Lucas already had another meeting set up with the bar owner. He figured going back in when the place wasn't slammed and noisy would be a better option, plus he'd wanted to give the guy some time to jog his memory. Now that Lucas had already questioned him, there was no doubt the old guy was thinking back.

The mind was just wired that way. Once the past was mentioned, people tended to dwell on it over the next several days, sometimes weeks, and other memories would come to them.

Lucas was banking on that happening. He wasn't letting up on this at all…no matter what the outcome.

He stepped up to the bar and ordered a beer on tap. A local brewery had worked a deal with the TCC clubhouse. Lucas was all for supporting local businesses… except for Sterling. Lucas hoped like hell that man didn't become the new president. Sterling was the last person who should be given more authority.

Lucas was already making mental notes about grabbing more boxes from Paisley's stash of her mother's things when a hand clamped down on his shoulder.

He glanced around to see Ethan Barringer, the CEO of Perry Construction. Sterling owned a multitude of companies through Perry Holdings, but Ethan was one of his main men.

"Haven't seen you around here," Ethan commented

as he settled on a stool next to Lucas. "Been keeping busy?"

Lucas nodded and accepted the frosty mug from the bartender. "Just now getting a chance to come back and see the place. It's really coming together."

Ethan nodded and curled his hands around his own beer. "This old building had some stumbling blocks, but we're definitely seeing the light at the end of the tunnel."

"Heard Sterling was out."

Ethan took a long pull of his drink, but Lucas kept his eyes on the guy. He liked Ethan well enough. It wasn't his fault his employer was a bastard.

"Yeah. House arrest," Ethan added. "He's determined to find out who set him up. I just heard a rumor that Roarke might actually be Ryder's son and not Sterling's. Sterling's just in a hell of a mess right now and I'm not sure when things will clear for him."

Lucas was glad he'd swallowed his drink before that little bombshell was dropped. What the hell kind of twists and turns did Sterling have in his life? His own son wasn't actually his son? And he may have an illegitimate daughter?

The man was a walking soap opera.

Lucas could hardly keep up with the chaos that seemed to always surround Sterling. Was this really a guy anyone would consider for president of the most elite club in Texas?

"That would certainly put a spin on things if that turned out to be true," Lucas muttered, taking another sip of his beer.

"Who knows what's going to happen," Ethan commented with a shake of his head. "I feel like the past few weeks have been all ups and downs and one surprise after another. For all of us, really."

Lucas shifted in his seat and nodded in agreement. Houston certainly had its share of drama lately and it seemed no one was left out.

"Is that a wedding band?" Ethan asked, gesturing toward Lucas's hand.

"Yeah. A little over a week ago, actually. I married Paisley Morgan."

A wide smile spread across Ethan's face. "Congrats, man. Let me buy your beer. Marriage is a wonderful thing when you find the right person. I couldn't imagine life without Aria Jensen."

Ethan and Aria had been friends turned lovers and they both played a huge roll in the Houston Club.

While he was thrilled for the happy couple, Lucas didn't really want to get into the whole marriage and love talk with Ethan...or with anyone, really. The arrangement he had with Paisley worked for them. They might not be in love, but they had a history, and they knew each other more than most married couples. They might be different people now, but they still had a bond that time and pain couldn't erase.

"You're a lucky man," Lucas stated, making sure to keep the topic on Ethan. "Not many people find their soul mate."

"I'd say we're both lucky," Ethan commented. "With all the chaos in this town, we need to cling to something good."

Lucas couldn't agree more. Only the "good" he

was clinging to was the promise that he'd seek justice against Sterling for all the crooked dealings and people he'd betrayed.

Paisley was in that mix, so in a sense he was seeking justice for her, too. He kept reminding himself of that so he didn't focus on the guilt he felt from using her to get to Sterling.

Lucas finished his beer, more than ready to get home to his wife. This new rumor could prove to be extremely useful in their journey, but Lucas still wasn't ready to confront Sterling. He wanted a better timeline and a way to put him and Lynette together before Paisley was born. Maybe the affairs coincided. Revenge affairs weren't uncommon.

Lucas couldn't imagine being married to one woman and wanting another. Loyalty meant everything to him.

Suddenly, Lucas was more eager to get home. He'd never had someone waiting for him before and he knew this was something he shouldn't get accustomed to… but that didn't stop him from enjoying what he had now.

Paisley kept saying this marriage was temporary, but he knew her and knew that was her defense mechanism. She was afraid, but what she didn't realize was that he was, too. Having her back in his life, back in his bed, terrified him. Because if she walked away again, he wasn't sure if he could rebuild his heart a second time.

Eleven

"What do you say we go away?"

Angela Perry slid her arms up around Ryder Currin's neck and threaded her fingers through his hair. She worried so much about the turmoil surrounding her family. But she and Ryder needed a chance to just be themselves without all the rest of the messy outside world getting in.

She was falling for him and she needed him to realize this was serious for her. Could they have a future together even though he was much older and his family and hers had been rivals for decades?

The rivalry didn't matter to her, though it mattered heavily to her father. Angela couldn't live her life to please her father.

Sterling had been released from prison last night

and Angela feared they'd go back into a verbal sparring match over her relationship with Ryder. She'd yet to visit him. While she fully believed in her father's innocence, she wanted him to understand that he couldn't control who she wanted to spend her time with.

"Just the two of us," she went on, loving how Ryder wrapped his arms around her waist and pulled her close. "Maybe fly to the mountains and get a cozy cabin. Or, if you prefer me in a skimpy suit, we could go to the beach."

Ryder pulled in a deep breath, and she knew from that second of hesitation that he would make an excuse or give a justifiable reason why they shouldn't go. She didn't want to hear all the reasons why this might be a bad idea. All she cared about was why they should escape and put their relationship above all else. But she didn't want to argue in the few stolen moments they had together.

"It's okay," she quickly continued. "I know there's so much going on and it's—"

"Not that I don't want to," he interjected. "I'd love nothing more than to get away with you for a few days and forget we have a whole host of issues."

"Then let's do it," she urged. "What's a few days? I swear, every issue will be waiting for us when we return, so we might as well ignore them for a bit."

Ryder reached up and smoothed her hair from her face. The wind kicked up and wrapped them in the evening summer air. What she wouldn't give to be somewhere else with him right this moment instead of in Houston where her father was out on bail and no doubt ready to fight, where there was an unidentified dead body that her father was framed in the murder of, and where the whole financial scheme seemed to touch everyone she knew.

When her father caused a mess, he caused a hell of a disaster. She honestly didn't believe he had killed someone—he wasn't vicious. He might be egotistical and greedy, but he wasn't a killer. Still, he had that black cloud looming over him, and she couldn't help but worry the drama would trickle down onto her.

The feud between her father and her lover...

Angela closed her eyes and rested her head in the crook of Ryder's neck. She inhaled the familiar scent she only associated with him and attempted to calm herself.

Would they ever just get peace? Could they ever truly be happy or would something, or someone, constantly be trying to pry them apart?

"I'll take you anywhere you want to go."

Angela jerked back, unable to stop the smile. "Seriously?"

Ryder covered her lips with his before easing away just enough to reply, "Yes. You deserve it. Hell, we deserve it. Pick the place and I'll have my jet ready."

Ryder Currin was a workaholic, but she also knew he'd do anything for her. She thought herself lucky that Ryder wanted to be with her, considering the feud, but that was just a testimony to how strong their bond was. Angela refused to let anyone come between them, including her powerful father. She and Ryder together were a dynamic couple and could forge through anything.

"Better yet," he amended, "I'll surprise you. Give me a few days to get things lined up and some work settled and I'll take you away."

Angela couldn't even explain the excitement that rushed through her. Finally, they were going to escape and just be a real couple with no problems. The idea of getting away with Ryder thrilled her and she couldn't wait to see where he decided to take her.

Her father had pointed out that Ryder was too old for her, but Angela didn't care about age. She cared about how a man treated her, how he put her first, and Ryder did just that. He was romantic and loving and selfless… exactly what Angela needed in her messy life right now. Not to mention what she wanted in her future.

But, now that her father was home, she couldn't guarantee he wouldn't double down his efforts to cause trouble and tear them apart. Even if he was under house arrest, Sterling Perry's arms reached far and wide. When he wanted something, people reacted swiftly and effectively.

Angela nuzzled back into Ryder and already started a mental countdown to their romantic getaway. She refused to let anyone or anything stand in their way of happiness.

The bastard was out on bail. How the hell could that have happened?

Oh, right. Money. Something I'd never have enough

of to simply pay off my sins and make people drop and obey my every command.

Sterling had to take the fall for murder. I wouldn't go down for something that I'd done only to protect myself.

Maybe Sterling hadn't done the actual crimes he was incarcerated for, but he'd sure as hell done plenty of others. He was a complete bastard and nearly everyone could agree to that.

I wouldn't get caught. I had a plan and nobody would get in my way. Not the police, not Sterling.

I was making my own way through life and it wouldn't be long before people took notice and respected me.

Paisley had just slid her satin gown over her head when she heard the chime from the elevator. She glanced to the clock and wondered what Lucas's version of late actually was. He'd told her she didn't have to wait up, but it was only eight o'clock.

She stepped into the living area just as the elevator door slid open. Lucas's eyes immediately met hers and she got that giddy, aroused feeling she always did when she saw him. Maybe that young girl who'd been in love with him was still inside there. She was hopeful something could come from this crazy arrangement.

But the woman who was married to him? Well, she had to be a bit more realistic. She enjoyed the sex and the living arrangement, but she also knew it would come to an end.

"Thanks for my surprise." Paisley gestured toward the coffee table with a giant bowl full of Sweetarts—hence the name he'd dubbed her years ago. "The Thai food was amazing and so was the candy. I also managed a glass of wine and a good book. It's been a great night."

He unbuttoned his sleeves and rolled them up his forearms, then undid the top two buttons of his shirt as he stalked toward her.

"So you're saying you didn't need me?" he joked with a naughty grin.

"I need you for other things," she told him, purposely raking her gaze down his lean body. "I thought you were going to be late," she added.

Lucas pulled the black Stetson off his head and ruffled a hand through his hair, leaving it messy, sexy.

"I went to the clubhouse hoping there would be some buzz about Sterling's release," he said. "Ethan Barringer was there and I found out something that could affect our plans."

Paisley reached for his arm and stared into his eyes. "What happened?"

"First of all, you know Sterling is out, but he's under house arrest. Clearly, he's not going anywhere, but that won't stop his cronies from coming to him."

"Okay. What else?"

Lucas's mouth twitched and she couldn't tell if he was amused or stunned. "There's a new rumor that Roarke isn't Sterling's son."

Paisley gasped. "What?"

"I don't know if it's true, but if it is, that would explain why Roarke wasn't at his father's side or working to free him."

"You think Roarke knows Sterling isn't his father?"

she asked, her mind trying to process what all this could mean.

Lucas trailed a fingertip up her arm and curled his hand over her shoulder. "I don't know anything yet, but I wanted to keep you informed. We need to figure out our next steps. I really need to find something that will put Sterling and your mom together before you were born. You and Roarke are about the same age, so maybe there's some backstory there that we're missing."

Paisley nodded in agreement, but she had no clue how to go about finding the truth about illicit affairs. Again, these were things only Sterling could reveal because everyone else—her mother and Sterling's wife—had passed on.

"Do you think Sterling cheated on his wife because she cheated on him first or vice versa?" she asked.

Good grief. Was nobody faithful? Were she and Roarke both love children spawned from lust and revenge?

"I think it's worth exploring," he told her as he slid his hand down her back and pulled her against him. "I planned on going back to the office and working more, but after I left the clubhouse, I just wanted to get home."

Paisley shouldn't let his charming words affect her so, but she couldn't help herself. Lucas was getting to her more and more each day. She wasn't even sure he was deliberately trying to use his charms to spin her farther into his web. He was just naturally appealing.

How could she not fall for the man he'd become? Successful, strong, protective…he was the entire package. And their past bond only pulled her in deeper.

"Well, I'm glad you're here," she admitted. "I wasn't looking forward to going to bed without you."

Those blue eyes raked down her body as he reached for the straps on her gown. "It's a bit too early for bed, isn't it?"

Paisley shivered as the satin slid over the swell of her breasts and grazed her sensitive nipples. She pulled in a deep breath and relished the instant arousal and the hunger in his eyes.

"I'm not tired," she told him. "Did you have something in mind?"

Lucas's lips twitched. "I have in mind to rip this gown off you, but I'm also enjoying your slow striptease."

"It's not a striptease if you're the one doing the stripping," she informed him.

Before he could say a word, Paisley stepped back. Keeping her eyes locked on his, she slid her thumbs into the fabric at her waist and very carefully, methodically, eased the material down. The gradual way it slid over her body only awakened her senses even more. She couldn't wait for him to get his hands on her.

They'd been intimate every single day since they'd married and the need to be with him continued to grow. Being physical was easy. The hard part was all the emotions that were going to hold her hostage in this marriage.

Paisley stepped out of the gown and stood before Lucas completely bare. Once again, he raked that hungry gaze over her and she couldn't begin to say who was actually in charge here. She may have him spellbound by being naked, but all he had to do was give her that heavy-lidded look or a crook of his finger and she turned into a puddle of desire.

"Do you ever wear anything under your clothes?" He took a step toward her. "Not that I'm complaining."

"Are you implying I'm not ladylike?" she retorted. "I love my teddies beneath my dresses. They're comfortable and keep all my rolls smoothed out, which works out well because I love candy, as you well know."

Lucas laughed as his hands circled her waist. "Your rolls are sexy, the teddies are sexy, though I realize you use them for other reasons than to drive me crazy."

"You feed me dinner every night, surprise me with my favorite candy, call my extra pounds sexy… Better watch it, Lucas. I might not want to end this marriage, after all."

Something shifted in his eyes, something she couldn't quite pinpoint. Did he truly want to stay married to her? What if she did remain in this marriage? What if they had children like they'd once dreamed? She wanted to know his thoughts on her, on the marriage. Could he see a real future here?

Just because their lives had changed drastically, did that mean their original goals when they'd been young had to change as well? Perhaps that twentysomething couple had been smarter than she gave them credit for. They'd had it all figured out…until she'd walked away.

"Maybe we can come to an agreement that works for both of us," he countered.

Before she could reply, Lucas leaned down and slid his lips over hers. The slow, easy way he made love to her mouth only added to the ever-growing anticipation and arousal. They'd typically been so hot for each other, their clothes were removed in a frantic flurry.

But right now, with his delicate touch, the way he seemed to explore her kiss as if for the first time, Paisley wondered what had overcome him. It was almost like he was getting to know her all over again.

In a move she didn't expect, Lucas removed his lips from hers and swept her up into his arms. She smiled as she looped her arms around his neck and threaded her fingers through his hair.

She thought he would take a few steps to the couch since they always just went with the closest surface, but he carried her down the hall toward their master suite.

The man was full of romance tonight and he was spoiling her for any type of a future without him.

Lucas set her down on her feet next to the side of the bed. With gentle hands, he forced her to lie down before he stepped back and started undressing. His gaze never wavered as he slowly exposed himself in all his magnificent, naked glory.

Lucas Ford was a stunning man. With his sculpted muscles in all the right places and that wicked grin, Paisley couldn't ignore the lust that slammed into her. But her attraction went beyond lust and she was well aware that love had entered back into the mix.

That was something she certainly would not be sharing with him. They had more pressing things to tend to than her emotions…which she doubted he reciprocated.

Lucas dropped to his knees before her and Paisley rose up on her elbows, eager to watch whatever he was about to do. He took one of her feet in hand and began massaging it. Not the body part she thought he was going for, but she certainly wasn't complaining.

His thumb slid over her arch and Paisley nearly groaned from the sensation. Nobody had ever given her a foot massage.

Oh, mercy, those hands were talented.

He thoroughly gave attention to one foot before releasing it and moving to the other. As she stared down at the top of his head, she couldn't believe this was the position she was in. Not literally this moment, but the marriage to Lucas, the fact that she wanted it to keep going and see if they could build on this shaky foundation.

Paisley's eyes nearly rolled back in her head when Lucas slid his hands up her calves and continued this amazing massage. Then he traveled up to the knee, where he placed a gentle kiss on the inside of each one.

He was driving her out of her ever loving mind and she wouldn't trade this for anything.

Lucas's eyes came up to meet hers as his hands grazed up to her thighs. There it was again—that naughty grin that had her squirming at his silent promise.

"You're going awfully slow tonight," she complained.

Those thumbs moved up again, closer to her core where she ached the most. He was enjoying this bout of torture.

"Have I ever left you hanging?" he asked, sliding one finger into her.

Paisley's hips bucked as she gripped handfuls of the

duvet. A moan was her only reply. Did he actually expect her to talk?

"That's what I thought," he murmured before he replaced that finger with his mouth.

Paisley thought she heard him mutter something about needing her, but she was too lost to comprehend anything but his touch.

Lucas grabbed hold of her hips as he pleasured her in a way he'd never done before. Paisley went between glancing down to him to tossing her head back and shutting her eyes to lock in the moment.

Her body responded in no time and she spiraled completely out of control. Lucas never let up as he continued meeting her every need and making love to her in a way that took their intimacy to a different level.

Finally, her body settled, the tremors ceased and Paisley was positive she'd never move again.

But Lucas crept up her body, placing kisses on her abdomen and massaging her breasts.

"Sorry about that," he muttered between kisses. "I was trying to give you a body massage and got sidetracked."

Paisley dropped onto her back and flung an arm over her eyes. "I've never had a massage quite like that."

He eventually came all the way up and pressed her deeper into the mattress with his weight. His arms rested on either side of her head as he smiled down at her.

"I'll be the only one giving you massages," he told her. "This body is all for me."

Paisley thrust her fingers through his coarse hair and

shifted her body to turn them over. Lucas went onto his back, and she straddled him. Her hair curtained them both as she looked down onto his surprised face.

"I think it's my turn to massage something," she warned. "Plus, I need to show you my thanks for the dinner, the candy and for working so hard on my case."

Lucas curled his fingers into her backside and urged her exactly where she wanted to be. The second she sank down onto him, every needy, achy emotion came rushing back.

"Do your thing, Tart." He smiled as he moved her hips with his. "I do love to be rewarded."

Paisley proceeded to show him just how grateful she was…and she tried to tell herself that falling for him again was a huge mistake.

Unfortunately, it was too late.

Twelve

"And if you want to remove the veil from the headpiece for the reception, that's always an option."

Paisley assisted the bride and showed her the transformation, which earned a gasp from the bride's mother and best friend who sat next to the stage and curved mirrors.

"You have to get it," the beaming friend said with a dramatic clap of her hands. "You look like royalty."

It was true. Paisley loved each of her customers and reveled in watching their dream wedding unfold before her eyes. Part of Paisley should be bitter for having been robbed of her special day, but that was all on her. She could've said no. She could've figured out another way.

But part of her still wanted Lucas after all these years. She'd never wanted to end things with him in the first place. If his father hadn't intervened and caught a naive young Paisley off guard, there was no doubt in her mind they'd be married…for the right reasons.

Perhaps even by this time they would have little baby Fords running around, probably even in school.

Even though they'd been separated, she had to admit being married to him was working out much better than she ever would've thought. She never felt used or like she was a burden to him. In fact, she'd swear that he had feelings for her, but she just couldn't bring that up.

Not when the case was hovering over them and he had made it quite clear he wanted her to have his child.

She'd first thought that idea was preposterous, but now…if she could clear out all the mess surrounding them and they could start with a solid foundation, Paisley would jump at the chance to start a family with Lucas.

"I want the veil and the dress," the bride gushed, pulling Paisley back into the moment. "They're so perfect for the venue and my style. Now, moving onto accessories and shoes."

Paisley smiled at the bride's reflection in the wall of mirrors. "I can pull some of my favorites and then we can go from there. What size shoe?"

"Eight."

While Paisley went to the accessory room, she heard the bell on the door chime. She poked her head out and was surprised to see her husband.

Her stomach did a flip and she hated that he looked way better than any man had a right to. It was just last night they'd made love and cuddled. That hadn't happened since they'd married. They'd only had fast, frantic sex and gone their separate ways. But last night was different. Last night had thrust her back to a time when nothing else had existed but the two of them. When she'd thought for sure she would spend her life with Lucas Ford.

As much as she wanted to believe that could be a possibility, she had to guard her heart until this ordeal was settled and she knew the truth about her father. She really didn't want to think of a future family when she didn't have her past family figured out.

As soon as Lucas spotted her, he crossed the space and kissed her cheek, then laid a quick, toe-curling kiss on her lips.

"What are you doing here?" she asked, trying to regain her mental balance.

"You're closing soon, so I thought I'd take you to dinner."

She glanced over her shoulder and spotted the party of three ladies all smiling and staring in her direction. No doubt they caught sight of the kisses.

"I might be a bit longer," she murmured. "I need to help this bride finalize her look."

Lucas shrugged and glanced around the shop. "No problem. I can just have a seat and wait. Don't rush."

Not that she wasn't thrilled he was taking her out, but having him hang around while she worked was a bit unnerving. Still, she knew it would be a vain attempt to get him to leave or wait somewhere else, so she didn't argue the point.

Paisley grabbed several earrings, bracelet and necklace options and took them back out to the bride.

"Is that your husband?" the mother of the bride asked.

Paisley nodded as she laid out the black velvet display board for everyone to see. She had her favorites, but she never said which until the bride made her opinion known.

"You are one lucky woman," the lady replied.

Paisley merely smiled. "Thank you."

"Newlyweds?" she guessed.

"We've been married two weeks."

The bride gasped. "Oh, congratulations! I already noticed your killer rings. They're stunning. I bet you had a gorgeous wedding, too."

Paisley resisted the urge to laugh, but merely nodded and smiled. "It was quite memorable."

After about thirty minutes of debating, Paisley finally got the bride all settled with her dress, veil, shoes and accessories. Once they were gone, Paisley turned the sign and flicked the lock on the door.

"You are remarkable."

She turned and tipped her head. "Excuse me?"

Lucas should look ridiculous all relaxed on the white chaise, but he looked…perfect. Damn it. The man always looked perfect. She likely looked haggard since he'd kept her up most of the night and she'd logged in a full ten hours at the shop.

"With your customer," he added. "She was clearly nervous and not taking advice from her mother and you somehow found a middle ground and made them both happy."

Paisley smoothed her hand down her red sheath dress and headed for the dressing room to start gathering up the gown rejects.

"That's what most of my job consists of, believe it or not. Moms always see their daughters as little girls playing dress up, so they have their own idea of what the gown should be. But the bride has been dreaming of this moment for her entire life and she has her own idea."

Paisley smoothed the heavy drapes aside and entered the oversize dressing area. There were only three gowns that needed to be put back. These were all the mother's top picks, unfortunately.

"Did you have dreams with your mother?" he asked, following her inside.

The slam of emotions hit her hard, and Paisley's hands stilled on the zipper. She drew in a deep breath and swallowed the lump in her throat.

"I've always had a dream about my wedding," she replied, going back to the task and not turning to face him. "My mother would've agreed to anything I wanted. She only wanted to see me happy."

If her mother could only see her now.

"She'd be proud of you," he told her. "She'd admire you for what you're doing to find the truth."

"If she'd told me the truth years ago, I wouldn't be in this position."

She realized how her words sounded the second they came out. Paisley spun around. "I didn't mean that."

Lucas shrugged. "You did, but it's okay."

"Fine, I did." No need in lying. "But I'm still grateful for all you've done so far. I know you'll get to the truth."

"I appreciate the faith." Lucas stepped in and glanced at the gowns. "Are these all worth thirty-thousand as well?"

Paisley groaned. "No. These are all under ten."

"Still sounds absurd for a dress," he muttered.

She turned back around and zipped the final dress in the protective bag. "Spoken like a true man."

A man who could buy every single dress in her shop and still not feel a dent in his bank account.

"I like that one," he said, pointing to the strapless fitted gown with intricate beading around the waist.

Paisley ran her hand over the bag. "That was my favorite out of the ones she tried on, but I can't tell my customers that. I can only guide them."

"Maybe you should've worn this."

Paisley glared at him. "Are you always going to bring up my wedding attire?"

He chuckled and took a step closer. "Not always. But when we renew our vows, you can get this one."

Paisley nearly choked on her breath. "Renew our vows? Are you insane?"

Lucas shoved his hands in his pockets as one corner of his mouth quirked up in a naughty grin. "Is our one-year anniversary too soon?"

"We're not renewing our vows. Ever."

Would they even be married in a year? She honestly didn't know if her sanity could hold out that long…or her heart. Yes, she was falling for him, but that didn't mean he felt the same. As much as she wanted this to turn to something real, she couldn't stay married if their union was loveless.

She still had some traditional values, even if she went about things in a nontraditional way.

"You don't want to have a chance to wear the gown of your dreams?" he asked, inching closer.

"Who says I won't have that chance?" she countered. "If this marriage ends, I want to find love."

Something akin to pain flashed in his eyes, but was just as quickly replaced by desire.

"You keep saying there's an expiration." Lucas reached up and tucked her hair behind her ears, trailing his fingers along her jawline. "I'm starting to think you don't like me around."

On the contrary, she liked having him around too much. And each day that passed only reminded her of what they could've had, what they could've been, had his father not intervened.

But she had nobody else to blame but herself. She should've stood her ground, fought for the life she and Lucas had dreamed of.

Perhaps this was her penance, being in a loveless marriage based on blackmail and revenge. She had to assume that was part of his angle. Revenge on her for leaving him the way she did.

Paisley reached up and eased his hands away from her face.

"Last night changed things," she told him. "I'm not sure where you stand, but you need to know that when you do things for me, and I'm not talking sex, it makes me remember how we were. It makes me remember the dreams we shared and how we never thought anything could come between us."

Lucas remained silent and she had no clue what he was thinking, so she used this momentum bursting through her to continue her honesty.

"When I left you that note before," she started, then swallowed as emotions clogged her throat. "Um…"

Lucas shoved his hands back in his pockets and stepped back. "There's no need to revisit the past."

"Our past has been the third party in this marriage and I think we do need to revisit it," she insisted, because now that she'd started, now that they'd grown closer, she needed him to know. "There's a resentment and anger in you that wasn't there before. I know all of that is my fault. I know I should've handled things differently. But I need you to understand—"

"That you handed me a damn note?" he yelled. "A note, Paisley."

He never called her by her real name unless he was upset. Bringing up their past upset her as well, but until they resurrected that time and talked about it, she didn't know how she could keep going. It was getting too difficult—the emotions, the memories. Her mind screamed at her to keep her distance, to not let this arrangement get any more complicated or emotional. But her heart, well, it had a mind of its own and had never fully closed back up from the gaping hole Lucas had left.

The void had been with her for years and now that she had him back, he filled that spot so perfectly. She'd always known there was nobody else, but how did she manage to hang on to what they had now? There was so much damage, so many variables out of her control.

She'd hurt him by leaving that note. But he had to understand, she'd ripped her own heart out as well.

"I couldn't do it face-to-face," she cried.

When he only stood there staring at her, Paisley grabbed the last gown and marched from the dressing room. With shaky hands, she hung it back on the rack and attempted to regain her composure.

"I never took you for a coward."

Lucas's low accusation had Paisley gasping and spinning to face him. "Maybe I was a coward, but maybe I was trying to put your needs ahead of my own. I know you don't want to believe that, but I could never forgive myself if I was the reason you didn't go after your dreams."

That bright blue gaze held her. "Did you ever think maybe you were my dream? Did you stop to think that had you told me what happened, I would've found a way to make things work between us? Who says I had to give up anything?"

Maybe bringing up all of this was a mistake. Even after all these years, the hurt wrapped all around her heart, squeezing out every single emotion she'd felt back then.

Paisley had thought discussing old feelings and tending those wounds would help for their present and their future, but clearly she'd made a mistake.

"You know what? Forget it." She held up her hands, admitting defeat because she simply couldn't do this. "I just wanted you to know where I came from. I thought since we were…well, married, that maybe I should try to get you to understand. I can't blame it all on your father for confronting me. I know I made the choice to break things off. But you have to know I did it because I loved you and I was scared."

She started walking by him, but he reached for her arm. Paisley came to a halt, but didn't turn to look at him.

"I didn't come here to fight," he murmured. "I really came to take you out to a nice dinner."

A piece of her heart melted. Maybe they couldn't rehash the past. Maybe at this point, all they could do was focus on who they were now and leave that young couple alone.

What if Lucas wasn't working another angle? What if his sole purpose was to get her to give him a child? Could that be all? Granted that was a huge deal, but he could've turned her away in his office and found another woman to start a family with. A successful, wealthy, sexy man like him would certainly have his choice.

"Where are we going?" she asked, trying to salvage their evening and end an argument.

Lucas smiled and her heart fluttered. "I have a surprise for you."

Thirteen

"I think these turned out rather great."

Lucas held up the colorful strip of photos and admired them. Well, they were a little off center, but what else did he expect from a shopping mall photo booth?

"Let me see." Paisley laughed as she reached for them. She took one look and laughed even harder. "Half of my face is missing from this one and the bottom picture looks like our mug shots."

He shifted to look over her shoulder. Honestly, he didn't care what they looked like. The intensity of their discussion at the bridal shop had made him change his mind on where they were going. He'd had reservations at his favorite steak house, but they both needed to unwind and do something utterly silly.

So they'd come to the mall.

"We didn't have wedding photos done, so these will have to do."

Paisley snorted. "Why not? Our wedding was tacky anyway, might as well have a photo booth as our photographer."

"These will look great on my desk," he told her, taking the photos back. He slid them into his shirt pocket and grabbed her hand. "Let's go grab something to eat."

"Wait," she said. "You're putting those on your desk?"

With a shrug, he led her toward the food court. "Why wouldn't I? Most people have a photo of their spouse at their office."

"We're not most couples and I don't know anyone who uses a photo booth to get a picture of his loved one."

That stopped him. Lucas kept his hold on her hand, but turned to face her. Love couldn't enter this marriage. At least not from her. She couldn't profess any such thing because, while he might not believe in love, it was clear she did and he didn't want her to be under any illusion that this would develop into what they once had.

Paisley's eyes widened as if she just realized the words she'd uttered. With a shaky smile, she shook her head and kept going.

"You know what I mean," she said in a rush. "I don't actually think you love me, but I'm at least hoping you don't hate me."

Was that what she thought? That he hated her? Despite the hurt he'd felt years ago, even at his darkest time after she'd left, he could never hate her.

Lucas stared at her another minute before turning to face her fully and taking her other hand. People milled about them in the busy area, but he didn't care. This was so much more important.

"I've never hated you," he corrected. "I wanted to, but I never did. Hate would've been easier to deal with."

Her eyes searched him, as if she wanted to hear more, but he had no more to give. That was all he could divulge about his feelings and still remain in control. The slithering guilt about using her to get to Sterling gnawed at his conscience.

"Well, that's something," she finally murmured. She tipped her chin and smiled. "So, are we really eating here?"

Lucas pushed aside everything outside this moment and let out a fake gasp. "You mean you don't want a salty pretzel with cheese dip or questionable pizza?"

"Hey, I'm always up for junk food. I just didn't think someone like you would eat in a place where you technically serve yourself."

Lucas squeezed her hand and headed toward the pretzel stand. "Did you just call me a snob?"

She fell in step with him and gave him a nudge with her shoulder. "More like…choosy."

Lucas stepped into the line and sighed. "You know, we may have grown up in a different type of household, but that doesn't mean I think I'm better than anyone and I sure as hell know good food."

Paisley laughed. "I wouldn't call a pretzel that's been sitting in a warmer cube good food."

Lucas pointed to the surrounding concessions. "We'll grab something from each one and then we'll judge whose food is the best."

"Where were you really taking me tonight?" she asked as they moved up in the line. "Because I'm sure you had fancy reservations that required you to wear a jacket and tie."

Which was why he'd shed them in the car before they'd arrived. He'd wanted her relaxed, he'd wanted to see her smile, and he'd figured the mall was probably as far removed as possible from what he had planned at an upscale restaurant.

"Plans change," he replied. "I wanted something simple, maybe like we used to have. There's so much going on. We both needed a break."

The smile she offered was like a punch to his gut, and Lucas wondered if he should've kept the stuffy old reservations. But thankfully the line moved and broke the moment.

They'd only been married a short time, but he realized then that Paisley wasn't that different from the young girl he'd once known.

She might own the poshest bridal boutique in the area, but she was a humble woman with big worries. He didn't want to feel guilty for his actions and he didn't want to get caught up in her again because all of this was so shaky. He had no clue how this was all going to end. At this point, he had to take this marriage like he did all of his cases. One day at a time.

"Maybe we could go to the movies after dinner?" she asked, her smile wide and hopeful.

Yeah, there went that punch to the gut again. Nobody ever affected him like Paisley…and he knew nobody ever would.

"I'm choosing the movie," he replied with a flirty wink. "Just try to keep your hands to yourself if we sit in the back row."

Paisley laughed. "My husband is the handsy one."

"Very true," he agreed. "So you better keep those moans to a minimum."

Paisley set the dish on the table and stood back to survey her work. Lucas had told her he'd be working late on another case he had to wrap up and his cooking duties weren't going to happen tonight. As soon as she'd closed up the boutique, she pulled up her cooking app and headed to the store.

She'd seriously considered re-creating the junk from the mall a few nights ago just as a joke, but opted to make a nice meal instead. He'd been working so hard on not just her case, but those of his other clients. She'd caught him sneaking out of bed in the middle of the night and poring over the rest of the boxes she'd brought from her home. The boxes were the last of her mother's belongings and they'd just been too painful for Paisley to search through.

At first, she'd started going through them, looking for any clue that would lead her toward Sterling, but nothing had stood out and emotions had always consumed her.

Warped as it might sound, Lucas had been amazing during this process and she wanted to show him how much she appreciated his hard work.

So here she stood two hours after getting home from the store, praying she'd managed a meal that was edible. She wanted to impress him, she wanted him to see her as something other than a painful past or a way to grow his lineage.

Damn, that sounded so absurd even in her own thoughts, but it was true. Part of her wanted him to start to feel more for her...because if she was having all of these feelings emerge, she certainly didn't want to be alone.

Yes, they'd been in love in the past, but that was where all of those emotions remained. Everything she felt now stemmed from the present. Being with him again only showed her that maybe he truly was the one for her. Life and obstacles had pulled them apart, but maybe they were meant to be together. Maybe they needed this growth, these trials to realize just how special they were.

Or maybe she was a complete and utter fool and a hopeless romantic. Lucas didn't believe in love. He'd basically put up an invisible barrier around his heart... not that she could blame him.

The bell sounded from the elevator and the nerves in her belly quickened. So silly. She shouldn't be worried about what he thought; she should be more concerned about him finding the truth about her father. That was the sole reason that led her to his office only a few short weeks ago.

Instead, she glanced to the living room where she'd de-Paisleyed the throw pillows and tried to incorporate more of his boringness.

Wasn't marriage all about balance?

The elevator slid open, and Lucas stepped out. The moment the door closed behind him, he pulled off his black Stetson and hung it on the peg near the door.

Paisley waited until he glanced up and she caught his attention. His eyes scanned the table behind her before he drew his brows in and crossed the penthouse.

"No naked chef tonight?" he asked.

"That was a onetime thing," she admitted. "I'd hate for you to think that was the norm."

"Such a shame." He moved right into her, utterly invading her space and wrapping his arms around her waist. "You didn't have to cook, but I'm glad you did. I skipped lunch and my last client wanted me to head for drinks after we wrapped up, but I bowed out. I'm beat."

He'd never really discussed his work with her, except that little bit that involved her mother. Maybe he did want to pull her a little more into his world.

"Well, I didn't test it first," she warned, placing her hands on his shoulders. "But I know you like steak, so I went from there."

He gave her a quick kiss on the lips before stepping around her and letting out a low whistle.

"I'm impressed."

"I'd hold back praise until you actually taste it."

Lucas glanced over his shoulder to her. "You went to a good bit of trouble for this meal."

Paisley wasn't great at dealing with compliments of the domestic goddess variety, so she skirted around him and grabbed the bottle of wine from the ice bucket.

"Don't get too excited," she told him as she poured him a glass of Chianti. "I had to look everything up. It's not like I was raised with a mom who showed me how to make homemade mashed potatoes with gravy or roll out fresh biscuits."

After she served herself some wine, she placed the bottle back in the bucket and risked glancing to Lucas. He remained in place, his eyes locked on her.

"Your mother didn't have to make homemade anything," he stated. "She had other areas she excelled at, I'm sure."

Paisley attempted a smile and started filling the plates. "I've never thought about it before," she told him. "I mean, she did work her butt off to support us. I didn't know any different than having her gone most of the time or there were days I had to go to work with her when she couldn't afford a sitter. By the time I was ten, she just started leaving me alone and would call on her breaks to check in."

Ten years old. Paisley couldn't imagine leaving a ten-year-old home alone, but then again, she wasn't a single parent with limited options. Never once did she doubt her mother's love. The woman just made life choices that made things more difficult at times.

"She never dated," Paisley went on. "Or if she did, I never met the men. It always seemed to just be the two of us. I guess that's why this is so hard. I had no clue she knew who my father was and purposely kept it from me."

Lucas took a seat next to her instead of across from her. Once she sat down, he took her hand and stared into her eyes.

"Maybe she didn't know," he defended. "That's still to be determined and I'm sure we'll find out more once we get proof on Sterling."

Paisley sighed. "Is that even possible at this point? I doubt he would even know unless my mother flat out told him, and if she did tell him, why didn't he claim me or ever reach out?"

Paisley had so many questions and there were only two people who could answer them: her mother, who was no longer living, and her real father, if he ever knew anything to begin with.

"It's hopeless, isn't it?" she asked.

"I've never given up on a client and I sure as hell am not about to start with my wife."

His conviction had her blossom of hope growing. She truly believed him. She just didn't know how he'd pull this off.

"I just want to go see him," she muttered.

Lucas's fork clattered to his plate a second before he reached for her hand and squeezed. "Patience. That's the one thing you have to have in my business. It's not easy, and can be downright maddening at times. But I promise, we will confront him. Together."

Together. Perhaps he did want them to be a team and maybe in more ways than just this case. Having dinner together every night seemed so familial and they'd settled right into a nice pattern.

Paisley couldn't help but feel that maybe this could work. She so badly wanted to tell him her true feelings, but she needed to be patient. Isn't that what he'd just told her?

Every part of her life now required the right timing— confronting Sterling and telling Lucas she'd fallen in love with him again.

Fourteen

Lucas had never been the best at sleeping all night. Clients and cases would wake him, and his mind never fully seemed to shut down.

Which was why he sat on the floor of his living room with another open box of Lynette's things. She wasn't the most organized person. He'd uncovered some planners that she seemed to have good intentions of completing. She'd start out the year with detailed accounts of events, only to taper off about May or June.

Nothing in any of those pointed toward any man, let alone Sterling. It truly did look like all she did was work and spend time with Paisley.

He pulled out a planner dated for the year Paisley would've been four. Lucas still flipped through each page, even knowing the end of the year would be blank, as per the usual, and found a set of pockets in the back.

Shifting in his seated position, Lucas turned toward the rustic coffee table and searched the pockets. A coupon fell out, overlooked bills and an envelope with a name on it. Jeb Smith. Lucas pulled out the folded piece of paper.

Jeb,
You are behind on your child support AGAIN! Why do I have to always remind you of this? It's bad enough you're her father and have dismissed her, but you could at least send what you owe so I can raise her without worrying about two or three jobs.

Don't think I won't contact an attorney if you keep ignoring me. You're six months behind now. Pay up!

Lucas read the letter through a second and third time. What the hell? Who was Jeb Smith? Why did Lynette never mail this? Clearly she was angry and obviously needed the money.

Lucas glanced over his shoulder toward the bedroom where Paisley slept. If this Jeb turned out to be her father, that would destroy any thoughts of Sterling.

So many mixed emotions swirled around inside him at this revelation. If Sterling was out of the picture, that meant Lucas wouldn't get his revenge through Paisley. But more importantly, she wouldn't have the Perry name. That sounded so selfish even to him, but if Paisley were a Perry, she would've had sisters and possibly a brother, if Roarke was actually Sterling's son.

If this letter, pointing toward Jeb Smith, proved to be truthful, Lucas had a sinking feeing he'd just found Paisley's biological father.

He quickly put everything back in the planner, keeping the letter and envelope to himself. After placing everything back in the box, Lucas came to his feet and stretched until his back popped. He really should get to bed, but this development had him more wired than ever to uncover the truth for Paisley.

Somewhere along the way this case shifted from pure revenge to wanting to do this for the woman he still cared about. Oh, he still wanted Sterling to pay for every crime he'd committed, but now he wanted Paisley to find that family she deserved.

What she didn't deserve was being kept in the dark, but that was exactly what he needed to do until he found Mr. Smith and talked to him.

Lucas went to the kitchen and made a cup of coffee. This was going to be a long night and an even longer day if he uncovered the location of this new player in the game.

He took the coffee to his office and closed the door. In no time he had his laptop up and was on the hunt. It didn't take long for him to find several Jeb Smiths in Texas, considering the first and last name were quite popular.

He was successful at his job for a reason and by six in the morning, after two more cups of coffee and before Paisley woke, Lucas had an address and he was just thankful Jeb was only in the next town over and alive and well.

He'd go pay him a visit, take this letter and Lynette's picture, and hopefully get the answers Paisley deserved.

And once Lucas had all the facts, he'd present them to her. Then they could decide what to do about this marriage. A sinking pit in his stomach had him wondering if she'd follow through with ending things or if she'd stay. While Lucas tried to remain emotionally distant, he couldn't deny he'd started developing more feelings for her than he would've liked.

He hadn't been able to avoid that heart tug years ago and now was no different. Having her in his bed every night, knowing how determined she was to remain on her feet and find the truth, seeing her passion for her work all made him realize the girl he'd wanted all those years ago had grown into the woman he didn't want to live without.

If she walked out again, Lucas wasn't sure he could handle the void again. All the more reason to never tell her how he truly felt.

Paisley turned side to side in the mirror and smoothed down her red cocktail dress. Lucas had planned on coming to Melinda's party, but he'd texted a few hours ago and said he was following a lead and couldn't get back in time. He told her to go enjoy herself and he'd meet her back at home.

When she'd asked if the lead was on her case, he never replied.

Paisley didn't want to go to the party. She wanted

to wait and see what was going on because his silence spoke volumes. He'd been so up-front with her so far, she had to believe everything he was doing was in her best interest.

She hoped the truth revealed itself soon. She was on the brink of telling him she loved him. There was only so long she could hold in her emotions and he deserved to know where she stood.

Plus, he loved the color red.

Paisley had chosen this slinky dress with her husband in mind. She'd imagined him slipping her out of this as soon as they made it back to the penthouse, or maybe he'd try in the elevator on the way up. Or maybe he'd give her another one of those toe-curling massages.

With one last glance to her hair and a swipe of pale shimmer gloss to her lips, Paisley grabbed her gold clutch and headed to the elevator. Lucas had ordered his driver to take Paisley to the party even though she insisted she could drive herself.

Arguing with that man was sometimes just a losing battle. But when he was being adorably sweet, she couldn't quite fault him.

The drive to Melinda's home didn't take long, but Paisley found herself looking at her phone, waiting for any update or clue as to what he'd found.

Paisley thanked the driver as he assisted her from the car, and he informed her he'd be out here waiting whenever she was ready to go. No doubt by her husband's orders.

This was a whole new lifestyle for her—living in a penthouse that was three times the size of her little town house, having a driver at her disposal, being made love to the way Lucas made love to her and having someone put her needs first.

There was no way Paisley could leave. She wanted to build a life with him; she wanted to give him that family he wanted. She had so much in her to give because when she'd left him all those years ago, she'd never given her heart to another man. There had been no one that even came close to Lucas.

Yes, he was harder now, more cautious, but that all stemmed from having been hurt. She'd made a mistake and she knew building anything new would take time… time she was more than willing to give because she'd already created their little family in her mind.

After this party, Paisley would tell him she loved him. She would tell him she wanted to move forward with a real marriage, a real family. He may not be ready to admit love yet, and that was fine. But she wasn't going anywhere, and he could take his time in coming to grips with his emotions.

With a renewed hope for her future, Paisley headed toward the limestone condo high-rise. The doorman greeted her, and the attendant at the elevator happily sent her on up to the twenty-fourth floor. Melinda and her sister Angela both lived in this stunning building, but on different floors. Paisley had to assume Angela would be at the party, too, and perhaps their other sister, Esme.

Nerves of anticipation curled low in her belly. These women could potentially be her half sisters. If Lucas came back with information confirming Sterling was her father, Paisley would have names to put with her new family.

What would it be like to have sisters?

The elevator opened on Melinda's floor and Paisley made her way to the condo unit. She'd barely knocked when the door swung wide and the hostess herself beamed a wide smile.

"You made it," Melinda exclaimed. "Come on in. Where's your husband?"

Trying to see if you and I share a father.

"He's away on business," Paisley replied.

She stepped into the suite and glanced around at the people mingling as trays of delicate finger foods passed by in the deft hands of uniformed waitstaff.

"Well, I'm glad you could make it anyway," Melinda stated. "Come out to the balcony. Esme and Angela are out there and I know they'd love to see you."

Paisley slid her clutch beneath her arm and followed Melinda out to the balcony, which overlooked Houston. The lights from the city were the perfect picturesque backdrop for the cocktail party.

"Paisley," Esme squealed. "It's so great to see you again."

The beautiful blonde stepped forward and gave a half hug so as not to spill her champagne glass.

"Great to see you," Paisley replied, smiling.

"Excuse me," Melinda said. "I'm going to grab you a drink."

Melinda stepped inside and plucked a fluted glass from a server's tray and returned, handing it to Paisley.

"I'm so glad you could come," Angela chimed in, sipping her own glass. "And that red dress is killer!"

"It's a shame Lucas isn't here with you," Melinda joked. "But maybe it's a good thing. No man could resist that."

"Lucas?" Esme asked, her brows drawn in. "Lucas Ford?"

Paisley smiled and gripped the stem of her glass. "Yes."

"Her new husband," Melinda added.

Angela's eyes darted to Paisley's hand, then back up. "It's a good thing he didn't come," she murmured.

"Excuse me?" Paisley asked.

"Getting him in a room full of Perrys is probably not the best idea," Esme added. "He has had a thing for our dad for years."

Paisley stared at the women, stunned by what she heard, but trying to process everything. Lucas hated Sterling that much? A hatred that spanned years and he'd failed to say one word to her when she first approached him?

No, that couldn't be right. He wouldn't hide something like that from her.

"I forgot about that," Melinda said, clearly surprised. "I mean, I knew Lucas hated Dad, but I didn't put it all together when you said you guys had married. I was just so happy for you. He still would've been welcome here."

"Of course," Angela added. "Lucas is a nice guy and his reputation is impeccable. But I'm not sure he would've liked it very much or felt comfortable here."

Paisley remained silent, confused, hurt, wondering if this was true. She wanted to believe him, she'd put so much faith in him. Lucas hadn't said a word when she'd told him whose party she was attending. Not. One. Word.

Surely this was all wrong information or gossip.

"You didn't know this, did you?" Melinda asked, sympathy lacing her tone.

Paisley took a sip of her drink, mostly to have something to do and to help push down that lump of emotions and doubt that clogged her throat.

"No, I wasn't aware," she admitted, suddenly feeling nauseated. "We were apart for years, so we both have things in our past that haven't come out yet."

Like the fact she'd never stopped loving him and he opted to deceive. Oh, she prayed that wasn't the truth, but the niggling in the back of her mind said she had to be realistic.

"Apparently our dad did something to Lucas's father years ago," Angela added. "I don't know all the details, but I do know Lucas has made it clear he's not a friend of the Perrys."

The women continued to discuss, reminding each other of what their father had indeed done to Lucas's. Something about a business deal gone wrong, lies, betrayal…all of that sounded like Sterling, and Paisley wasn't doubting all of that had happened.

What she was doubting, however, was her husband's devotion to her. If all this was true, was Lucas using her as a stepping-stone to get closer to Sterling and serve justice for his father's wrongdoings?

The idea made her tremble—out of fear, anger, the unknown.

Paisley's cell vibrated in her clutch beneath her arm. She'd been waiting for Lucas to get back to her. Could that be him now? Had he found the truth he'd been looking for?

"Paisley, I drove by your shop earlier and that is a gorgeous strapless gown in the window," Melinda stated, obviously trying to turn the conversation around. "If I marry, I want that one."

Paisley attempted a smile. "I will be happy to set you up. You would make a stunning bride."

"I just want to come in and try everything on," Esme said with a laugh. "Your shop is so elegant and every wedding you've done that I've been to has been like a fairy tale."

"I love my job and I hope every bride feels special when she's there."

Paisley did not want to stand around and make small talk, not even when the chatter involved her beloved boutique. She wanted to make haste and get back home. She wanted to know if Lucas had deceived her purposefully. If he'd married her only as a way to seek the ultimate revenge.

But if she left now, the ladies would know why and she really didn't want anyone to have an insight into her sham of a marriage.

As much as this bombshell hurt, she wanted to hash it out in private with Lucas and at least give him a chance to defend himself. It would be so easy to rush into judgment and lay into him about how much it hurt that he hadn't told her about his hatred for Sterling.

But she wanted to hear his side because she prayed he hadn't married her as some warped way to get revenge on Sterling for doing his father wrong...and for her leaving him years ago.

Fifteen

After about an hour, Paisley couldn't stand any more small talk. She checked her phone, seeing a message from Lucas, and feigned a need to get home.

The ladies assumed she was just in a hurry to get home to her husband, but her reasons for rushing home were far removed from what they were winking and hinting at.

Paisley took the elevator and rushed out the front door. She didn't have to say a word to the driver. He had been standing next to the car and immediately opened the back door for her so she could slide in.

She settled back against the seat and glanced at Lucas's text again. He'd simply said he was home and he'd wait up for her, but hoped she was having fun. There was no mention of his findings, nothing that hinted as to what he'd been doing.

Paisley tried to relax her breathing, to calm herself so she didn't just go in and explode all over him. She truly did want to give him a chance to defend himself.

The idea that she was a pawn in his grand scheme to get to Sterling sickened her. After all they'd been through in the past, all they'd been through just in the past few weeks, she didn't want to believe the worst.

The car pulled in front of Lucas's condo building, and Paisley didn't wait on the driver. The car had barely rolled to a stop before she jerked the door handle and bolted out. She headed into the building and typed in the code at the elevator with shaky hands. When the doors opened, she clutched her purse to still her nerves and watched the numbers light up as she ascended to the penthouse.

The moment the doors slid open, Paisley pulled in a deep breath and stepped into the suite, placing her clutch on the table next to the elevator. Lucas came from the hallway, his hair a mess from his hat, his shirt unbuttoned, sleeves rolled up on his forearms. There was a wariness to his heavy-lidded gaze, but he offered her a smile that never failed to curl all around her heart.

"Had I known you were going out looking so sexy, I would've made sure I was back in time." He reached her and slid his hands up her bare arms. "Red is your color."

When he started to pull her in, Paisley flattened her palms against his chest and took a step back. Suspicion quickly replaced the exhaustion.

"Something wrong?" he asked.

"Where were you today?"

He stared at her for a moment, then shook his head and raked a hand over the back of his neck.

"I was working," he murmured. "There's something you need to know."

Paisley's heart quickened as nerves like she'd never known consumed her. She knew. She knew before she even opened her mouth, but she had to hear him say it.

"Does this have anything to do with your revenge against Sterling?"

Lucas didn't flinch, he didn't look surprised, he didn't even attempt to deny the allegation. The truth settled heavily between them.

"My work today had to do with you," he stated, as if that explained all the missing pieces he'd conveniently kept from her.

"Which I'm sure just pushes your agenda to bring justice to Sterling."

Lucas nodded, a dark look clouding his eyes. "I hate the man. He ruined my father's business and I won't apologize for seeking justice or for trying to honor my father."

Paisley let out a humorless laugh. "You must've really loved it when I stepped into your office and wanted you to research him. I just handed you a golden ticket to get the ultimate revenge if I was his daughter."

He stared at her for another minute before blowing out a sigh and turning from her, muttering something beneath his breath.

Paisley watched as he paced in front of the wall of living room windows. The dark night behind him only added to the mystery of this man. The man she'd thought she'd known so well…but she'd been so blinded by love. Or was it foolishness? At this point, weren't they the same emotion?

Maybe that was what sickened her most. She'd wanted to believe there was no hidden agenda. She'd wanted to believe that when he'd said he wanted a child, that maybe that was the only stipulation.

Like a damn fool, she'd been ready to give everything to him. Her heart, her life, her future.

Lucas had his back to her, staring out into the night. She wanted to know what was going through his mind, but at the same time, she didn't know if he'd just spout off more lies and keep the real truth hidden like he'd been doing.

"Sterling is a bastard and, yes, I did see you as a way to get back at him if you turned out to be his daughter."

He turned to face her, shoving his hands in his pockets. "But so much changed between us and… Damn it. He's not your father."

Paisley heard the words, attempted to process them, but could she believe anything he said at this point? How could he be so sure about Sterling? Who had he spoken to?

She had so many questions, but would he give her the answers she wanted, the ones she deserved?

On shaky legs, Paisley made her way across the room and rested her hands on the back of the leather chair. As much as she felt she needed to take a seat, she wanted to look like she was strong, in control—though she felt anything but.

"Why should I believe you?" she asked.

"I've been going through the boxes you've brought," he started. "I searched through some of Lynette's old planners last night and another letter slipped out. She wrote it to a Jeb Smith, but never mailed it. The letter said—"

"I want to see it," she demanded, barely holding her emotions together.

"Paisley—"

"Now."

Lucas stared at her a minute before he crossed the room toward her and pulled a folded paper from his pocket. Without a word he handed it over. Paisley attempted to calm her breathing and will her hands to stop shaking before she opened the note. Anything inside here was clearly going to alter her future, and now that it came down to it, she wasn't sure if she was ready to know the truth.

Carefully, she unfolded the letter and read each word her mother had written. The emotions flooded her from so many angles. Seeing her mother's beautiful cursive writing had a knot of loss forming in her gut. But Paisley pushed through that pain as she experienced another round from the fact this Jeb Smith could be her father.

Paisley had never heard that name in her life, but from the way her mother demanded child support, Paisley wondered if this was real. At this point, she wasn't sure if even her mother knew who the father was.

The only thing that was clear now was that Lucas had lied to her and that hurt more than not knowing the truth about her father.

"I don't believe this or you," she stated, refolding

the paper and tossing it into the chair in front of her. "Sterling makes sense. He's the type of guy my mother would've gravitated toward and he's already been rumored to have had affairs."

The muscle in Lucas's jaw ticked, his lips thinned. "He's not your father. I went to see Jeb today and he was fully aware of you. He even had photos of you as a child. Apparently Lynette had given them to him."

Paisley's vision wavered. Black dots swam before her. She shook her head, gripping the seat back and closing her eyes. There was a man out there who knew he was her father...and hadn't sought her out. There was a man her mother had known for sure and hadn't said a word about to Paisley.

The emotions were too strong, her heart too raw to attempt to process what all of this meant. Had anyone in her life been truthful? It hit her then, hard, that she truly was alone.

Lucas reached out to her and his hand rested on her arm. Paisley jerked away as she focused on him.

"Don't touch me," she murmured.

The last thing she wanted was attention out of pity. She was alone, right? There was no need to lean on someone who was just using her. She would get through all of this, somehow, and come out stronger.

But first she needed to go home, be by herself and have a much-needed breakdown.

"You looked like you were about to pass out on me."

She rubbed at her temples, then shoved her hair from her face. "I don't need your help with anything anymore. Not the truth, not my health, nothing."

The light glinted off the rock on her hand and Paisley wasted no time twisting the bands off. She held them out, but Lucas merely glanced at them and back up to her.

"They're yours."

Paisley laughed. "I don't want them. Save them for the next woman you use or return them. I don't give a damn, but they will not be leaving with me."

Lucas shook his head. "You're not leaving."

Backing up a step, Paisley let out a mock laugh. "Like hell I'm not. If this Jeb Smith is my father, then we're done. I told you from the beginning that this wasn't permanent."

Yeah, she'd said those words, but she'd ignored them and had fallen face-first in love. She hadn't taken her own advice and had totally ignored all the red flags as to why getting too emotionally attached was a bad idea.

So here she was. Brokenhearted, barely holding herself together, and the daughter of a man she'd never heard of…and clearly a man who wanted nothing to do with her since he'd known of her existence.

Paisley bit her quivering lip and turned away. She did not need a witness to her vulnerability and agony.

"Paisley, don't shut me out," Lucas pleaded. "I wanted to find all the facts before I came to you. I was trying to make this process as painless as possible."

She whirled back around, swiping at the tear that had the nerve to escape. "What process? Finding my father or you lying to my face night after night as we made love? Did you even feel guilty for using me? After all we shared before, after what we were building now, where the hell was your conscience in all of this? Because I would never use someone I love."

His brows rose as he stared back at her without a word.

"That's right. I love you." Another tear escaped and she didn't bother wiping it away. She wanted him to see the damage he'd caused. "At least when I broke your heart years ago, I did it so you'd have a better life. I did it because I loved you so much. I never lied to you, not one time."

Lucas pursed his lips and gave a clipped nod. He glanced away, but not before Paisley saw a shimmer in his eyes.

Could he actually have a heart, after all?

"I won't be staying here," she told him. "I'll come back and get my things and my mother's boxes when you're at work. My attorney will be in touch regarding the divorce."

His eyes darted right back to hers. "Don't make any decisions out of anger. We need to talk about this."

"We've been talking," she reminded him. "The story won't change. You lied to me and used me. I thought we could actually have something together again. I was foolish enough to want to give you that family you mentioned. I was hopeful that you'd grow to love me again and maybe this would all work out. But that was all too naive and I can see exactly what this is and what this isn't."

She started to turn, but he reached for her.

"At least let me tell you about your real father," he stated. "You have his face shape and the same mouth, the same dimple to the right of your lips."

Paisley stared down at her gold, strappy sandals on the glossy hardwood floors. She didn't want to look at him, didn't want him to see the impact of everything he said.

"He never wanted children," Lucas went on. "He was paying your mother at first for child support, but then he got laid off from his job in construction. He kept telling her to just move on and leave him out of it. He thought you'd be better off without him as a father. Surely you can understand that."

Paisley didn't miss his hint at the similarities between this man thinking she was better off without him and her doing the same to Lucas years ago.

But this wasn't the same. This wasn't some young love trying to figure out their future. This was her life, her past, the part that shaped her into who she was today.

"You can text me all of his information and I'll take it from here," she told him, heading to the elevator. She grabbed her clutch and hit the button. "My lawyer will contact you this week."

She didn't turn around, didn't want to look into his eyes again. The pain she felt… She couldn't even put a label on such emotions, but she didn't want him to see. Yes, she'd wanted him to know he'd hurt her, but now that pain bordered on soul crushing and heartbreaking, and she didn't want to be seen as weak.

The doors slid open and she fully expected him to call out her name, to come up behind her and try to convince her to stay. But the doors slid open and Paisley stepped in.

The second she turned, her eyes locked with his. Damn it. She hadn't wanted him to be the last thing she saw as she left.

But maybe this was what she needed to finalize this chapter on her life. The anguish on his face almost had her pausing, but no. He was good at manipulating people, manipulating her. If he had pain or angst, that was all on him.

She had her own life to piece back together. As much as she still loved him, she just didn't have the energy to play this marriage game any longer.

Sixteen

Silence was deafening.

Lucas had heard the term before, but never fully comprehended those words until Paisley walked out of his penthouse.

That had been five hours ago.

Lucas stared out into the night from his living room. He still held on to the tumbler of bourbon he'd poured an hour ago. He had no clue what to do, how to be. He wasn't himself without Paisley and he'd severed any chance of having her in his life.

But he had no heart to give her. One time he'd thought he had, but he wouldn't have treated her this way if he'd truly loved her. Using her had been a mistake, but for years he'd hated Sterling and the second she stepped into his office, Lucas had seen a clever way in.

What he hadn't seen was the woman he'd loved once, the woman who'd had the ability to hurt him. Instead, he'd seen anger and resentment.

He was a damn fool.

Lucas stared down at the glass in his hand and had every desire to throw it and hear the shatter, but that would solve nothing. Who the hell was he angry at? He was the only one who'd made a mess of this entire ordeal.

But he'd found the answers for Paisley. That was most important. After all she'd been through, she deserved to know the truth.

He hadn't gotten a chance to tell her that her biological father was sick, but from here on out, that part of her life was out of his hands. He'd texted her the information she'd wanted and had gotten no reply—not that he expected one.

Lucas turned from the view that had once been lit up with lights from the city, but now, in the middle of the night, was mostly dark. There was probably some correlation between that and his life, but right now he couldn't figure it out.

He took the glass to the bar and headed toward the bedroom. The second he stepped through the doorway, he realized his mistake. He couldn't sleep in here. Paisley was everywhere. Her satin robe draped across the bottom of the bed, her heels placed near the closet where she'd stepped out of them yesterday, the perfume... damn. That floral scent was everywhere.

Lucas stared at the bed they'd been sleeping in and

knew he wouldn't be back in this room for a long, long time.

He marched across to the other side of the penthouse, unbuttoning his shirt as he went. One of the guest rooms would have to do. Maybe he wouldn't see her there, maybe he'd sleep, maybe he'd actually be able to move on without her.

But he knew the truth. Paisley had infiltrated his life on two separate occasions and both times when she'd walked out, he'd been left feeling completely gutted with no hope of what tomorrow would bring.

Paisley stared across the street at the simple bungalow owned by Jeb Smith. She'd barely slept last night because she'd been so nervous about today and confronting the man who supposedly was her father.

Though if she was being honest with herself, she couldn't sleep because she'd been back in her town house, alone in her bed and trying to get the ache in her heart to subside.

But she couldn't think about Lucas right now. Not that he was ever fully out of her thoughts, but she had to push him to the back. This day was too important. The man inside that house could truly be her father.

Inside her heart, she knew he was. Lucas wouldn't have told her if he wasn't 100 percent certain. Yes, he'd lied to her about Sterling to try to seek his own revenge, but Paisley couldn't question this.

She gripped her door handle and stepped from her car. Pulling in a deep breath, she smoothed down her maxidress and glanced both ways before setting off across the street. Maybe she should've worn jeans. Was a dress too formal? What did one wear to meet a parent for the first time?

Nerves curled all through her, sending doubts shooting off in all directions. There was no turning back. She wanted to know, she deserved to know. She'd already lost one parent and she wanted the opportunity to get to know the other.

She had no clue why her mother hadn't just come out and told her who her father was or why she didn't state his name in the letter. Perhaps she was trying to save him after all this time or maybe she was ashamed of her past. Paisley truly had no idea and she might never know her mother's reasoning. All she knew was she was about to meet her father at long last.

Paisley climbed the porch steps and glanced to the homey wooden swing on the opposite end. With a shaky finger, she pressed the doorbell and stepped back to wait.

The click of a lock and twist of the handle had her pasting on a smile and ready to face whomever was on the other side of that door.

A middle-aged man with silver hair and kind eyes stood on the other side of the glass door. The second his gaze locked with hers, his brows shot up, his mouth dropped in surprise. He quickly opened the door.

"Paisley?" he asked, his tone laced with uncertainty.

She nodded, trying not to let her emotions get the best of her. "Jeb Smith?"

He didn't confirm as he gestured her to come in. "I thought after your husband came by, you might follow."

Paisley stepped into the foyer and stood awkwardly as he closed the door behind her. When he turned to face her once again, he smiled and a piece of her fear melted away.

"Come in and sit down," he told her. "I—I don't even know what to say or…maybe I should get you something to drink?"

Paisley laughed. "I'm fine. I'd say we're both nervous."

He stared at her another minute before shaking his head and blowing out a sigh. "You've grown into such a beautiful young lady."

"It's been a long time since someone called me a young lady," she replied with a slight laugh. "But thank you."

He pointed toward the arched doorway. "Let's go into the living room."

She stepped into the cozy space and took a seat on the sofa as Jeb carefully eased himself into a worn recliner. Paisley's fears returned.

"Are you all right?"

His eyes snapped to hers.

"Sorry," she added. "It's none of my business."

"Don't be sorry," he stated, resting his arms on the edge of the chair. "As I told Lucas, I have a heart issue that's messed up my way of living. I'm tired easy. I have a caregiver that comes in a few times a week to help around the house and get my meds. I'm just…not quite as spry as I used to be."

Heart issue? Paisley crossed her ankles and leaned forward in her seat.

"What can I do to help?"

Jeb shook his head. "Unless you're a miracle worker, there's nothing that can be done. I'm…terminal."

"That can't be," she cried. "I just found you."

Then she remembered what all Lucas had said.

"But you knew about me all along, didn't you?"

Jeb nodded. "I did. Lynette and I weren't necessarily a couple. We dated a few times, but never anything serious. I kept getting laid off work so when she said she was pregnant, I did what I could financially, but it wasn't much. I'd hoped she'd find someone who could provide for you both, but she never did."

"You didn't want me, though." The words hurt, but she came here for answers.

"I wasn't fit to be a father," he corrected. "I'm old enough now to realize I made mistakes where you were concerned. I thought Lynette would find someone and start a real family. I guess I thought if I just paid her what I could and left her alone, you both would be better off."

Paisley listened to him, and had she read this in a letter or email, she'd be furious and assume he was merely making lame excuses. But she heard the remorse in his voice. She could tell by the way he looked at her that he had regrets.

She had a few of her own.

"If I had to do it over, I'd fight to see you, to be part of your life," he added.

"Lucas said you had photos of me," Paisley said.

Jeb nodded. "Your mother would give me pictures every now and then. When I came with a check she would give me one. I only have a few. I…wasn't the best father figure and she had every right to hate me."

Paisley crossed her legs and smoothed her dress down. "Why didn't you get in touch with me in later years?"

"I was ashamed, embarrassed, afraid." He shrugged and glanced out the window as if gathering his thoughts. "I'd say you were about fifteen when I really thought about approaching you, but then I figured you and Lynette were set in your ways. If she hadn't told you about me, there was a reason. I couldn't just come waltzing in and blow up the only world you knew. Then after she passed away…"

His focus came back to her. "I wasn't sure you'd want anything to do with me. I had no clue what she ever told you about your father and I didn't want to disrupt your life."

He might have had a terrible excuse when she'd been young, but as time went on, Paisley fully believed he'd stayed away out of shame and fear.

"Maybe we could have a relationship now," she suggested.

Jeb smiled, the gesture crinkling the corners of his eyes and enhancing the deep lines around his mouth.

"There's nothing I'd like more," he told her. "I hate that I'm sick, that we may not have years left. I've missed a lifetime."

Paisley's throat clogged with emotions, but she truly wanted to be strong for him. "Then we'll have to cram in a lifetime of memories in the time we have."

His smile widened. "Do you have dinner plans?"

Finally, hope spread through her. "I'm having dinner with my dad."

Seventeen

Lucas stared at the computer screen, but the words kept blurring. He'd been focused on the same sentence for the past hour and he was getting absolutely nowhere.

His cases were not taking top priority like they always had. He couldn't focus, couldn't sleep, couldn't function, because his entire world had blown up and he was wading through the bits and pieces trying to find his new normal.

And if this was it, he wasn't going to make it.

The penthouse was too quiet, so he'd been staying in his office. But on his desk sat the mall photos they'd had done in the photo booth and he couldn't stop staring at them.

He and Paisley looked so ridiculously happy—like the couple they'd once been.

Lucas pushed away from his desk and came to his feet. He shoved his hands in his pockets and glared down at the photo mocking him. This was what he could've had, this was what he'd thrown away all for the sake of revenge.

Now he was left with no revenge and no wife. Well, she was technically his wife until the divorce was finalized. He hadn't heard from her attorney and she'd left his home four days ago.

Four damn days. The longest days of his life.

If he thought he'd been crushed and broken the first time she walked out, that was nothing compared to this time. Both occasions had not been her fault, but she'd been pushed out just the same. Both instances she'd trusted him, confided in him…loved him.

Lucas's eyes started to burn and he blinked as he glanced away from the pictures. Apologizing didn't seem to be enough. How could the words *I'm sorry* cover a multitude of sins?

But he couldn't go on like this. He couldn't go on without her or let her walk out of his life again, because he knew this time would be for good.

Lucas closed out the case he was reading on his computer and sent an email to one of his top guys to take over. The company wouldn't suffer—he'd spent too long making a reputation for himself, but he couldn't put himself on any job right now and give it his all.

The only job he wanted was that of husband to Paisley Ford. She hadn't actually changed her name, but damn it, he liked the sound of it. He wanted to be married to her, for real, without any pretenses or lies. He wanted to build that life they'd dreamed of so long ago. He wanted kids with her, not just because he wanted a child to pass his legacy to, but because he wanted children with the woman he loved more than the world.

A viselike grip clenched his heart. There was nothing he wouldn't do to win Paisley back. Nothing he wouldn't sacrifice, including his pride. His life meant nothing without her. Even if he'd gotten the revenge he wanted on Sterling, it would have been an empty victory because he'd lost Paisley and she took precedence over everything else.

He scooped up his keys and headed out the back office door. His driver had taken Paisley home the other night and Lucas had ordered the guy to hang around since then for anything she needed.

Lucas couldn't believe she hadn't texted to tell him to back off, but perhaps she was that angry she didn't even want to talk. Or maybe she was using the driver, who knew.

There was nothing Lucas wouldn't give her to make her life easier. He somehow had to get her to understand his actions, and that he'd cared for her, even though he had a poor way of showing it.

Lucas climbed into his SUV and headed toward her town house. He wasn't giving her a heads-up; he didn't want her to make excuses to leave or talk him out of not coming. He needed to see her, needed to just tell his side. Hell, he'd beg, plead, sell his soul to get her back.

He wasn't too proud to admit he'd been a bastard. He wasn't too proud to lay his heart on the line for the woman that he loved. Once he put everything out there, he'd respect her enough to back away and let her think. Walking away would kill him, but he had to let her come to him on her own if that was what she decided.

Baring his heart, laying it before her, and then walking away and leaving all control to her was going to be pure hell. But nothing could be worse than not having her at all.

Four days was too long to be without his wife. It was time to reclaim his life, *their* life, and find a way to make things right.

Sundays were meant for relaxing, but Paisley felt anything but relaxed.

She'd received an insane amount of money in her business account, more than enough to order any dress she'd ever want in her shop, more than enough to pay off her building, and more than enough if she wanted to throw a new car into the mix.

So how could she relax when her soon-to-be ex-husband was trying to buy his way back into her life?

Not that she wasn't thankful for the exorbitant amount of money, but she couldn't keep it. She was filing for divorce and she wasn't going to take something that wasn't hers…the money or the man.

Paisley tightened the belt on her robe and started to head to the master bedroom for a shower when her doorbell rang. Who on earth would be here on a Sunday morning? She didn't just get drop-in visitors and she certainly hadn't invited anyone over. With the mood she'd been in, she tried to keep to herself for fear of lashing out at anyone who asked how she was doing.

She'd had to save every bit of patience and smiles for her customers. Today, though, she'd wanted to do absolutely nothing. She wanted to give her mind time to rest, her heart time to heal, but none of that would happen anytime soon.

She'd never gotten over Lucas when she'd left him years ago—how the hell did she think she'd get over him after becoming his wife and spending every night in his bed?

Paisley smoothed her bed head away from her face as she padded barefoot to the front door. From the silhouette she could make out through the etched glass, she knew exactly who stood on the other side.

Well, it took him long enough and he'd better be here groveling and down on his knees. Not that she'd take him back. She was going to be strong, stand her ground and not let anyone take advantage of her again.

But she wasn't going to turn down an apology. Tears would help, too. At least she'd know she wasn't in the land of misery alone.

Did he even cry? She'd never seen him show such emotions or anything really other than passion and greed.

No, that wasn't true. He'd shown so much more, but right now, anger and pain fueled her thoughts.

The doorbell chimed again, followed by a knock.

"Tart, I know you're in there."

Damn that nickname.

Paisley flicked the lock on the door and swung it open. Taking in his rumpled hair, his wrinkled shirt that looked like it was from yesterday and the dark circles beneath his eyes, she couldn't help but feel a little sorry for him.

"You look like hell."

Well, that was not exactly what she'd meant to say, but it was the truth. She'd never seen him so frazzled and forlorn, but he'd brought everything upon himself… so why did she feel bad?

"I've been sleeping in my office and I can't focus on work," he told her. "I don't deserve five minutes of your time, but I'm asking for it anyway."

Not only had she never seen him look like this, she'd never heard that tone before. Oh, he still had a strength to his words, but the underlying vibe was definitely broken.

Still, after all he'd put her through, she refused to go easy on him. Why should she? She'd put herself out there from the second she'd walked into his office and he'd taken advantage without even an ounce of guilt. Well, he probably had guilt once he got caught, but he'd slept with her night after night. At any point he could've told her about his father and Sterling.

But he chose to keep her in the dark and continue the lie.

"I know you want to slam that door in my face," he went on. "Do what you have to do, but I'm just asking for a chance to explain my actions. Just like I gave you the chance to explain yours about what happened years ago."

"I call bullshit on that." Paisley gripped the doorknob and seriously thought about slamming the door as he suggested. "You didn't let me fully explain. I attempted and you brushed it aside as a maybe truth because you didn't want to believe your father would lie to you. That hurts, doesn't it? Knowing someone you love, someone you trust with your entire life has betrayed you?"

"I believe what happened with my dad," he told her. "I know you loved me then and I know you love me now. Can I just have five minutes?"

"I think you need quite a bit longer than that to offer a proper apology." She pursed her lips and considered, though her heart was breaking and she wanted to ignore all the red flags and invite him in…straight to her bed. "You have four and a half minutes. Go."

"Can I come in?"

She shifted her stance and leaned against the door. "No."

He stared at her for a minute before he finally nodded and glanced down to his feet. For the first time in her life she wondered if he'd ever been in this position before. He had no control and they both knew it.

Lucas raised his head and focused back on her as his shoulders squared and eyes held hers. "I messed up. There's really no way to sugarcoat that and I want you to know that I'm not here just because I want a child or I want to keep up this arrangement we had. I'm here because I want you back for good. I want a real wedding, I want a real future, no secrets. I want everything with you, Paisley."

She listened, trying to ignore the pull of her heartstrings, but how could she? Each word sounded so heartfelt, not rehearsed at all. Still…

"It's not that simple," she explained. "You can't just

come here because you're lonely. You're supposed to hurt. That's your punishment."

He took a step closer, sliding a hand around the dip in her waist and making her shiver. Damn that man for making her feel when she tried so hard not to.

"I'm not here because I hurt," he murmured, staring into her eyes. "I'm here because you're hurt."

Tears pricked her eyes. Why did he know the right words? Why did he have so much charm that he made it impossible for her to hate him?

Paisley blinked back the unshed tears. "Yes, I'm hurting," she admitted. "But words won't just make that pain go away. I've never been used before, Lucas. And I never thought I'd be used by someone so close to me."

The warmth from his hand had her softening her words, and Paisley could feel herself melting little by little. The wall of defense she had so firmly in place was slowly slipping away.

"I never intended to hurt you," he stated. "Yes, I saw you as a way to get to Sterling, but the man is a complete bastard. I volleyed between wanting him to be your dad so you'd have closure and wanting him to not be your dad because I didn't want you to have anything to do with the jerk."

He slid his free hand to the other side of her waist and pulled her closer until their torsos aligned. Even rumpled and haggard, Lucas Ford was the sexiest man she'd ever seen.

Sexy wasn't going to win her heart over, though. But that pain in his eyes, a look that she'd never experienced, and the pleading were doing a damn good job of getting her attention.

So much for being made of steel and making him grovel.

"I went and saw my real dad," she told him. "He's... sick."

"I know, but I'm glad you're getting time together now."

Paisley closed her eyes and pulled in a deep breath. "I can't be with you if I can't trust you."

"I know that, too," he countered. "But I plan on spending every day for the rest of our lives making you see that I love you more than anything."

Paisley's heart clenched. "What?"

"I love you," he repeated.

He dipped his head and captured her mouth, gently at first, then he coaxed her lips apart. Paisley arched against him and opened, her body instantly responding to his touch. All warning flags dropped. She didn't want to focus on the negative. She only wanted to focus on the fact Lucas had come because she was hurting—and to tell her he loved her.

His hands slid around the silky robe and beneath the hem to her bare backside.

"Damn, Tart," he muttered against her mouth. "You're naked."

"I was going to get in the shower," she whispered. "I didn't plan on company."

He rested his forehead against hers. "Let me in," he commanded. "Your neighbors are getting a show."

Totally caught up in the moment, in the man, she'd

forgotten they were standing in her doorway for the whole street and anyone walking by to see.

Paisley gripped his shirtfront and tugged him into her foyer. He dove right back in, devouring her mouth as his hands went to the tie on her robe. The material parted and his hands were on her. Finally.

"I've missed you," he growled against her mouth. "I need you so much."

Yeah, she had some pretty desperate needs of her own.

Lucas gripped her ass and lifted her against him. Paisley wrapped her legs around his waist, then held on as he turned and sat her on the accent table at the base of the staircase. He immediately stepped between her spread legs and yanked the robe down to her elbows, trapping her arms against her sides.

"Tell me you want this," he demanded. "I want to hear you say it."

Paisley nodded, trying to form a sentence when her body was aching. "I want you, Lucas. Now."

He released the robe and palmed her breasts as she laced her fingers through his hair. She scooted forward on the cool tabletop and locked her ankles behind his back.

His hands fell away and she felt him fidgeting between her legs followed by the sound of his zipper. He circled her waist with his large, strong hands and stared into her eyes as he joined their bodies.

Paisley cried out as her body arched, her head dropping back. Lucas slid a hand around to the small of her back for support as he pumped his hips and murmured something she couldn't make out.

His lips grazed over her breasts, along her neck, and she tipped her head back so he could take her lips. Her fingertips dug into his shoulders and she gripped the fabric of his shirt, wishing he would've removed it so she could fully touch him.

"Paisley," he murmured.

Hearing her name on his lips, seeing that tightening of his jaw as if he was barely holding on to his control, had her body spiraling out of control. She tightened all around him and let the moment consume her.

Seconds later, Lucas tightened his hold on her waist and dropped his head to the crook in her neck. Paisley ran her hands over his shoulders, to his neck, and into his hair, cradling him as his pleasure took hold.

After several moments, when their bodies settled, only their breathing filled the space. Paisley wondered if she'd made a mistake letting him in so soon. She hadn't made him grovel too much and she was pretty sure she hadn't even made him use the four and a half minutes.

She'd always been weak where Lucas was concerned, but now she had to figure out how to handle this. Yes, she wanted him, but she had to trust him.

"Don't start having doubts."

Lucas felt her pulling away. Oh, not physically. She was still wrapped all around him. Emotionally and mentally, she was already rewinding and trying to come up with something to say and some way to protect herself.

"This can work," he added. "I know I made a mistake that could cost me everything, but I'm here to tell you that I won't put anything above you ever again."

He eased back and smoothed the hair away from her face. The thought of letting her go hurt him to a level he couldn't describe and didn't want to comprehend. He didn't even want to go there in his own mind because he was going to do anything in his power to show her he was in love with her.

"I'll buy you a wedding dress." The words were out before he thought twice, but then he realized she deserved so much more. "Any dress. I don't care if it's hand-beaded, or whatever that expensive one was, or if you want to recycle that lace thing. I want to give you the wedding of your dreams."

Paisley laughed. "I'm never wearing that jumpsuit again and you put so much money in my business account, I don't need you to buy me anything."

He'd put that money in her account because he didn't want her to worry about finances even for a second. He'd secretly contacted the jilted bride and he knew the insane wedding gown had ultimately been paid for in full after he'd reminded the customer she was in breach of contract.

If Paisley ultimately decided to leave him, Lucas would be absolutely devastated, but he still wanted to provide a solid security for her and pave a smooth path in her life.

Paisley sighed. "I can't keep that money, you know. And great sex won't fix our problems."

Lucas took a half step back and adjusted his pants,

but left them unbuttoned. He eased the silky robe back up her arms and covered her breasts.

"I swear I did not come here for sex." He wanted her to know she was so much more to him. "You're everything to me. I'm here because I wanted to fix your hurt, if that's even possible. I know I did damage, but tell me what I can do to make it right. There's nothing I wouldn't do for you."

Paisley bit on her bottom lip as her eyes darted away. She eased off the table, causing him to take another step back to give her space. Lucas watched as she righted her robe, but the silence was absolutely maddening.

He had nobody to be angry with but himself, but he couldn't go back in time and have a redo. At this point, all he could hope to accomplish was to get through to Paisley that he really did have good intentions, he just executed everything the wrong way.

"Family is everything to me," he told her. "I wanted vengeance for my father. I had been waiting for the right opportunity to get back at Sterling, so when he went to jail, I was thinking that would have to suffice, though I had nothing to do with that. But then you walked in and my first thought was, what if it's true? What if you do belong to him? I won't lie, I wanted you in my bed. I was more than eager to have you all to myself while I investigated."

Paisley crossed her arms over her chest, but didn't make a move to step away or shut him out. Lucas took that as a good sign and kept going.

"But then you moved in," he said. "Having you in my space, even with the yellow throw pillows and those pic-

tures you call art, I realized I wanted all of that there because that's who you are. I wasn't still hung up on some
young love. I was falling for the woman you are now."

Her eyes misted and she glanced down, but Lucas
took his hand and lifted her attention back to him.

"Don't hide from me," he said. "When you feel something, anything, I want you to share it with me. And I'll
do the same. There's nothing I want to do alone anymore.
Tell me you'll think about us, think about not leaving for
good. I'm willing to start over, I'm willing—"

"Shut up."

Lucas froze. "Excuse me?"

Paisley blinked, causing a tear to slide down her
cheek. "I told myself to let you grovel for a long time,
but I can't handle it anymore."

She'd told herself…

What the hell?

Lucas framed her face and swiped at the tear with the
pad of his thumb. "Did I grovel long enough?"

Paisley shrugged. "I'm not sure yet. But I needed
a break."

He kissed her lips, quickly, softly. "I'll spend the rest
of my life groveling if you give me the chance. Let's
make this a real marriage and start a family."

She smiled. For the first time since he'd set foot in
the door, she offered a true, genuine smile.

"I wouldn't have let you in, let alone had sex with
you, if I didn't want to give you another chance."

Paisley's delicate arms came up around his neck and
Lucas wasted no time in pulling her closer. "I don't deserve you," he murmured.

"You don't," she agreed with a laugh. "But we're legally bound, so you're stuck with me."

"Fine by me." He nipped at her lips once again. "I believe you said something about a shower earlier. Do you have room for one more?"

"In my shower and in my heart."

Lucas swept her up into his arms and carried her up to the second floor. This next chapter of his life was going to be the best yet. He may not have gotten revenge like he'd wanted, but he got something so much more fulfilling. He had the only woman he'd ever loved and soon, they'd have their own family.

Nothing compared to that.

Epilogue

Angela swept into the café and weaved her way through the tables. Lavinia sat in the back and lifted a hand to wave Angela over.

"So sorry I'm late," Angela said as she pulled her chair out. "Traffic was a nightmare."

The waiter came by and Angela ordered a water as she set her bag beneath the table and took a seat. She inhaled deeply and stared across the table at her friend.

"It's so good to see you," Angela stated. "We don't do lunch often enough."

"We don't," Lavinia agreed. "So much has been going on with your dad and then there's that body that has still not been identified. Everything is so crazy lately."

Angela cringed. "I can't even wrap my mind around

that poor person who died. I mean, they had a family somewhere that is no doubt wondering where their loved one is. Nobody deserves to just…"

"I know," Lavinia muttered her agreement.

The waiter came back with water and took their order before leaving them alone again.

"On a brighter note," Lavinia said. "You're absolutely beaming. Something must be going right for you."

Angela pulled the cloth napkin from the table and smoothed it over her lap. "You could say that. With all the upheaval in my life, Ryder and I have decided to get away from it all and take a trip. Just the two of us. We really need the time alone to just reset."

Lavinia gasped. "Oh, my. You are one strong woman. I admire that. I don't know what I'd do if the man I was dating was rumored to have fathered my brother."

Angela stilled, and her heart clenched as the breath caught in her throat. "What?"

"You haven't heard?" Lavinia asked, her eyes wide. She took a sip of her water and leaned forward as she spoke lower. "Ryder is rumored to have had an affair with your mother and he's actually Roarke's father, not Sterling."

Angela gripped her napkin in her lap, suddenly feeling quite nauseated. The affairs were nothing new, but she hadn't heard the most damning rumor. No doubt Lavinia, the town gossip, was all too eager to share the tidbits she knew.

This couldn't be true. There was no way Ryder was

Roarke's father. That couldn't be. There had to be some mistake.

Angela couldn't even gather all her thoughts that were swirling through her head. She needed to talk to her father; she needed to talk to Ryder.

"Angela, darling. Are you all right?" Lavinia asked. "I truly thought you'd heard. When I spoke with Sterling the other day, he acted as if this was public knowledge."

"You spoke to my father about this?" Angela asked. She tossed the napkin onto the table. "I have to go. We'll do lunch another time."

"Don't go," Lavinia pleaded. "Sit down and we can talk. You shouldn't drive when you're upset."

Upset? That didn't even come close to what she was feeling. Upset was scuffing your favorite shoe. Finding out your boyfriend might have slept with your mother was sickening...it was destroying.

"I'm not too upset to drive," Angela retorted. "I'm determined to find out the truth."

She turned, nearly knocking over a waiter with a tray of food, and fled out the door. There was no way in hell she could stay in a relationship with Ryder if this was true.

How had he overlooked the fact he'd had a relationship with her mother? That was something he definitely should've brought up when they started getting closer.

Angela's hands shook as she started her car. She gripped the steering wheel and stared straight ahead. She forced herself to breath slowly in and out, trying to remain calm, but the attempt was in vain. There was no calming down from this.

She couldn't even wrap her mind fully around what she wanted to say to Ryder, but she knew one thing, there would be no romantic getaway for them.

* * * * *

RED HOT RANCHER

MAUREEN CHILD

To my kids,
Jason and Sarah,
who have added so much love
and laughter to our lives.
I wouldn't have missed a minute of it.

One

"She's back."

"She *who*?" Caden Hale looked up at his foreman, Jack Franklin. No one knew him better than Jack, which was why Caden was surprised to see the man now.

Everyone on the ranch knew not to disturb Caden when he was engulfed by the dreaded paperwork needed to keep the Double H ranch running. Caden would much rather be out in the corral or riding fence-line, checking for breaks. Hell, to be honest, he'd rather be in the stables, mucking out stalls. But at least once a week, he was forced to sentence himself to hours behind the desk that had once been his father's.

Jack stood opposite that desk now and the foreman's expression was a weird mixture of dread and shock. Caden braced himself, leaning back in the chair, tapping one finger against the desktop.

Caden didn't have a clue who could have put that look on his oldest friend's face. He and Jack had been pals since grade school and when Caden took over the family ranch ten years ago, Jack had come on board, too. Usually, the man was unshakable. Not today.

"Come on, Jack. What's going on? You look like somebody died."

"Not yet," his friend muttered, then swept off his Stetson, curled his fingers around the brim and tapped the hat against his upper thigh.

Caden straightened in the chair, leaned both forearms on the desk and stared at his friend. "Just spit it out. Who the hell are you talking about and why should I care?"

"You shouldn't care," Jack said. "But you will."

"Enough. Just tell me."

"It's Emma, Caden," Jack told him flatly. "Emma Williams is back."

And just like that, the day went from annoying to a crap-fest. Caden's chest was tight, and he didn't even notice how hard he was clenching his teeth until his jaw ached in response. Deliberately, he took a long, deep breath and willed the sudden tension in his body to drain away.

Damned if he'd let a woman he hadn't seen or spoken to in five long years get under his skin. And yet, he had to admit, just the mention of her name had done it. Caden closed his eyes briefly to fight the wave of tangled emotions rising up inside him. Anger and betrayal were tied for first place, but the rest weren't far behind. Lust, the remnants of a love he thought would live forever and just enough pleasure to worry him.

Emma was back.

Why? For how long?

And damn it, why did he care? He hadn't spoken to her in five years. She'd tried to call a few times, but he'd never answered. Why the hell should he?

"Did you see her?" he finally asked.

"No," Jack said with a sharp shake of his head. "Gwen did. She was in town this morning, getting some groceries. Saw Emma wandering the aisles. Caden," he added, "she had a baby with her."

Another sucker punch and now breathing was becoming a hell of a lot harder than it should have been. A *baby*? She'd had a baby while she was gone? With who? Was the baby's father here with them? "Damn it."

"Yeah," Jack said. "When Gwen told me I knew this wasn't going to go well."

"Good call."

Caden exhaled roughly, hoping to ease the raging tide of conflicting emotions rising inside him. Yeah, he was still furious over how Emma had ended things between them, but through it all, there was a hot, thick wave of need he'd never been able to shake. Just thinking about Emma Williams was enough to make his body hard as stone and his mind an empty cavern. Which was why, he reminded himself, he'd tried to avoid all thought of her for the past five years. It was only in his dreams that she came back to haunt him. Every damn night.

"Did Gwen talk to her?" Jack's wife knew everything that had happened between Caden and Emma. Hell, everyone for miles around knew the story. It's what happened in a small town.

Cache, Montana, had a population that hovered around five thousand. If you needed a big city once in a while, Kalispell was only thirty miles away. But

Cache was large enough for Caden. It had everything he needed. There were stores and schools and Main Street was dotted with buildings that were built more than a hundred years ago. It was small, but it was his. A tiny town, where everyone felt free to share their opinion on just about anything.

"Yeah." Jack pushed one hand through his hair. "She says Emma got home last night. Didn't tell anyone she was coming..."

Which explained why Emma's sister Gracie hadn't said anything about this to Caden when he saw her yesterday. And he was willing to bet that Gracie was no happier about this than he was.

"Says she's home to stay. She's done with Hollywood."

"Is that right?" Teeth clenched, he thought about what this would mean for him. He'd have to see her all the damn time now. The town would resurrect old stories and he'd catch people watching him with mocking eyes—or worse yet, sympathy.

Still, she'd left once before. Why should he believe that she would stay now?

"Caden," Jack advised, "just let it be."

He shot a look at his oldest friend. Jack looked worried but he couldn't help the man with that. If Emma was home, then he was going to face her and get a few things out in the open. "Not going to happen. She's back and we're going to talk. Set things straight right away."

"What's left to set straight? You guys ended it five years ago."

"*She* ended it," Caden reminded the other man. "Now it's *my* turn."

* * *

"What exactly is your problem, Gracie?" Emma Williams caught her younger sister's arm to stop her before she could flounce out of the room Emma had just entered.

The living room was as it had always been. Wide windows overlooking the front yard and the long driveway leading up to the Williams' ranch. Furniture chosen for its comfort rather than style and now threadbare rugs that her mother had hooked before Emma was born. Watery October sunlight pushed its way through the grime on the windows and spotlighted dust motes floating in the still air.

Gracie yanked her arm free. "You, Em. You're my problem."

Her sister had been avoiding her since the night before, when Emma had walked into the house as if she'd been gone an hour instead of five years.

"How?" Emma threw both hands high. "I just got home last night."

"Exactly." Gracie tossed her short, curly hair back from her face. "You've been gone a long time, Emma. Then you show up and we're all supposed to act like you've been here all along? Like nothing's changed? Like the ranch isn't falling apart and Dad has hardly gotten out of bed in the last year?"

Gracie's green eyes, so much like Emma's own, were flashing with fury, and at least, Emma told herself, that was honest. Since the night before, Gracie had been shut down, refusing to speak to her. Well, angry shouts were at least communication of a sort.

And everything her sister was saying jabbed at her like hot needles. She'd had time to look around the ranch this morning and Gracie was right. The place looked as though it was struggling and their father was grayer and slower then she remembered. But even as she felt that quick jolt of guilt, she defended herself.

"You never told me Dad was sick," she countered. And worry twisted with guilt inside her.

"He wasn't," her sister retorted. "Isn't. He just gave up. Because *you* walked away."

That hurt and she really hoped it wasn't true. But it felt true and Emma's pain rose up to choke her. She hadn't meant to leave a trail of destruction in her wake when she left. Hadn't meant a lot of things. And that changed nothing. "You should have told me."

"In an email?" Gracie asked hotly. "Or one of your famous two-minute phone calls? Yeah, lots of time for a chat then, huh, Em?"

More guilt. Great.

"You can't lay this all on me, Gracie," Emma argued. "You were here. You knew what was happening."

"And couldn't change it," her sister said as tears filled her eyes. She took a deep breath, blinked the tears away and when she spoke again, her voice was low, but controlled. "I was trying to hold the ranch together and all Dad could do was worry about you. 'All alone in California.' While I was all alone right here."

Stung, Emma swayed at the impact of her sister's words. It was true that she hadn't thought about what would happen here at home when she left. Maybe she hadn't *allowed* herself to think of it.

Five years ago, she'd seen her future laid out in front of her and something inside her had just *snapped*. She'd had to go. Had to *try*.

"Gracie…" She didn't know what she might have said, but it didn't matter when her sister cut her off.

"Don't say you're sorry. It doesn't matter and besides, you're really not." She swiped away a solitary angry tear. "You did what you wanted to do. Just like you always have."

For the first time in this conversation, Emma felt a quick blast of anger. She was willing to take a little bit of bitterness from her sister, but damned if she'd stand there and be a target for whatever Gracie wanted to throw at her.

"Seriously? What the hell is that supposed to mean?" Emma moved in closer, kept her voice low so their father wouldn't overhear them. "When Mom died, who was it who held this place together, taking care of you and Dad? Besides, you *don't* do what you want? Since when? You stole Dad's truck for a joyride, remember? And, you ditched school and hitched a ride to a concert in Billings—"

"When I was a kid," Gracie cut her off. "Don't have any new stories to tell, though, do you, Em? Because you weren't *here*."

This was getting old, fast. "A lot of people leave home, Gracie."

"Most of them at least visit."

"If they can *afford it*," Emma argued.

"You were on TV," Gracie shot back.

"For one season," Emma reminded her and on one level, she couldn't believe they were having this argument. God, she hadn't even been home for twenty-four hours.

Apparently Thomas Wolfe was wrong. You *could* go home again, you just couldn't make anyone happy to see you.

For some reason, Emma had expected it to be easier to slide back into her old life. While she was in Hollywood, this ranch, her family, had become her mental security blanket. When she was worried or scared or whatever, she'd close her eyes and let her memories soothe her.

This was *home*. It was the one place she'd told herself that was there, waiting for her if the world turned on her. She'd always told herself that she could go home if her dreams crashed and burned. But home wasn't what it had been when she left five years ago. Now that she was back in Cache, she had to admit that it wasn't what she'd remembered. What she'd hoped to find. But even as that thought settled in her mind, Emma wondered if that was true. Maybe it wasn't home that had changed, after all. It was *her*.

But how could she not? So much had happened to her in California that Montana had begun to seem like a dream world to her. She'd written and emailed and video chatted, but the longer she was away, the bigger the chasm between her and her family had grown. And how could it have been different, when she wasn't really telling them what her life was like in California? She didn't want them worried about her making rent on that dumpy little apartment in Hollywood. Didn't want them knowing that she was hungry often and anxious all the time. So she'd been bright and happy and brief in those calls that had become less and less frequent.

Her father, Frank, had always been happy to hear from her. But Gracie had slowly shut down, pulled away. And now her little sister could barely stand to be in the same room with her.

And maybe she had it coming. Emma's world was

now divided into two separate entities. Before she left Montana and *now*. She preferred the before because dealing with the now was harder than anything she'd ever done. *Now* meant she had a sick father, a sister who hated her and a baby who depended on her.

What felt like boulders dropped onto Emma's shoulders and she almost sagged under the emotional weight of it all. But the truth was, none of those burdens were as crushing as the knowledge that she still had to see Caden again. And everything in her was torn.

It had been five years since she'd seen him and five minutes since she'd thought of him. He'd been in her mind forever. Since the moment they'd met in high school, Caden Hale was all she'd been able to see. All she'd *wanted* to see. Until the night he had laid out their future together. Marriage, kids, the ranch, everything they used to talk about. Everything that Emma had come to believe was somehow *destined*.

But that same night, it had become clear to her that if she stayed in Montana with him and never tried to chase down her own dreams, she'd end up resenting him and hating herself. So she'd left. Walked away. And she had the feeling he'd be even less happy to see her than Gracie was.

Since the evening before, when she'd walked in the door of her family home, Emma had been dreading and anticipating the moment when she'd face *him* again.

"Emma! Come on in here." Her father's voice splintered her thoughts and dragged her back to the moment.

"Coming, Dad!"

"Bring a bottle," he shouted, "I think my granddaughter's getting hungry!"

Emma frowned as one more weight settled on her

shoulders, but she told herself that was a problem for another day. She looked at her sister and said, "We'll finish this later."

"Oh," Gracie told her, "we're finished."

Taking a breath, hoping for patience, Emma headed to the kitchen.

The drive from the Double H ranch to the Williamses' place only took about twenty minutes. Once upon a time, he and Emma had talked about one day cutting a road directly across their adjoining fields, to directly link the ranches. But that, like so many other things, had never happened.

At any other time, Caden might have noticed the fall colors erupting on the trees lining the wide road. But now, all he could see were the images replaying in his mind, of Emma's eyes the night she said goodbye.

"I have to go, Caden," she said plaintively, trying to make him understand. "I have to try. I can't do what my mom did. She gave up on her dreams. You remember what a great singer she was, right?"

"I do, but—"

"She never did anything with it and before she died, she told me that was her one regret. That she'd never found out if she could make it or not."

Panic was rising in his chest, but Caden fought it down. He and Emma had been together a long time. He'd always believed that they were working toward the same goals. This had come out of nowhere for him and he didn't know what the hell to think. "What about the dream of building up my family ranch?"

"That's your dream, Caden," she said simply and tore a hole in his heart.

That was a slap. She'd had plenty of ideas, had jumped in enthusiastically with plans. "We've been talking about this for years," he reminded her. "We were going to do it together. Create something special."

"I know." She touched him and her hand on his arm was like a fire that was bone chilling. "But this is important to me, too, Caden. I have to find out if I'm good enough."

Couldn't she see that she'd never be as important in Hollywood as she was right here? To him?

"So you're just leaving."

"You could come with me..."

He laughed at her. "I can't leave."

"And I can't stay," she said. "If I don't go now, neither one of us will be happy."

He cut off the memories and buried them under a layer of fury. She'd made it seem like she was doing him a favor by walking away. As if the dreams they'd forged together for years hadn't been as important as the ones she'd nurtured all to herself.

Well, she'd ripped his heart out that night and he'd had to shut himself down to get through it. But he had. He'd made a damn good life without Emma and it was only going to get better. And once he'd faced her and had his say, he could get back to it.

When he steered his top-of-the-line, black Dodge Ram truck up the drive to her father's ranch, he noted the peeling paint on the fence rails and the weeds choking out the front flower bed. The Williams place had been slowly going to hell since Emma left. Just another black mark against her.

Frank Williams had pretty much given up when his oldest girl had run off to Hollywood. He'd expected her to take over, to merge their ranch with Caden's as they'd always planned.

Emma had torn up a lot of dreams when she left to find her own.

Still, Caden felt a pang of guilt. He should make more time to check in on Frank and do what he could to help out. Frowning to himself, he made a mental note to send a few of his ranch hands over in a day or two to paint the corral fence. Get it done before winter, he told himself, or the damn wood would rot and warp and the whole fence would have to be replaced.

"The perfect metaphor," he muttered. When Emma left, they'd all had to rebuild. She'd taken off to chase a dream and left the rest of them wondering what the hell had happened. Now she was back.

With a baby.

He parked the truck, turned off the engine and just sat there for a minute, staring at the house where he'd spent so much of his life. It was old and sturdy, yellow, with white trim because that's how Emma's mother had liked it best. There was a big front porch and a second story where the bedrooms were. He knew this house as well as he knew his own.

He and Emma had been a couple since the year she was a freshman in high school. He'd been a "manly" junior and took substantial mocking from his friends for being interested in a "kid," but he hadn't cared.

Emma was all he'd been able to see back then and until the night she'd walked away, that hadn't changed.

But things were different now. Emma had left once before. Why should he believe she was here to stay *now*? No, what was between them had curled up and died five years ago.

Yet even as that thought rose up in his mind, his body was tightening at the prospect of being near her again.

While he sat there, watching the house, the front door flew open and Gracie, Emma's younger sister, raced toward him. Caden got out of the truck in time to catch her when Gracie threw herself at him.

"I can't believe this," she muttered against his chest. "She just showed up last night like it was *nothing* and we're supposed to be happy she's here." She pulled her head back and glared up at him. "I'm not. I'm furious."

At twenty-five, Gracie was a beauty, with short, curly brown hair and green eyes a shade paler than her sister's. He'd been a big brother to Gracie all their lives and he could see that there was pain as well as fury in her eyes.

He knew how she felt. "Gwen ran into her at the market this morning. Said she's come back to stay."

Gracie let him go, took a step back and swiped a solitary tear off her cheek. "That's what she says, but why should we believe her? She left before, didn't she?"

He didn't know if it was good or bad that Gracie was pretty much echoing his own thoughts on the matter.

"Dad's happy to see her anyway." She shoved her hands into her jeans pockets and tossed her windblown hair off her forehead. "He actually got out of bed this morning."

That was news. Frank had given up on life about a year after Emma left. Little by little, he'd withdrawn more and more from everyday life. He'd started out hoping Emma would see she'd made a mistake and come running home. But finally, the older man had realized that his girl was probably gone forever and all the life in him had just drained away. Not even Gracie had been able to coax him out of the depression he'd dropped into.

If Emma left again, it'd probably kill her father this time.

"She can't be here, Caden," Gracie was saying. "What if she finds out? She'll tell Dad and then—"

"*You* should tell your dad," Caden whispered. He was the only person Gracie had trusted with her secrets and he'd never betray her. But he did think she was handling them all wrong and didn't mind saying so.

"I can't," she said, shaking her head. "Especially not now."

"Hello, Caden."

Just like that, everything in him went still and cold. He hadn't heard that low-pitched, sultry voice in too damn long, but it had the same effect on him it always had. He turned to look, saw Emma standing in the open doorway and his mouth went dry. His jeans were suddenly too tight and drawing a breath seemed near impossible.

The last time he'd seen her was on his television screen. Emma had been starring in a vapid, ridiculous sitcom, and as hard as it had been for Caden to admit, she had been really good in it. So good, he'd watched the show exactly once, got stinking drunk and never turned the damn TV on again. She'd left him for Hollywood and it burned his ass that she'd done well.

Now she was back, and why did she have to look so damn tempting?

Her dark brown hair was longer, falling well past

her shoulders now, in the wild, thick curls she'd always hated. She wore a long-sleeved red flannel shirt and a pair of black jeans that hugged her hips and long, shapely legs. Her old boots completed the outfit and somehow it felt to Caden as if she'd donned a costume to fit in.

Maybe the Hollywood Emma was the real person now and this woman in front of him was the one acting out a part.

And as much as he wanted her, Caden braced himself against old emotions, desires and faced her now with the cold, empty memories flooding his mind. Her greenish-gold eyes were still as clear and beautiful as ever, but as he met her gaze, Caden saw secrets there. Something he'd never seen before.

He didn't like it.

"You're not going to say hello?" she asked.

The voice that had haunted his dreams. The woman who had haunted *everything* in his life. Caden felt a sharp stab of betrayal. She'd walked out on him five years ago and never looked back. Now she said hello like nothing had changed between them? Were they supposed to go have a drink? Catch up on old times? Maybe she'd ask him to babysit. Well, screw that.

Beside him, Gracie had a death grip on his arm, her fingers digging into his skin right through the fabric of his heavy brown coat. Reminding him where his loyalties lay now. Gracie had stayed. Had taken care of everything that Emma had walked away from. So he'd stand with her against the woman who had left them both.

"What're you doing here, Emma?"

She lifted her chin, kept her gaze fixed on his and said simply, "This is my home."

"Not for five years."

She chewed at her bottom lip and that action tugged at something inside him, too. Heat bubbled in his gut but Caden ignored it.

"I'm back now," Emma told him. "I'm not leaving again."

"Is that right?" He didn't believe her.

"It is. I'm done with Hollywood." Her chin was still lifted in self-defense mode.

She'd had success, though he didn't want to admit it. So what had changed her mind? What had chased her home? And why the hell did he still care after all this time?

"What changed?" he asked, before he could stop himself.

"I guess I did," she said.

He nodded. "Right. You changed five years ago. And now you've changed again. When's the next change coming?"

"There won't be one."

"Don't believe her," Gracie murmured.

"Oh, I don't," Caden assured her and had the satisfaction of seeing Emma's eyes flash. Anger? Insult? Didn't matter which. As long as she knew where he stood.

Even knowing he couldn't trust her didn't stop Caden from wanting her with a bone-deep desire that had never really left him. "Why don't you go inside, Gracie? I want to talk to Emma."

She gave him a long, speculative look, then did as he asked, skirting past her sister still standing in the doorway.

"Wow." Emma's gaze locked on him. "You and Gracie must be really close these days. She's taking orders from you now?"

"It wasn't an order," he told her. "It was a request."

"That she hopped to fulfill." Tipping her head to one side, she kept her eyes on him. "What's going on between you two?"

Caden stared right back, and folded his arms across his chest. He hadn't missed the temper in her tone. "You don't get to ask that question, Emma. It's none of your business."

"She's my sister."

He laughed shortly. "You've been gone for years, Emma. All of a sudden now, you're sisters?"

"I didn't leave the family, Caden," she argued and her chin lifted a little higher. "I left Montana."

"And *me*."

She took a breath, nodded and said, "Yeah. And you. But I explained why I had to go."

Anger whipped through him like a lightning bolt. "That makes it okay that you took off? As long as you 'explained'?"

She took a breath, stuffed her hands into her jeans pockets and stared at him for a long moment before asking, "What is it you want from me, Caden?"

Well, now, that was the question, wasn't it? He'd come here to have his say. To set things straight with Emma and let her know exactly where he stood. But being here, with her, was making it hard to think.

He looked her up and down, felt a stir of need and squashed it. When he held her gaze again, he leaned in and whispered, *"Absolutely nothing."*

Two

Absolutely nothing.

For the next several days, those two words echoed in Emma's brain. There was a lot to do around the ranch and yet she couldn't shake Caden's voice.

"No surprise there," she muttered as she shuffled equipment around in the tack room. Caden had never been far from her mind. Yes, she'd walked away from him, but she'd had to follow her heart, right? Fight for her dream or end up an old woman, eaten by regret.

"You'd think he'd understand that," she said tightly. "The man has a one-track mind when it comes to *his* dreams. What? I'm not allowed to chase mine? Is that it? I can only have the dreams that don't inconvenience him?"

Absolutely nothing.

But it seemed he wanted *something* from Emma's

sister. Gracie had gone to Caden's place nearly every day. Why? Jealousy bristled in her chest and twisted around her heart, giving it a hard squeeze. Was Gracie sleeping with him? Had he moved from one sister to another without missing a beat? Was Gracie the one sharing in Caden's dreams now?

She had no way of knowing since her sister hadn't really spoken to her since that first day. The two of them passed each other in the house locked in a strained silence that their father was either not noticing or actively ignoring.

Frank was completely in love with baby Molly, though, and every day, he seemed to return a bit more to the man that Emma remembered. His granddaughter had given him a new lease on life, he claimed, and that worried Emma, too. There was simply too much going on. Too many things to feel. To think. To be anxious over.

Why had she ever thought that coming home would be easy?

She grabbed two shovels and slammed them into the corner. This whole ranch was a mess. The barn, the stable, the house. Oh, it was all still standing, but it looked to Emma like no one had been paying attention to what needed doing. Except Caden, apparently. A couple of men from his ranch had been over two days ago, to repaint the corral fences, and when she had told them they didn't need his help, they'd ignored her, too. Said that they took orders from Caden and if she had a problem with it, she should take it up with him.

As if she could.

So now the fences had been painted, but the grass was too high, and the railing on the wraparound porch was wobbly. And the tack room was in shambles. "There are *shelves* for God's sake. Why aren't they using them?"

Anger guided Emma as she picked up saddle soap, cloths and a million other little supplies that were tossed around. One by one, she straightened them out, lining them up on the shelves and giving it all a nod of satisfaction when she was finished. For a soul as organized as Emma, this place was torture.

"And why is there an old saddle on the desk?" she asked no one.

"It's waiting to be repaired."

Emma spun around to see her younger sister standing in the doorway. "How long's it been waiting?"

Gracie shrugged. "A few months I guess."

"Months?" Emma shook her head, exasperated at the mess and her sister's nonchalant attitude. "Why hasn't Buck fixed it?"

"Buck quit six months ago."

"What?" Buck Simpson had worked for them since Emma was a girl. He was a master at saddlery and had kept the ranch equipment in tip-top shape. "Why?"

Gracie shrugged again and leaned one shoulder against the doorjamb. "He said he was getting too old to deal with ranching in winter. He went to live with his daughter and her husband on their ranch outside Billings. It still snows, but he doesn't have to get out and work in it every day."

Another change she hadn't known about and she didn't like it. "Why didn't you tell me? You could've emailed or something."

"Yeah, because we've been so close."

Emma sighed, shoved her hands into the back pockets of her jeans and looked at the little sister who used to follow her around like a puppy. "You know, I tried to stay close. I left the ranch, I didn't leave the *family*. I wrote to you, Gracie. I called. *You* never did."

"What was I supposed to say?" Gracie countered, pushing off the doorjamb. "Happy trails? Good luck with your perfect life while I'm here trying to hold a ranch together?"

God. She would have laughed at that if she hadn't felt like screeching.

"Perfect? You think my life was perfect?" Emma actually felt her eyes roll. "Going to auditions and never getting the part? Being told that if you sleep with the producer, he'll *consider* hiring you?

"Being on your feet for a twelve-hour shift at a restaurant because the landlord just jacked your rent higher? *Again?* Having your ass patted by an old man when you bring his lunch order?"

"Wait," Gracie said, holding up one hand and looking around the room for effect. "Let me find a tissue."

"God, you're a bitch."

"Said the queen bitch of the universe."

Frustration rippled through her. She kept trying and kept getting shut down. Her life in Hollywood hadn't been *anyone's* idea of a dream and there was plenty more that she wasn't telling Gracie. Dark, hard things that she'd never told anyone and wouldn't use to get a glimmer of sympathy now.

"What the hell, Gracie?" Emma threw her hands up, faced her sister and demanded, "What is going on with you? This isn't all about me moving to California. You can't be this mad about me being gone for a few years. There's something else going on."

Gracie's features tightened, then went deliberately blank. "You don't know me, Emma. Not anymore. And just so you know? Everything else is fine. Just stop expecting me to be happy to have you home."

"You didn't want me leaving and now you don't want me here." Emma shook her head, then tossed her hair back behind her shoulders. "What the hell *do* you want?"

For just a split second, something flashed in Gracie's eyes, but it was gone an instant later. Emma had the distinct feeling she'd almost reached the real Gracie. The little sister she'd missed for so long.

"Nothing," Gracie said. "Look. I only came out here to tell you your daughter woke up. She's crying."

Emma drew her head back as if she'd been slapped. "And you couldn't pick her up?"

For a second, her sister's eyes shone with shame, but it didn't last long. Defiant, she lifted her chin. "I'm not your babysitter, Em. And neither is Dad."

Emma gave her a hard look. "I didn't say you were. And Dad takes care of her because he *wants* to. I haven't heard him complain about Molly."

"Of course not." Gracie took a breath and lifted one hand to push her hair back from her face. "He'd never say anything to you. You think he wants to risk you leaving again?"

"I told you. And him. I'm not leaving."

"And we should believe you," Gracie said wryly, quirking a brow.

"Damn it, Gracie, is it going to be like this between us all the time now?"

"I don't know. If it is, will you leave?"

"No."

"We'll see, won't we," Gracie said, then turned away before Emma could speak. The anger and hurt in her sister's eyes was impossible to miss.

"Wow. Welcome home, Emma."

"Right. I'll get the balloons." Gracie turned on her heel, then looked back over her shoulder. "By the way, the vet's coming over later. I'd appreciate it if you'd leave us alone."

She was gone before Emma could respond and maybe it was just as well. These "conversations" with Gracie were exhausting and sort of circular. No matter which direction they went, it eventually returned to *you left us.* And there was no argument to that because Emma had left her old life behind to try for something else. Something she'd dreamed of doing since she was a kid. No one seemed to understand that and for the millionth time, Emma found herself wishing her mom were still alive. Maggie Williams would have understood.

Emma fumed for another minute or two. Just long enough to make sure she wouldn't have to walk alongside Gracie back to the house. She'd had no idea when she left Montana that she would completely shatter the relationship she had with her sister. Emma was five years older than her sister and so she'd always looked after Gracie—especially since their mother died when Gracie was fourteen. And now it felt as if they were armed camps on opposite sides of a battle.

She blew out a breath, finished organizing the shelves and then swept the floor, focusing the burning energy inside toward getting *something* in her life straightened out. Coming home was turning into a big-scale drama. Her father was deteriorating, her sister was furious and her old boyfriend could barely stand to look at her. If she'd had the energy, Emma might have thrown herself a little pity party. But since she didn't, she headed for the house and the baby girl who needed her instead.

Molly was nearly five months old and her personality was, thank God, happy. The tiny girl welcomed everyone with a toothless smile and only cried when she was hungry or wet. You just couldn't ask for much more than that. Having Molly in her life had been a surprise, but Emma was determined to protect that baby girl. To give Molly the kind of life she'd had, growing up.

Which was the main reason she was back in Montana taking a mountain of crap from everyone.

She found her father and Molly in the living room. The baby was on his lap, laughing as Frank made silly faces. Was it her imagination, or did her dad look better today than he had when she'd arrived just a few days before? His eyes were brighter, his hair was combed and he'd shaved. All good signs that Gracie hadn't bothered to mention. Plus, her little sister had made it sound as if Frank was aggrieved at taking care of the baby but it looked to Emma as if he was having a great time.

Gracie and she were going to have to have a long talk. Soon.

"Dad?"

He turned to grin at her. "Hello, honey, what're you up to?"

"Oh, I was just…" She waved one hand toward the outside. "Straightening out the tack room."

He chuckled. "You always did have your mother's neat streak."

Emma walked up to him and sat down on the chair closest to him. "Gracie told me Buck quit."

He frowned. "He did, but couldn't blame him any. He's older than I am and damned if I'm out working the ranch every day."

The baby slapped both of her little hands on top of his and then played with his fingers.

"Got to remember to watch my language now, don't I?" He grinned down at Molly. "This little darling reminds me so much of you at her age."

Emma felt a tiny pang that she refused to identify or acknowledge. "Does she?"

"Always happy, always looking for the next thing…" His smile faded a bit, but his eyes were still shining. "I'm glad to have you home, Emma, and that's the truth."

She leaned forward, reached out and squeezed his hand briefly. "I'm glad somebody is." She blew out a breath in frustration. "Gracie sneers at me every time we pass by each other."

He laughed. "Well, Gracie's just put out. She's done her best these last five years, but she doesn't have your confidence. Never has. So she doubts everything she does."

Emma didn't like the sound of that. "Well, she shouldn't. She's always seemed so sure of herself to me. Even in school, she went her own way no matter what anyone else had to say."

"All true," he mused. "But at the heart of it, she questions herself."

"She hates me now." Emma picked at a fraying thread on the arm of the couch.

Frank laughed again. "No, she doesn't. She's just afraid to enjoy having you back. Probably thinking you're not going to stay."

Gracie wouldn't be worried about that in the slightest if she knew what had been a huge motivating factor in driving Emma home in the first place. Oh, she had been planning on coming back to Montana, but she'd pushed her schedule up fast for one reason only. But that wasn't something she could talk about. Not even with her family.

Watching her, Frank asked quietly, "Is she right? Are you just stopping by for a visit before you take off again?"

She couldn't blame her father for the question. When she left, Emma had had big plans. She'd done her best, and put everything she had into making those plans a reality. None of it had worked out and by the end of her time in California she had been wondering why she'd ever left Montana in the first place. Now she'd come home to build different dreams. And this time, she would succeed.

But it wasn't only her family and her home that had pulled her back to Montana. It was Caden. The cowboy she'd left behind. The man who could set her body ablaze with a look. The man who starred in her dreams nightly. The man she'd never been able to forget—not that she'd really tried.

"No, Dad," she said, leaning forward to lay her hand on his forearm. She wanted him to see her resolve. To feel that she was really back for good. Her gaze locked with his and she willed him to believe her. "Molly and I are home to stay."

He studied her for a long moment or two, then pleasure shone on his face. "Relieved to hear that, Em," he said. "Don't think I could stand watching you leave again and taking this little nugget with you."

"You don't have to worry," she assured him.

"And Molly's daddy?" Frank asked, sliding her a glance. "What's he have to say about all of this? Doesn't he mind you bringing his daughter to Montana?"

Emma went completely still, then forced her mouth to curve slightly. Molly's father wasn't someone she could talk about. This was dangerous territory. She hated lying to her own father, but there were some things she couldn't tell him. At least not now.

"Molly's father isn't involved with her at all, Dad. He doesn't know where we are and that's the way I hope it stays."

"Did he hurt you?" Instantly, her affable, loving dad went into grizzly mode.

Emma's heart swelled, relishing the feeling of being loved so fiercely. She actually didn't need protection, but it was lovely to have it offered so freely. And she was grateful that she could at least tell him the truth about this.

"No. He didn't." She got up, kissed his forehead and said, "Nothing like that. I swear."

"All right, then." He stroked one hand down Molly's silky black hair. "As long as you two are here and safe. That's all that's important."

"Just how I feel." And as long as Molly was safe, Emma could deal with just about anything. Then her father spoke up and tested that thought.

"Caden called me this morning."

Her gaze snapped to his. Warily, she asked, "What did he want?"

"Oh, just to tell me he was going to send some of his men over to mow the meadow behind the barn."

Frowning, Emma thought about that. Every year,

they mowed the meadow, to protect it. The fallen grasses acted as mulch and the clipped-off seedpods planted themselves for the following spring. But since when did her ex take care of that?

"Why?" She straightened up and looked down at her father in disbelief. "First his men come and paint our fence. Now they're mowing our meadow?"

"Well," Frank mused, barely hiding the curve of his lips, "let's think about that. Could be, it's just him being neighborly. Could be, he's trying to impress you."

A choked-off laugh shot from her throat as she remembered clearly the look on his face when he'd murmured, *Absolutely nothing.* "No, it's not that, trust me."

"Seem awful sure."

"You didn't see him when he was here." She stalked over to the fireplace and idly noted that it had been turned into a gas hearth sometime while she was gone. Easier, probably. But she'd always loved the hiss and snap of real flames over real wood.

"No, but I saw him after you left for California."

She closed her eyes briefly, then looked back over her shoulder at her father. "I know I hurt him."

"Crushed him, more like."

Guilt reared up and took a bite of her heart. She knew her father was right. She'd known it then. It hadn't stopped her because she hadn't allowed it to. If she'd let herself acknowledge what she was doing to Caden— heck, to *herself*—by leaving, she might not have gone. And if she'd stayed, she'd still be wondering. Still be dreaming. Maybe Hollywood wasn't for her, but at least now, she knew that for herself. Still, she admitted silently, maybe she could have handled it better. "I had to go, Dad."

"I know that," Frank said, giving her an under-standing smile. "Didn't make it any easier to lose you. I know why you had to leave, too. You think I didn't realize what your mother gave up to marry me and have our family?" He shook his head and sighed. "She had dreams, too, Emma, and she died not knowing if they could have come true. That still tears at me."

Emma instantly felt guilty for the pain she saw in her father's eyes. "Oh, Dad, Mom loved you. Loved us."

He snorted. "Hell, I know that. Doesn't mean a part of her wasn't wishing that she'd gone to Nash-ville and tried her hand at singing professionally." Frank smoothed the baby's hair and wistfully said, "That's why I was glad you tried, honey. As bad as it was with you gone, I was glad you were trying."

Tears stung her eyes and Emma blinked them back. At least her dad was glad to have her home. In the quiet, the baby cooed and gurgled in Frank's arms. Outside the windows, the October sky was leaden and a hard gust shook the turning leaves on the trees. A week ago, she'd been in Southern California, where the only sign of fall was the pumpkin spice lattes for sale on every corner. Here in Montana, the wind was cold, the trees golden and red and you could smell winter in the air.

It was good to be back. But, since she was here to stay, she would have to have a talk with Caden.

Absolutely nothing.

His voice repeated in Emma's mind again and she scowled to herself. Coming home was never going to be easy. She hadn't expected it to be. And she'd known that facing Caden again would be one of the hardest things she'd ever done, but she hadn't realized how hard it would be to not touch him. To not be touched by him.

Seeing him again, hearing his voice had brought everything inside her back to life—only to be slapped down
by his dismissal. She'd thought she was ready to see
him again. Apparently, she'd been wrong.

"Things'll get better," her father said and she turned
around to face him. He shifted the baby in his arms so
that little Molly was looking directly at her. Emma's
heart squeezed in her chest. That tiny girl had become
all-important and there was simply nothing she wouldn't
do to protect her. Bringing her here had assured that
Molly would be cared for. Loved. It was up to Emma
to see that she stayed that way.

"You'll find your path, and you brought my granddaughter home, too," Frank was saying and Emma's
heart gave another hard lurch. "Your sister will get past
what she's feeling. You two will work it out."

Emma wasn't so sure, but all right.

"As for me, though," Frank said, pushing up out
of his chair and cradling Molly against his chest, "I
couldn't be happier. Now I'm going to go give our girl
here some lunch—"

"Dad," she said, remembering some of what Gracie
had said just a while ago, "I didn't bring the baby here
expecting you to babysit."

Insult stamped itself on his features. "Spending time
with my granddaughter isn't 'babysitting,'" he told her.
"Besides, makes me remember when my own girls were
little. Your mother and I were hopping every minute."

A soft smile curved her mouth. "I still miss her."

"So do I, darling. Every damn day." Frank sighed a
little, then grinned when Molly slapped her hands together. "She'd have loved this little one. So don't you

worry about me and Molly. We're fine. You go and do something useful."

Something useful. Was talking to Caden a waste of time? Or a chance to set them both on a different path?

She watched her father walk away and thought about it. She could go back and finish cleaning out the tack room. Or she could go over the ranch books and see exactly where they stood financially. Or maybe go and talk to the cowboys and hear their opinions.

But she wasn't going to do any of that, Emma realized.

"Dad?"

He stopped and looked back at her, waiting.

Decision made, she said, "If it's okay with you, I'm going over to Caden's. Maybe settle a few things."

Her father winked. "That's a good idea, honey. You go ahead. Take your time."

When he left, Emma walked across the room and grabbed her heavy brown jacket off the coat tree in the hall. Take her time. That was assuming that Caden would speak to her at all. But even as she considered that, she remembered that she'd always been able to talk her way around that stubborn cowboy. Today would be no different.

They would get everything out in the open and find a way to deal with each other. Or, she considered, this would blow up in her face and she'd be no further along than she was right now.

Pulling her coat on, Emma stepped out onto the wide porch. There was a lot to do around here and she'd barely made a dent in any of it in the past few days.

But facing Caden was more important. All of the work would still be here waiting for her when she got

back, she reminded herself. Digging her car keys out
of her jacket pocket, she headed for the old and cranky
SUV that had brought her and Molly all the way from
Los Angeles.

She climbed in, fired it up and threw it into gear.
Out by the stable, she saw Gracie talking to a woman
with long, braided red hair and a face full of freckles.
Must be the vet, she thought, then waved when Gracie
turned to fire a glare at her. If her sister was mad, she
only had herself to blame. She'd actually told Emma to
stay away. So she would.

Turning the car around, she headed down the drive
to the road that would take her to Caden's house. They
were going to talk, damn it. And she wasn't going to
take no for an answer.

Dirt and gravel flew up in her wake like the tail of a
dragon and she barely noticed Gracie, standing in the
yard, staring after her.

Three

Caden helped load the mare into a fancy horse trailer big enough for four horses. His buyer's teenage daughter was thrilled to be getting her own horse and he was pleased to have another satisfied customer.

Once the mare was inside and the back was closed, Caden walked to the front, opened the door and stepped inside. The mare tossed her pretty head when he entered and he had to smile.

"Yeah, you're a beauty and I'm sorry to lose you," he whispered, running his hands up and down her long, elegant neck. "But that girl out there is going to love you like crazy and spoil you even more than I do."

He stroked the star-shaped blaze on her forehead and just for a moment, allowed himself to remember the night this mare was born. Eight years ago. He and Emma had stayed up all night with Star's mother, talking, comforting, and they had been there when Star was born. Emma had been the one to name her and they'd planned to have Star be the first of a herd of beauties they would breed and build together.

Then they'd celebrated by making love in the loft above the stable.

God, he could still feel the heat, the magic of touching her, of being inside her, of having Emma's hands on his body.

Star whickered as if even the horse could judge his shift in mood. Well, hell, damned if he'd be so transparent an *animal* could read him. Shaking his head, Caden stroked her forehead one last time and said, "You be good to that girl and she'll love you all her life."

Just for a second, he thought about how ironic it was that he was selling Star now. Caden had thought that in letting the horse go, he'd be getting rid of the last real reminder of Emma on the ranch. Was it cosmic or karmic or just fate with a sense of humor to send Emma home now?

"It's a kick in the ass for damn sure," he muttered.

Then he turned his back on the past and walked out of the trailer and into an icy wind. Shaking hands with Matt Fraser, he said, "You've got a good horse there."

"We'll take care of her," the other man said.

Nodding, Caden looked at the man's daughter. About fourteen years old, she was practically vibrating with excitement.

"Your dad says you'll take good care of Star. Is that right?"

"I will," she said solemnly, her eyes locked on his face. "I promise I will."

He nodded. "If you do, that horse will love you forever."

"Thank you!" The words rushed from her and she impulsively gave Caden a hard hug. When she let him go, she looked up at him, eyes dazzled. "This is the best day of my whole life."

Caden smiled, despite the pang of regret he felt in losing Star. There was nothing quite like the relationship between a person and a horse.

And now, this young girl was clearly seeing a long, happy future ahead of her and Star. He hoped she had half the fun he'd had with River. "Well, you'd better get her home so you two can have a ride."

The girl raced to close the door on the trailer and jump into the front seat of her dad's truck. A few minutes later, the Frasers and Star were gone in a swirl of dust and wind.

Caden watched them go and realized that it was easier now to say goodbye. To let go. When Emma had left him, she'd ripped the earth out from beneath his feet. But she'd taught him something, too. He'd learned that he could survive loss.

And most importantly, he'd learned he couldn't trust Emma.

Gracie watched Emma drive off and a part of her wondered if she'd be back. She hated feeling the way she did, but Emma had hurt her deeply by leaving and that pain was still with her. How could she just forget? Forgive?

She huddled deeper into her jacket and pulled the collar up to protect her neck. Every winter, she thought about growing her hair out just because it would be warmer. Then in the summer, she was grateful it was short.

She tipped her head back to look at the sky and shivered a little at the gunmetal-gray clouds swarming in. Brightly colored leaves were ripped from the trees and sent tumbling on the icy afternoon wind.

"The place looks nice," Madison Peters said. "You got the corral fence painted."

Gracie smiled. "That was Caden. He sent some of his guys over to take care of it a couple days ago."

"He's a good friend," Madison mused.

"Yeah," Gracie said, "he is." Caden was someone she could always count on. He'd promised he'd take care of it and he had. When Caden gave his word, you could put money on it. That was something Gracie had really come to appreciate over the past five years. When she needed help, he was there. Unlike Emma.

Fresh anger erupted and bubbled in the pit of her stomach. She didn't like it. Didn't want to be so furious with the sister she'd loved so desperately most of her life. But how was she supposed to get past what she was feeling?

"Gracie, you've got to get over this thing with your sister."

She turned her head to look at the other woman, not even surprised that Madison had read what she was feeling. Her long red hair was pulled back in a braid, to keep it out of her way while she was working. Her pretty face was dotted with golden freckles and her green eyes shone like twin emeralds when she smiled. Which she wasn't doing at the moment.

"How'm I supposed to do that?"

Madison threw both hands up. "I don't know. Be

grateful you have someone else here to help you with the ranch?" She tipped her head to one side and asked, "Aren't you always telling me that you need extra help here? Well, now Emma's home and you'll have it."

"Will I?" Gracie's mouth twisted. "She was in here straightening out the tack room earlier and now no one's going to be able to find anything."

Madison laughed. "I'm willing to thank her for bringing a little order into that room. And you should, too."

"Now I should thank her?" Disgusted with Mad and with herself, Gracie turned her face into the wind. "No. She can't slide back into her own life like nothing ever happened."

"Is she really trying to do that?"

"Yeah," Gracie said, staring at the other woman. "She's acting like she never left! She's back in her old bedroom and she's taken over mom's sewing room for the baby…"

"You weren't using it for anything."

"You don't get it, Mad," Gracie said, shaking her head and pushing her own hair out of her eyes.

"Gracie…"

"She just does whatever the hell she feels like and screw what anyone else thinks about it."

Madison sighed. "You're just mad at her. Still."

"Of course I am."

Irritated that her friend wasn't able to understand what she was feeling, Gracie had to bite back a quick burst of anger. It wasn't surprising that she couldn't see this. Madison was new to Cache. She'd only moved there three years ago to take over the retiring vet's office. And almost from the moment they met, Mad and Gracie had been thick as thieves.

Taking a breath, Gracie now told herself to relax. Usually, she really appreciated Mad's optimistic, sunshiny attitude. But today, she'd really like her best friend to be on her side. "You weren't here when Emma left town. You don't know how hard it was. On everybody."

"You're right. I wasn't here," Madison agreed. "But you've told me about it. You've also told me how close you and Emma always were. So why're you so mad that she finally came home?"

"Whose side are you on?" Gracie asked, a little wounded that Madison was being so damn impartial.

The redhead laughed shortly. "Yours. I'm always on your side, Gracie. I just think maybe you should cut her a small break."

"Okay, what about this?" Gracie stepped in closer to Madison. "What if Emma's going to Caden's? What if he *tells* her?"

Worry flashed across Madison's eyes briefly and didn't do a thing to lessen Gracie's anxiety.

"Do you think he would?"

"No, but I didn't think Emma would ever come home, either, so don't go by my opinion."

"All right." Madison nodded sharply. "Let's say he *does* tell her. Would that really be so bad? Don't you have to tell her and your dad at some point?"

"Sure I do. But when I'm ready."

"And when will that be?" Madison's voice was small and Gracie winced.

"Soon. I swear, soon," she said and reached out to briefly squeeze Madison's hand.

"Secrets never stay secret, Gracie," Madison said.

"And I don't want it to," Gracie took a breath and chewed at her bottom lip. "Right now, I don't know how to tell them. But I'm going to figure it out. I swear."

"I know you will. And when you're ready, remember that I'm here for you." Madison gave her a smile. "But I'm not the only one who cares about you. You've got your dad. And now your sister. And the baby's here. You can't fool me, Gracie. I know how much you love kids. So let yourself love that baby."

Gracie sighed a little. She already did love that tiny girl, but she was afraid to let it show because what if Emma left? Again?

"How about," Madison continued, "when Emma comes home, you talk to her. Sit down, have a beer and just get it all out."

She laughed shortly. "Never thought I'd say this, but a beer can't solve everything."

"It's a start…"

"Why do you have to be so understanding all the time?"

"Because someone has to be." Madison asked, "Are you mad she left? Or mad she came home?"

"Both." Gracie waved one hand before Madison could say anything. "And yes, I know that makes zero sense."

Madison grinned. "Well, at least you know it."

Scowling, Gracie looked at the other woman. "You're not helping."

"I don't know how to help." She shrugged, and grabbed her bag before heading into the stable. Gracie stuck with her and Madison kept talking. "You and Emma used to be close."

"Key words there being *used to be*."

They walked into the stable and Madison headed for the far stall, where Diamond, an aging stallion, was waiting. "Uh-huh, but she's back. And the only thing stopping the two of you from being close again, is *you*."

"It's not the only thing," Gracie muttered darkly. She was feeling like a temperamental child throwing a tantrum. And speaking of child… "And she's got a baby she never bothered to tell us about. Who does that, Mad? Who doesn't tell her family that she's pregnant?"

Madison glanced at her before stepping into the stall. "We all have secrets, don't we, Gracie?"

She flushed and didn't like it. "Okay, good point. But she's clearly expecting Dad and I to take care of Molly."

"You love kids." Madison cooed and soothed the horse, then slowly bent to inspect the small nick on his foreleg.

"Not the point."

"What *is* the point, Gracie?"

Irritated, frustrated and just feeling so not herself, Gracie snapped, "The point is, Queen Emma has arrived and all of us peasants are expected to toss confetti her way."

Madison straightened up, looked at her for a long second or two, then burst out laughing. "Honestly, you're really going over the top here, Gracie. She's your sister. She came home. Sure, you can be upset, but she's *family*. That hasn't changed."

Gracie stuffed both hands into her jacket pockets and faced her friend. "I can't forget that she left."

"No one's asking you to," Madison said, bent down again, to medicate and wrap the small cut on the horse's leg. When she was finished, she stood up, and looked at Gracie across the half-door of the stall. "All I'm say-

ing is that maybe you set the last five years aside—"
she held up one hand when Gracie would have spoken
"—and try to find your way from here."

"I don't know…" Gracie turned her head to look
toward the open double doors and the darkening day
outside. "She wasn't here, Mad. When I really needed
her, she wasn't here."

Sighing a little, Madison left the stall, and set her bag
down. Then she hugged Gracie tightly before taking a
step back and meeting her eyes. "I know, honey. And
it was hard for you. But you got through. And maybe
it was a good thing that you had to face things on your
own. Make the hard decisions and learn what you really wanted."

Giving her a wry smile, Gracie said, "Have I told you
that I really hate it when you're so rational?"

"That's why I do it," Mad told her with a quick grin.

Gracie gave her a hard hug, then let her go. "Fine.
I'll try." She narrowed her eyes. "I make no promises,
but I'll try."

"That's good enough," Madison said. "Now, Diamond should be fine, but I'll be back tomorrow to check
on him."

"That's the best news I've had today. I like when
you're here."

"I'm glad," Madison said with a quick, impish grin.
"Now, why don't you walk me out to my truck?"

"Sure." Gracie fell into step beside her. "Are we still
on for dinner tonight?"

"As long as the Callahan's cow doesn't go into labor,"
Madison said. "Fingers crossed. I'll call you if I can't
make it. Otherwise, I'll meet you at the Little River
Diner at five."

Gracie opened the door and held it while Madison climbed in. "Thanks for listening to me rant."

Madison grinned again and her bright green eyes sparkled. "Not a problem. Now you owe me the next time I need to vent."

"Deal."

She patted Gracie's hand. "Don't be so hard on Emma. She might surprise you."

"Yeah. That's what I'm afraid of," Gracie admitted.

On the short ride to Caden's Emma rehearsed what she wanted to say. Not that it would help. The minute she saw him again, her mouth would go dry and her heart would hammer in her chest. Caden had been having that effect on her for as long as she could remember.

And during the years she was in California, surrounded by men who were deliberately gorgeous and continually posing to put themselves in the best possible light, she hadn't met a single one as amazing as the cowboy she'd left behind.

"This is such a bad idea," she told herself sternly, driving along the narrow road.

Seeing him, being with him, was only going to stir up more of the feelings he'd made it clear he wasn't interested in reviving. But she was home now. She wasn't leaving again. Caden's ranch was so close to hers and Cache was such a small town, they'd be seeing each other all the time. So they had to find a way to be together without a constant state of war between them. "That would just be exhausting."

She glanced into the rearview mirror and wished she'd taken the time to put on some eye makeup or something. But if she'd waited, she might have avoided facing Caden at all. So she was going to face down her former lover without a shred of makeup and with her hair in a tangle from the wild, cold wind rushing across Montana.

She gave her reflection a quick glare. "Why do you care what you look like? It's not as if you're going over there to seduce him."

Though that thought set up a flicker of fire that had her shifting uncomfortably in her seat. A moment later, her mind lit up with memories. God, sex with Caden had spoiled her for any other man. Not that she'd lived like a vestal virgin for the five years she was gone. But no one had come close to making her feel what Caden could with a single touch.

Images raced through her mind, one after another. Moonlit nights in Caden's arms. The two of them, naked and wrapped around each other in a sunlit meadow. Sex in a canoe that had ended up being sex in the lake once they'd capsized the narrow boat. Her lips twisted into a reluctant smile, but in the next instant, that smile faded.

Everything was different now.

Familiar countryside stretched out on either side of the road. Trees, meadows, the last lingering wild-flowers, already bent in half by the cold wind bringing winter. So much was the same, and yet so much had changed.

Caden had once been not only her lover, but her best friend. The one person she could go to with anything. He had been her touchstone.

Now he was a stranger to her and seemingly way too close to her little sister. Gracie had gone running over to Caden's three times in the few days Emma had been home. Why? What was going on there?

She remembered how Gracie had thrown herself into Caden's arms two days ago. She'd also heard her sister on the phone with him several times since then and late last night, Gracie had gone to Caden's place again to "talk." Anger bubbled inside and with it, some jealousy, as well. Was Gracie going after Caden because he'd once been Emma's? Was Caden doing the same thing?

She chewed at her bottom lip and ignored the swarms of what felt like dragons in the pit of her stomach.

Her hands tightened on the steering wheel. "If he's using Gracie to get back at me, that's going to stop today."

She made the turn into the Double H drive and familiarity stirred inside. How many times had she come down this road, to this ranch, running to Caden? She couldn't even count them all.

And Emma remembered that she and Caden had once planned to lay out a road linking their two ranches. Going straight across their land, it would be a private road, cutting ten minutes off the trip, making sure their families could always reach each other in a hurry.

But that plan had died along with so many others when she'd left Montana. Oaks, elms and aspen trees lined the drive and the fall jewel tones of gold and red and orange were bright splashes of color in a gray day. The wind drove fallen leaves into mini-tornadoes that drifted across the front of her SUV and temporarily blinded her.

Once they'd passed, Emma spotted the ranch house and came to a dead stop.

This was not the house she remembered. Five years ago, Caden's place had been big, but not palatial. *This* house was a Western palace.

Two stories, with a steep roof for the snow to slide off, the front was a wall of glass that would provide a spectacular view of Flathead Lake. River stone and golden oak planks made up the walls and lined the wide balcony off the first floor where several chairs were gathered around what she assumed was a gas firepit. The front porch was flanked by black iron sconces and the surrounding trees stood like soldiers on guard duty.

Simply staggered by the beauty of it all, Emma wondered what had happened while she was gone to allow Caden to build this place.

After a second or two, she continued on and noted the much bigger barn and an even larger stable with a corral that seemed to take up almost an acre of land. Caden had done just what he'd always planned to do. Taken his father's ranch and expanded it, made it something extraordinary. Of course, the plan was always that Emma would be a part of it. They'd both had dreams for this place and something tugged at her insides when she had to admit that he'd done it all without her.

She parked the SUV outside the house and got out, hunching deeper into her jacket. The wind was more fierce now and the icy chill was slicing into her bones. It had been a long time since she'd faced a Montana fall and winter, but she'd been raised here and so she knew that the weather could turn on you in a heartbeat. She glanced up at the leaden sky and told herself it would probably be best not to stay long. Of course, that might not be an issue. Caden might not be here. And if he was, he could refuse to talk to her.

"Emma, is that you?"

She looked up and smiled, grateful for the reprieve from her thoughts. "Hi, Jack. Good to see you."

Jack Franklin. Caden's best friend and foreman. Of course, once upon a time, Jack and his wife, Gwen, had been *her* friends, too. Now she wasn't so sure. "Is Caden around?"

"Yeah." He frowned a little, tugged the brim of his hat down on his forehead and glanced over his shoulder at the stable. "He's with one of our pregnant mares."

Her gaze drifted to the stables as well, as if she could see through the dark green wood walls to the man inside. "Everything all right?"

"Oh, sure," Jack said. "You know Caden, though. He takes care of what's his."

She shifted her gaze to the man and wondered if he was trying for some subtext. But he looked innocent enough. Hard to tell, though. Jack's loyalty would be to his friend. "I saw Gwen at the grocery store the other day."

"Yeah, she told me." He smiled at her and shook his head. "Feels weird, having you back. But good, at the same time. It's hard, isn't it?"

"Really is," she agreed, taking a little hope from Jack's attitude. "Look, I'm home to stay, Jack. I know Caden's not happy with me…"

He snorted.

She winced. "I just want to make things right, you know?"

"I get it Emma." His smile faded, but his eyes were still kind. "But it's not going to be easy."

She shrugged and said, "When was talking to Caden about something he didn't want to, *ever* easy?"

He nodded. "Good point. Okay, tell you what. Why don't you go on in the house? I'll let Caden know you're here."

She glanced at the big, beautiful building behind her, then back to Jack. "Okay, I will. Thanks."

"Not a problem." He turned to go and stopped when she spoke up again.

"Jack? Say hi to Gwen for me."

He grinned. "I will. And if it helps…she's really glad you're home again."

"It does. Thanks." She didn't watch him go. Instead, Emma walked up the steps to the wide front door and silently admired the carving of pines dug deeply into the wood. Entering the house, she had to stop again to admire it all. The floors were wide planked oak, with colorful rugs tossed here and there to break up the stark-ness. The great room held brown leather couches and chairs, heavy, wide tables and a few lamps that would spill golden light across the entire room when turned on.

The fireplace was river stone, with a thick slab of carved oak as a mantel. On the mantel was a windup clock she remembered Caden's mother had bought on a trip to Germany one year and on either side of that, were silver candlestick holders that had been in Caden's father's family for generations. The painting over the hearth was of the original ranch house and only served to bring home how much the Hale ranch had changed over the last few years.

The view of the lake was spectacular, that wall of windows displaying the amazing landscape like an oversize painting. But she turned from that view and walked toward the French doors on the far wall that opened onto the balcony. Inside the beautiful house, it was warm and luxurious and downright cozy, but Emma couldn't take it. The unfamiliarity of the place. The knowledge that Caden had done all of this without her. That he'd done so well on his own while her adventure in dream chasing had ended with a mind-numbing thud.

Shaking her head, she pushed through one of the doors into the icy wind that slapped at her and some-how felt more welcoming than the warmth of the house. Her boots sounded softly against the deck as she walked to the railing and watched the ranch at work. Cowboys were in the corral, working several horses. She could smell a fire and noted smoke lifting out of the chim-ney of what she guessed was Jack and Gwen's house.

And then he stepped out of the stable, a tall, muscled cowboy and all Emma could think was *Caden*.

Four

Caden stopped dead and looked across the yard to the house. To *her*.

Ridiculous to even think it, but Emma could have sworn he was looking directly into her eyes. She felt the solid punch of his stare even from a distance and knew that she still wanted him. More than anything else in her life, she wanted his hands on her. His mouth on hers. Remembering the fire that rose up between them made her hunger for that heat.

In spite of everything—or hell, maybe *because* of everything that had happened to her since she'd been gone, that need for Caden was as sharp as ever.

He was headed her way, a tall man, with broad shoulders, narrow hips and long legs. His black hair hung over the collar of his jacket and gave him a piratical look that did absolutely wicked things to Emma. But

then, looking at Caden had always made her want...
too much.

He kept his gaze fixed on her as he strode across the
yard and as he came closer, her heartbeat quickened and
her mouth went dry. *Seriously?* She'd come here furious that he might be using her sister. She'd come here
hurt that he was so willing to have nothing to do with
her. She'd arrived ready to have it out with him—and
now all she wanted was to *have* him.

Coming here might not have been such a good idea.

She turned, went inside and was standing beside the
cold hearth when he walked into the room. How one
cowboy could completely take over a huge space simply by standing there was a question for the ages. But
the simple truth was, Caden could.

"What're you doing here, Emma?"

Good question. Watching him now, so close, yet so
far away, tore at her and made Emma want all kinds of
things from this moment. She wanted to rewind time
and have the years separating them simply disapper.
Yet, at the same time, she couldn't wish it away and instead she wanted him to accept what she'd done. And
mostly, she wanted him to want her.

None of that was happening at the moment, though,
so she gave herself a mental kick and said, "We have
to talk, Caden."

"No, we really don't." He took his hat off and sailed
it like a tan Frisbee to the nearest couch. Shrugging
out of his green jacket, he dropped that on a chair and
stalked to the bar across the room.

"Caden—"

"I mean it," he said, tossing a quick look at her. "We
don't have anything to talk about, Em."

Em. He used to call her that and stupidly, she took heart from the use of that casual nickname now. There was nothing on his gorgeous face that should encourage her and yet…apparently *hope* was a hard kill.

She took her jacket off too and dropped it onto a chair before walking over to him. He grabbed a beer from the bar fridge, opened it and took a long drink. No friendly offer of one for her, so Emma didn't wait. She got one for herself and ignored his raised eyebrow. After a sip of beer, she looked up at him. "I want to know what's going on between you and Gracie."

"And I want you to go home," he said flatly. "Guess we're both going to be disappointed."

Turning his back on her, he headed to the fireplace and hit a switch tucked away behind one of the river stones used to frame it. Gas flames shot up instantly and danced along faux logs.

Surprised, she said, "You always liked real fireplaces better."

He shot her a look. "Things change."

That was plain enough.

Caden shook his head, took another drink of his beer and shrugged. "It's both. I can change it to a wood burner when I want to."

Was that a concession? Really? Was that how sad she was now? Taking a casual statement about a fireplace as a sign that maybe he didn't hate her? She looked into his eyes and felt flames lick at her insides. Didn't seem to matter that he hadn't welcomed her with open arms.

Caden was dynamite to her match.

He turned away and studied the dancing flames in a taut silence that scraped at her raw nerves.

Cradling her beer between her hands, she welcomed

the cold and silently hoped it would ease the heat engulfing her. Emma glanced at the glass French doors separating them from the outside world and reminded herself that every cowboy on this ranch could look through that glass and see whatever happened in this room. Not that anything *was* happening.

She dropped onto one of the leather couches to watch him. It took a few more minutes of strained silence, but finally, he turned to look down at her. "You're not leaving, are you?"

Emma shook her head. "Not until we talk."

Both of his eyebrows shot up. "Hope you brought some luggage with you, because that's going to be a while."

Irritation had her blurting, "Caden, you can't just ignore me."

"Why the hell not? Just what you did to me for five years."

Guilt pinged inside her, but she squashed it. No, she hadn't written to him or called, but she'd done that deliberately at first. Moving away from him, from Montana, hadn't been easy and she'd convinced herself that talking to Caden or clinging to the memory of him would only make the move that much harder. And then she'd found work and lost it and found something else and got in trouble and she hadn't wanted to talk to him. To tell him that she'd made a mistake by going to California. That she'd failed. Because what would have been the point?

"I left because I had to," she said quietly.

"Yeah, I remember the speech, thanks." He took another drink of his beer.

"But I'm back now."

"And what do you expect me to do? Handsprings?"

"And did you expect me to stay away?"

"Why wouldn't I?" he demanded and slammed his beer bottle down on the mantel hard enough to rattle the silver candlesticks. "You walked out on everything, Emma. Why should I think you'd come back? And now that we're down to it, why *did* you come back? Hollywood not living up to your expectations?"

Not even close, she thought but didn't say.

"I had to bring Molly home," she said instead.

He shook his head, then pushed both hands through his hair. God, just watching his muscles shift and move beneath his white long-sleeved shirt was earth-shattering. Her fingers actually itched to rip his shirt open and slide her hands across that muscled chest. To feel his heartbeat. To watch fire explode in his eyes.

"That's right," he said with a snort. "You came home with a *baby*. Who's the lucky father, Emma? Where the hell is he? Did he walk out on you like you walked out on me? Or did you leave him, too?"

Emma stiffened, then forced herself to relax so he wouldn't see. Wouldn't notice her reaction to the mention of Molly's father. She wouldn't talk about the baby. Not now.

Instead, she picked up on the last thing he'd said and argued the point. "Damn it, Caden, I didn't just walk out." Ready to defend herself, she stood up and faced him. "I talked to you about it. I *told* you that I had to do this. Hell, I asked you to go to California *with* me. Or did you forget that part?"

"I remember. Everything," he added, meeting her gaze with a cold stare that sent shivers along her spine. "You asked me to go with you but you knew I couldn't."

"Couldn't?" she argued. "Or *wouldn't?*"

"Both." He kept his eyes locked with hers and when he spoke again, his voice was so deep, so soft, it seemed to vibrate inside her, plucking every nerve.

"I had to be here, Emma," he said. "And you knew that. My life is here. This ranch. Building it into something special. That was my dream. Used to be yours, too. Or did you forget how many nights we spent planning what we'd build here?"

"I remember. Everything." She used his own words to make her point. "And you're right, Caden. It was my dream, too," she said quietly, owing him that much. To let him know she hadn't been pretending all those nights when the two of them would talk and plan and dream. "It was just that—"

"Other dreams came first?"

"Why don't you understand why I had to try?" She'd come here wanting to have it out with him, but it seemed they were just talking in circles, not solving anything, just dredging up more misery.

"I didn't want to understand, Emma. All I needed to know was, you left."

"And how long are you going to be throwing that in my face?"

"How long you going to be here?"

A verbal slap that set her back a step or two. She didn't remember him being this shut down. This cold. Or hard. Was she supposed to take the blame for that, as well?

"This was a mistake. So fine. I'll go." She grabbed her coat.

"Leaving must get easier the more you do it," he mused, still with that quiet, cold tone.

"Damn it, Caden," she argued, tossing her hair back behind her shoulders. "You just *told* me to go."

"Don't."

She dropped her coat again and stared at him. "Why?"

He crossed his arms over his broad chest and stood tall and gorgeous, staring at her. "You came here to talk, right?"

"Yeah."

"Then let's talk."

"Quick turnaround," she mused, wondering why he was being so reasonable all of a sudden.

"Living in Hollywood cause you to be this suspicious?" he asked.

Yes. "No," she said, tipping her head to one side to study him. "I just know you, Caden, and—"

He cut her off neatly. "You used to know me, Emma. Things change."

Pain tugged at her heart. "Yeah, I've noticed."

His jaw clenched and the muscle there twitched. "Come on back to the kitchen. I'm hungry and if we're going to have one of our 'conversations,' I'm gonna need my strength."

He headed out of the room and Emma followed him. True, they used to have some wonderful arguments back in the day. They were both stubborn and unwilling to admit when they were wrong, so those fights could go on for hours. And back then, they'd usually ended one of their *talks*, in bed—or on the ground, against a wall, in a hay loft...

The thought of that happening today sent a jolt of anticipation through her. She wondered if he was remembering. Wondered if he was wanting as badly as she was. Maybe he was right about needing strength.

As she walked behind him, Emma tried to keep her gaze off of his butt, so she distracted herself by looking at the rest of his amazing house. A long hallway led past a dining room with a hand-carved table big enough to seat twenty. There were paintings on the wall, depicting different sections of the ranch, the town of Cache and the river that cut through Caden's property and led up to the mountains. It was a showplace. Everything he'd ever dreamed of building and more.

Then she followed him into the kitchen and just stopped in the doorway to admire it.

For the past five years, she'd been sharing a tiny two-bedroom apartment in West Hollywood with her roommate, Terry. Their kitchen counter had been the size of a breadboard with a sink barely big enough to set a plate down into it. In fact, you could have fit the entire apartment in Caden's kitchen.

The cupboards were a pale oak with copper pulls. There was open shelving on the walls as well, where pitchers, platters and coffee mugs were stored. A huge island in the center of the room was topped with a slab of dark brown and white granite so huge that it must have taken ten men to carry in and install. An immense, hammered copper range hood over the eight-burner stove and an oversize refrigerator also covered in that same burnished copper.

Eight stools were pulled up to the island and a window over the sink that was wide enough to provide a glorious view of the lake. At one end of the room, there was a big round table with six chairs sitting in front of another window, this one with a view of the ranch yard and the pines that stood guard behind the buildings.

"This is…" she said on a breathy sigh, *"perfect."*

He glanced at her and she saw the flash of pride in his eyes before he buried it. "Yeah, had this place built a few years ago. Figured to make the kitchen as big as possible, since we sometimes end up with all the hands in here, looking for a hot meal."

A few years ago. How had he done all of this so quickly? The old ranch house had been small and cozy, the place where Caden had grown up, and now it had been displaced by a mansion that was simply breathtaking.

He tossed her a quick look as he opened the fridge and pulled out a covered plate of sandwiches.

Her eyes went wide. "Wow, the refrigerator is magic, too? You're hungry and it provides readymade food?"

One corner of his mouth twitched. "No, this is courtesy of my housekeeper."

She'd guessed that of course. "Does she live here?" Emma really hoped not. If they were going to be able to really argue and get everything between them out in the open—then she didn't want to have to worry about someone overhearing them.

"No," he said, setting the plate onto the island and reaching back into the fridge for a beer. He held it up. "Do you want one?"

"Sure." She grabbed a couple of paper towels, then took a seat on one of the island stools. "So she drives in from Cache every day? That's got to be challenging in winter." When that long, two-lane road became so packed with snow it could sometimes take *days* for the county to plow it.

He took a seat opposite her, twisted off the caps on the beer bottles and handed one to her. "No, Victoria lives on the ranch. Her husband, Micah Taylor, is the barn boss."

She nodded, understanding. A barn boss took care of the hiring and firing of people, though he'd work with the foreman on making those decisions. Plus he ran the schedules, ordered feed and made sure work was getting done.

The foreman oversaw *everything*. The men, the horses, the ranch itself. They also used both recognized and innovative breeding practices to improve the animal stock. Plus the foreman was in charge of the employees, and maintaining the ranch itself.

She handed Caden one of the paper towels as he peeled the plastic wrap off the plate. "Help yourself. Looks like there's ham and turkey today."

"Your favorite," she mused, and took a half a sandwich.

One eyebrow lifted. "You remember."

It wasn't a question. "We've known each other most of our lives," she pointed out. "Hard to not know."

"Uh-huh." He took a bite of his sandwich and while he chewed, he studied her.

Emma just barely managed to not shift positions beneath that steady stare. Fire was licking at her bloodstream and her heartbeat was accelerating with every breath she drew. Her skin felt electric, as if her body was pumping out a low-level buzz. Her gaze drifted from his eyes to his mouth, his strong jaw and then his Adam's apple as he swallowed, then took a swig of beer.

What was it about this man? How could she be reacting *exactly* as she had when she'd walked away from him all those years ago? Shouldn't this feeling have gotten fainter? Instead, it was as if her body had only been waiting for her to get close to him again to remind her just what she was capable of.

"You're staring," he said.

"You started it," she countered and lifted her gaze to his again.

She wished she could read his eyes as easily as she used to be able to. But apparently, he'd gotten better at hiding what he was thinking because all she saw in those lake-blue depths was a deliberate distance—and the hint of a smoldering fire. God, she'd missed that fire.

Setting his beer down onto the granite with a soft click, he said, "You wanted to talk, Emma."

"Yeah, I do." But where to start? Trying to explain *again* why she'd left Montana—and him? Demanding an explanation of what was going on between him and her sister? Even as she considered it, she realized that *demanding* was never the way to go with Caden. Any more than it was with her. Should she ask how he'd managed to build his dream ranch in the same amount of time that she was in California seeing her dreams die?

He was watching her. Waiting. And before she could stop herself, Emma blurted something she hadn't planned to say. "I missed you, Caden."

He looked surprised, though why he should have been, she couldn't have said.

"You didn't *have* to miss me, Emma."

"Maybe I did," she said. "Maybe I had to find out what was really important to me before I could appreciate what I had."

Wow. Was that true? It felt true. Being in Hollywood, surrounded by strangers, at first, she'd avoided thinking of him, of this place, her family, so she wouldn't miss them all so deeply. But as time passed, she'd dredged up memories of Caden, and her home and family, to keep her sane.

He shook his head, stood up and stalked a few paces away from her as if he couldn't sit still another minute. "You're not really going to try to convince me that you leaving was a *good* thing."

"No." He'd never believe it, but Emma did. She'd discovered a lot of truths about herself while she was gone. She'd learned that she wasn't cut out to live in the fast lane no matter what her dreams had been. The mountains and lakes and rivers were where she belonged. She'd learned what was important and what she could toss aside.

Most important, she'd realized that Caden was still at the heart of what she wanted. Needed. But why would he believe that?

"Caden, the important thing is I'm back now. And I'm not going anywhere."

He shoved one hand through his hair with an impatient gesture. "And I should take your word for that."

"You don't have to." She stood up, too, and walked toward him, stopping just out of reach. "You'll see it. I'll be right there at the ranch. I'll be in town. At the diner. In church. We'll be seeing a lot of each other whether you like it or not, so you're going to have to find a way to deal with it. With *me*."

"Think so, do you?"

"Well, what else?" she snapped, throwing both hands high. "Are you going to actively ignore me? Come and go from my family's ranch and not look at me? Play house with my sister and not give me a thought?"

His eyes narrowed. "I told you what's between me and Gracie is none of your business."

"You're wrong about that," Emma argued, feeling her temper spike along with her lust. "Gracie's my business and you used to be—"

"Key words there being *used to be*."

"Right. Fine. But damned if I'll watch you go from me to Gracie."

"Oh?" One dark eyebrow lifted and he gave her a sardonic smile. "Who put you in charge of who I sleep with?"

She sucked in a gulp of air. "So you're admitting it? You're having sex with my *sister*?"

"My sex life is none of your damn business, Emma. How many times do I have to say it?"

Emma was appalled. And yet…he hadn't really said he was, had he? Was he screwing with her just to make her crazier? That completely sounded like Caden. And really, as pissed as Gracie had been for days, if she was having sex with Emma's old boyfriend, she would have thrown the fact in Emma's face long before now.

Okay, maybe she was overreacting here.

"Were you celibate in California?" he taunted, taking a step to close the distance between them. "No guys coming to your bed? No Hollywood pretty men getting you naked and on your back?"

Did the thought of her with other men bother him? Sure seemed to. That was a good sign, wasn't it? If he didn't care, he wouldn't give a damn who she'd been with.

"I never said I was celibate and you weren't, either—" She didn't know that for sure, of course, but she couldn't imagine that Caden had stayed faithful to the memory of a woman who had walked out on him. Though damn it, she hated the images floating in her mind.

Of Caden's muscled, strong body covering some other woman, burying himself inside her, driving her to the brink of insanity as he'd once done to her. She *hated* that. Especially if that woman was Gracie.

"Damn straight I wasn't," he ground out and moved even closer, looking down at her, forcing her to look up to meet his eyes. "When you left, I lost myself in so many women I damn near couldn't keep track of them all."

She swallowed a knot of bitterness clogging her throat, but even at that, she realized that he hadn't had just *one* woman who had meant something to him. "You needed dozens of women to take *my* place, did you?"

"Yes." He snapped the word and he didn't look happy about the admission. "Like knowing that? Like knowing that you left such a gaping hole inside me that the more I tried to fill it, the emptier I felt?"

"Of course not," she whispered, caught by his gaze. There were fires there now, not smoldering, but hot, licking flames that swept over her skin, igniting every nerve ending until she felt as if she was bristling with sexual need.

"I was empty, too, Caden."

"By choice, Emma."

True again. She swallowed hard, and reached for him, half-afraid that he'd step away from her, leaving her shattered just to teach her a lesson. But he didn't move. If anything, he went completely still.

She hadn't come here for this, at least not consciously. But maybe this was what had been driving her since she got home. The need to touch him and be touched. To remember what it felt like to be so alive that she practically glowed. She wanted him more than she ever had before and if he pushed her away, the pain of it might kill her.

Emma moved up to him and kept her gaze locked with his. Laying both hands on his shoulders, she looked into his lake-blue eyes and said, "We've been empty too long, Caden. Fill me up. Fill us both."

"Damn you for leaving, Emma." His gaze moved over her face, then met her eyes. "And damn you for coming back."

Then he grabbed her, pulled her in close and bent his head to hers. His eyes locked with hers, his heated stare seemed to burn right through her. "This could be a mistake. For both of us. Are you sure you want to do this?"

"More sure than I've ever been about anything in my life," she told him breathlessly.

"Me, too," he admitted. "Damn it."

Five years fell away and once again it was just the two of them, combustible, eagerly leaping into the flames. Emma looked up into his eyes and saw hunger there. That need was something she'd always responded to. Now was no different.

She went up on her toes and took his mouth with hers. For one brief, shining moment, there were fireworks inside. And God how she'd missed them. Then he broke that kiss, pulled away and she was left staring at him, breathing hard.

"What're you doing?"

He walked to the wall, hit a switch and glanced back at her. "Damned if I'm putting on a show for the cowboys out there."

"What?" Confusion clouded her mind even more than the desire swirling through her.

"The windows," he said, coming back to her. "Got a lot of them."

"I noticed."

"Well, that switch I just threw darkens the glass so no one sees in."

Truth be told she hadn't given the walls of glass in this palace a single thought. She would have jumped him right here and never realized that the whole world could be watching—and maybe she wouldn't have cared. As long as she had his hands on her again.

"Good thinking." Then she stopped talking when he kissed her again, taking her mouth with a frenzied need that fired up everything she was already feeling. His hunger was as sharp and insistent as hers.

His tongue parted her lips, swept into her mouth and made her knees weak. Emma actually slumped against him and Caden pulled her in close and tight, his arms coming around her like steel bands.

He tasted her over and over again, never giving her a chance to catch her breath. And Emma didn't care. Breathing didn't matter. Nothing mattered but this moment. *Him.* His hands swept up and down her spine, then down to her butt so he could pull her hard against him. So she would feel his erection pressing into her. So she would want him even more than she did already. And just when she was ready to tear both of their clothes off and stretch out on the kitchen floor, Caden broke the kiss again.

"Are you doing that on purpose?" she asked as she swayed unsteadily.

"What?"

"Kissing me senseless then abruptly stopping. Because if you're doing it to make me crazy, you should know…it's working." She tossed her hair back from her face and looked up at him in time to see a flash of humor that quickened and died in his eyes in a heartbeat.

"No," he assured her, hooking one arm around her waist and leading her out of the room. He kept her pressed tightly to his side as he said, "But damned if we're doing this on the floor."

"It's a nice floor," she argued.

"Not as nice as my bed."

Five

Emma's stomach fluttered and her pulse jumped into a jackhammer beat. He led her down the hall, and she hurried to keep up with his long-legged stride. The main staircase loomed up in the foyer, with hand-turned spindles and a carved oak banister that made it look like one long branch sprouting thousands of leaves. There was a dark red runner in the middle of the stairs that muffled their steps and as they moved, Emma glanced at the windows and saw that they'd all darkened at the flip of the switch Caden had turned on.

"Everyone out there will guess what we're doing, won't they?" she wondered aloud, still hurrying alongside him.

He shrugged, kept her close and stepped up his pace. "Do you care?"

"Not a bit."

"Good." At the top of the staircase, he turned right, headed for the door at the end of the hall.

Pulling her into his bedroom, Caden kicked the door closed behind them and Emma took a quick look around. The wall facing the lake was glass here as well, but it too was dark, muting the already weak October sunlight until it was barely noticeable. The pines surrounding the lake were bending with the wind, the gray, stormy skies had lowered threateningly and the lake itself looked like a sheet of molten silver.

She barely had time to notice the stone fireplace on one wall, the chests and dressers against two other walls and the massive bed that was clearly the centerpiece of the room. Here, too, he'd had someone carve a head- and footboard with scenes of the lake, the pines and the horses Caden raised and trained. The bed itself was gigantic and covered in a forest green comforter accompanied by what looked like dozens of pillows.

Then his hands were on her and she couldn't have cared less about the furniture.

"After five years without you, this is gonna be fast, Emma," he warned, cupping her breasts, and all she could think about was she wanted her clothes gone so she could feel his skin against hers.

"Nothing wrong with fast," she assured him and tore at her clothes. He did the same and in just a few seconds, they were naked, wrapped together and tumbling back onto the big bed. His body was hot, muscled and strong. He was hard and ready and she didn't want to waste another minute, so Emma rolled with him until she was straddling him, then went up on her knees.

Smiling, she would have taken him inside her in the

next instant, but his big hands settled at her waist, lifted her and tossed her to one side.

Emma slapped one hand down on the bed. "Damn it, Caden, stop stopping!"

"You always were too bossy for your own good," he muttered and reached out to the bedside table. He yanked the top drawer open, pulled out a condom and ripped the foil packet open.

Emma blew out a breath. God, she was an idiot. Running on hormones and want, she'd have had unprotected sex just to feel him inside her again. "I hate when you're right."

He glanced at her and grinned. "Well, then, I guess some things *don't* change."

"Funny." She went up on her elbows, cocked her head to one side and asked, "Ready now?"

"You gonna argue our way through this, like old times?"

"I will if you don't get inside me in the next ten seconds."

"Like I said, bossy," Caden rasped, then grabbed her, pulled her close and spread her thighs. "Always liked that about you."

His fingers smoothed up and down her heated, damp core and with every caress, Emma squirmed, shifted, even whimpered a little. Planting her feet on the mattress, she rocked her hips to the rhythm of his touch and felt that hidden, coiled spring inside her tighten further.

"You're still not inside me," she ground out.

"You're still not the boss of me," he told her, then scooped his hands beneath her butt and lifted her off the mattress.

"Caden!" Emma's eyes glazed over as his mouth

closed over her center. His tongue stroked her, dipped inside and then stroked again. His lips and teeth nibbled at her and when he tasted that one hard, hot nub of sensation, Emma nearly flew off the mattress.

Helpless, her hips rocked spasmodically as he took her, forcing her to feel, to accept, to give herself up to what he could do to her body. It had always been like this between them, a small part of Emma's brain acknowledged. No matter what, Caden touched her and it was magic. She'd never found this with anyone else. It was him. Only Caden could break through her own sense of self to make her admit that they were more together than they were apart.

That had scared her five years ago.

Now, she just wanted more.

When the first ripples of release hit her, she screamed his name, gripped her fingers into the comforter and held on as her world rocked around her. And before her body had stopped trembling, Caden was there, pushing himself into her depths, claiming her in the most intimate way possible.

She gasped at that first invasion. He was so big, she could feel her body stretching to accommodate him and the marvelous friction he created when he moved within her, stoked the fire between them.

Emma moved with him, locked her legs around his hips and drew him higher, deeper, wanting all of him. Wanting him to be such a part of her that she wouldn't be able to let him go again.

His hips pistoned against her in a fierce rhythm that stole her breath even while it encouraged her to match his frantic moves. Emma did, racing toward completion, loving the feel of him, reeling in the memories and the now, tangling together in her mind and heart and body. He levered himself up, to look into her eyes as her body tightened further. As if he could sense she was close and he wanted to watch her take that wild ride.

"Come on, Emma, let go."

Then she did. What he'd made her feel only moments ago, paled in comparison to what exploded within her body now. She shrieked his name, clung to him and moved with the force of the climax slamming into her. It seemed to roll on and on, taking her higher and higher and Caden kept her firmly tethered to him while she soared. Finally, after what felt like forever, she heard him shout her name and when his body shattered, she clung to him, and they took the hard fall together.

A few minutes later, Caden had to silently admit that he felt energized in a way he hadn't in far too long to think about. Making love with Emma again had felt like…coming home. The two of them shared a connection he'd never found with anyone else. And while his body was happy, his mind was racing with all kinds of warning bells and a tiny voice shouting *red alert*!

He didn't need that voice, though. He already knew that sex with Emma solved nothing. Changed nothing. There were still five long years between them and the betrayal that had begun it all. That he couldn't bring himself to forget.

She was home now, but for how long? Was she just here in Montana as a pit stop before hitting the road again? How was he supposed to know? How could he ever trust her again?

He rolled away from her onto his back and tossed one

arm across his eyes. Beside him, he heard her breath rushing in and out of her lungs and felt the heat of her body reaching out for him.

And he wanted her again.

To fight that urge, he got out of bed, crossed to the bathroom to clean up, then gave himself a hard-eyed stare in the mirror. *Remember who you're dealing with*, he warned himself. *Keep your guard up.*

"Caden?" Her voice, still slightly breathless, called to him. "Everything okay?"

Still glaring at himself, he answered, "Fine."

He stepped out of the bathroom and paused on the threshold, looking at the bed where Emma lay sprawled across the mattress. She was a wonder, he thought idly, as he might if he were looking at a beautiful painting.

Her tantalizing mouth was curved in a secretive smile and that amazing hair of hers spilled across his pillows and then drifted down across her breasts, giving her nipples a peekaboo effect.

Her body was slim and strong, and if he didn't know she'd had a baby just a few months ago, he'd never have guessed. A baby. Emma had a daughter. She'd gotten pregnant by some other man. A rush of fury filled him, then drained away again. Who was he? *Where* was he? Why had she run from him?

"Wow," she mused softly. "For a man who just got lucky, you don't look very happy."

He blew out a breath. "Sex doesn't change anything, Emma."

She went up on her elbows, cocked her head to one side and said, "I don't know. I think it changed *something*." Pushing higher up, she stretched her arms over her head in a slow, languorous movement that sent Caden's gaze to her breasts, still peeking through the long silky curls of her hair.

His body stirred and he looked down at his own dick as if it were a traitor. The problem was, he considered, that a man's penis didn't give a damn what he was *thinking*. It only *wanted*.

And his wanted Emma. Now.

Her gaze dropped to his erection and that smile on her mouth curved higher. "Looks like at least a part of you agrees with me."

"At least you didn't say a 'small' part of me," he drawled and could have bitten off his own tongue when she laughed.

Damn, he'd missed that laugh. Musical, deep, infectious. Emma had always thrown herself into laughter and Caden had spent a huge amount of time trying to make her laugh just so he could listen to it. Now she was here, in his house, in his bed, and he was silently arguing with himself about what this would mean going forward.

Well, who the hell cared?

Enjoy what you had while you had it and let go of the rest of it.

With that thought firmly in mind, he absently flipped a switch alongside the fireplace and heard the gas flames kick into life. She sighed and that soft sound fed the heat inside him until Caden was sure he would simply spontaneously combust.

That burning need forced him across the room in a damn hurry. He was drawn to her like metal shavings to a magnet. He always had been. Emma was the one thing in his life that had always defied description.

What she was to him was too complex to label and too overpowering to ignore.

The light in the room was fading, but she seemed lit from within. Firelight danced across her bare skin, flickering shadows that defined every curve. Emma was watching him and her green eyes shone with anticipation as he paused long enough to grab a fresh condom and slide it on. He'd spent a lot of sleepless nights over the past five years, thinking about this moment. This woman. *No more thinking.*

He turned to her and she smiled up at him, lifted her arms in welcome and parted her lips for his kiss. He took what was offered and claimed her mouth with his. The taste of her exploded and spread through him on a river of heat. Their tongues tangled in a frantic burst of need—need that roared and clawed at his insides as if that climax only moments ago hadn't happened.

Caden ran his hands up and down her body, then settled on those breasts that had been driving him crazy. He cupped them both and she sighed into his mouth. His thumbs moved across her hard, dark pink nipples and she shivered. Then he tore his mouth from hers and lowered his head to those beautiful breasts and the sensitive, rigid nipples that tempted him so.

First one, then the other, he kissed and licked and nibbled, loving the taste of her. The sound of her sighs. The choked-off whimper that shot from her throat when he dropped one hand to her center and cupped the damp heat there. Her hips moved against his hand as she rocked helplessly, reaching for release from the tension rocketing up inside them both.

Caden was nearly blind with need. He lifted his head, stared down into her eyes and smiled. She was his again. His for now. His for however long he could keep her in this bed.

"Caden," she whispered, still moving her hips restlessly, "enough with the foreplay. Be in me."

"Plan to," he assured her, then sat back.

"You're stopping again and it's making me crazy." Confused, she pushed her hair back and stared at him.

"Not stopping," he said tightly, reaching for her. "Just rearranging."

With one quick move, he flipped her onto her stomach and then cupped her behind with his palms. Squeezing, kneading, he watched her squirm, heard the catch in her throat as she said again, "Come on, Caden. You're killing me."

He laughed shortly. "That is *not* the plan."

How many times had he lain awake in bed, picturing this moment, remembering others? How many nights had he simply given up on sleep and stalked through the quiet dark house like a man looking for something to remind him he was alive? Now she was here, with him, and he couldn't get enough of her. Didn't think he'd *ever* have enough of her. And that should worry him, Caden thought. He couldn't trust her to stay. Couldn't believe that she was really *back*. So, as much as he wanted her, as much as he loved having her here, he wouldn't allow himself to feel again what had once been the driving force in his life.

He wouldn't love her again.

Wouldn't risk that again.

But he could be with her, take what she offered and give what he could.

Taking hold of her hips, he lifted her off the mattress and said softly, "Come up to your knees, Emma…"

She threw a quick, surprised look at him over her shoulder. Licking her lips, she did as he asked, moving slowly, deliberately. When she was on her knees, her gorgeous behind in the air, Caden moved in behind her. He held her butt still when she would have moved again and as she looked back at him, studying him through clear green eyes, Caden pushed his body into hers with one long, satisfying stroke.

She groaned and her fingers curled into the comforter. Tossing her head back, she moved into him as he took her with a fast, hard rhythm. Sighs and moans slid from her throat as he kept them both at a frantic pace. Again and again, he took her, reclaiming what had once been between them. Reminding her of what they'd had. Reminding her what she'd tossed aside. Reminding himself.

"Caden…" His name was a plea. A command. A wish. He heard all of that and more in her voice and he responded.

Reaching down between them, he used his thumb to stroke that hard nub of sensation at her center. And still, he slammed himself home over and over again, feeding the growing tension within him.

"Caden!" She screamed his name and it was like music. She pushed back against him, trembling, rocking, shuddering as her release crashed into her.

An instant later, Caden claimed his own prize and nearly howled as his body erupted into an avalanche of satisfaction.

Breathing wasn't easy. He collapsed onto the bed, keeping her pinned to him, her back to his front. Bodies still joined, he rode the last of those tremors, waiting for his heartbeat to slow.

Against him, she squirmed a little, creating another ripple effect of sensation. In response, Caden held her still. "Now you're killing me."

Chucking gently, she took a breath and let it out on a sigh. "That was…" Emma shook her head as if she couldn't find the right word for what they'd just experienced. He knew how she felt. Hell, he'd been with plenty of women since Emma left Montana. He'd found satisfaction with most of them, but he'd never known the kind of earth-shattering climax that was only found in her arms.

He could have hated her for that alone.

Why should she still have any kind of hold on him? Well, that was a question he'd asked himself a lot. To this day, he didn't have an answer.

"…new," she finally finished and it took him a second to connect that word to the beginning of her statement.

She turned her head on the pillow and looked back at him. "You've got some new moves since the last time we were together, Caden."

He couldn't help himself; he smoothed a long strand of dark hair from her eyes. "The world didn't stand still while you were gone, Emma. I didn't stand still, either."

He disentangled their bodies because he'd learned long ago that a conversation with Emma required him to focus. And how the hell could he concentrate on a conversation when he was already hardening inside her again? He got up, took care of the condom issue, then went back to his bed, lying down beside her, but separate.

She didn't let that stand for long. Turning around, she went up on her elbows and looked at him. He didn't have a clue what she was thinking. Emma had always been partly a mystery to him and maybe that had been a draw back in the day. It was exciting, never being able to predict what his woman would do from one moment to the next. But it didn't make for easy conversations.

"So where'd you learn all these new tricks?" she asked in a way-too-quiet voice. "My sister?"

He threw her a hot look. "What?"

"Gracie. You remember her, right?" Temper was sounding in her voice now and in response, Caden's did the same. "Are you having sex with my sister?"

"None of your business, Emma." How many times would he have to say that?

She sat up on and stared down at him. "Tell me. Should I be getting dressed and leaving to make room for my little sister? When's the shift change here?"

His gaze pierced hers. "You're being an idiot."

"And you're not denying anything."

"Because like I said, not your business."

"Gracie's my business," she argued.

"And she's my friend," he countered.

"I was your friend, too," she reminded him, "when we were having sex out in your barn."

Was she jealous? That thought almost made him smile but the daggers she was shooting him told Caden that would be a big mistake.

"You left, Emma. You don't get an opinion on what we did after you were gone."

"So you did do something." She nodded sharply and he wondered how a woman could look so dangerous and so appealing all at the same time. "And believe me when I say I really do have an opinion."

Hell, it was tempting to let this go on. To let her wonder and fuss over what was between him and Gracie. Didn't she deserve a little torture for what she'd put him through? After all, Caden had done plenty of wondering himself about what Emma was up to out in California. But even as he considered it, he let it go. Caden wasn't going to play games with her. And if he was, he wouldn't use Gracie to do it.

"Damn it, Caden…" She pushed him, both hands on his chest, as if demanding his attention.

He caught her hands in his. His gaze locked on hers. "We did nothing, Emma. *Nothing* is between me and Gracie. I'm her friend. That's all."

She studied him for a few long seconds before he could see the tension slide from her system. "Really?"

"Really." He let her go, pushed one hand through his hair and then bunched the pillow under his head. "When you left, she needed a friend and I was there. I'll always be there for her. Hell, she's as much *my* little sister as she is yours."

The last of her anger slid away. He watched her let it go and had to admit that as quickly as she was to boil, Emma could let it go just as fast. She didn't hold grudges. She apologized when she was wrong and she was someone he could always count on. Well, he corrected, she used to be.

"Okay," she muttered. "I'm sorry. I know she must have needed you and I'm grateful you helped her out."

Scowling at her, he said, "I didn't do it for you, Emma."

"I know that, but I still appreciate it." She blew out a breath. "And I'm really glad you didn't sleep with Gracie because that would just be too weird. With a huge side of *ew*."

He snorted. Trust Emma to make him laugh at the oddest moments.

"But there is something going on with her, isn't there?"

And just like that, he wasn't laughing anymore. Instead, he walked around the bed, grabbed his jeans and yanked them on.

When he didn't say anything, she just stared at him. "That nonanswer was actually an answer, you get that, right?"

He lifted his gaze to her and nearly tore his jeans off again. She looked like temptation personified. Sitting there, bare-ass naked, that glorious hair of hers spilling over her shoulders and across her breasts and those forest green eyes fixed on him.

"I didn't say a thing," he muttered, shaking his head in an attempt to clear it.

"Exactly. If there was nothing going on, you would have said so, but because you didn't, I know there *is* something she's not telling me."

"Amazing how you do that circle speak," he murmured, and tossed his shirt to her.

"I have my own clothes," she said as she caught it.

"Takes too long and I'm really hungry for those sandwiches now."

"And for changing the subject…"

"Well, I guess you *do* know me, don't you?"

"I do, so I recognize the tactics to throw me off."

He shoved both hands into his jeans pockets, rocked back on his heels and looked down at her. She was shrugging into his shirt and something about her wearing his clothes made him hard again. Hell, everything about Emma Williams made him hard. Damn it.

"I'm not talking about it," he ground out. "If Gracie wants you to know, she'll tell you."

"No, she won't. She's so mad I'm home, she only speaks to me when she's got a good barb to shoot my way."

He headed out of the bedroom, expecting her to follow and she did. He could feel her right behind him. Their bare feet didn't make a sound on the stair runner and as they walked down the long hall to the kitchen, Emma hurried to keep up.

"I'm worried about her, Caden," she admitted, grabbing his arm to pull him to a stop. "Is she in trouble? Can you at least tell me that?"

He could see the anxiety in her eyes and a small piece of the ice she'd draped over his heart so long ago chipped off and fell away. He understood worry for family and though Gracie's secret wasn't his to tell, he could give Emma this. "She's not in trouble. She's just working some stuff out. When she's ready, she'll tell you."

"There was a time she told me everything," Emma mused quietly.

"Times change," he said.

"Yeah, I know that. And I know it's because of me. Doesn't make it any easier to accept."

He walked on toward the kitchen and Emma kept step with him. How many times had he pictured her here, in this house that his dream had built?

Now she was here—but he didn't trust her to stay.

Six

At the Little River Diner, Gracie sat across from Madison in a window booth at the back. The wall of windows showcased the river that ran through Cache and the trees that shrouded it. Aspens were bright gold and the maples were a deep scarlet. The pines were a rich, dark green and the diner felt as if it was in a secluded forest rather than at the edge of a bustling small town.

The diner itself had been in that spot for forty years. The wood tables had been polished so many times they were as smooth as glass. The red booth seats were comfortable, inviting people to sit and stay for a while and sooner or later, the whole town passed through this small restaurant, so it was a sure place to catch up on local gossip.

Shifting her gaze from the view to the woman across from her, Gracie silently admitted that she loved watching Madison. The way she grinned, the way she stirred her coffee long after it was cool enough to drink. The way she tucked stray strands of red hair behind her ear where silver leaves dangled from her lobes.

Since she first moved to Cache, Madison had become a sort of safe space for Gracie. She knew that she could tell Mad anything and it would be protected. She knew that her friend would always understand and would always be on her side.

"What're you thinking?" Madison took a sip of her coffee and waited.

"I was just thinking how glad I am that you moved to Cache."

"Hey, me, too." Reaching out, Madison grabbed Gracie's hand and squeezed briefly. "And, while you're still so pleased to have me, I'm going to test it by asking if you had a chance to talk to Emma after I left the ranch."

"Well, there went my nice little glow," Gracie muttered and slumped back against the booth. "No, I didn't. You saw her leave. And she hadn't come back by the time I left to meet up with you."

Madison shrugged. "Well, talk later tonight. Or tomorrow."

And say what? *You shouldn't have left?* What would be the point? "Talking won't solve anything."

"Nothing gets solved *without* talking."

"Boy," Gracie mused, with an accompanying eye roll, "I used to think Emma had the hardest head in the world. But you're coming in a close second."

Madison sighed in clear disappointment. "I just want you to get past this, Gracie."

"Why's it so important to you?" Madison had never

even met Emma, so why did it matter so much to her what Gracie's relationship with her sister was?

"Because I care about you, dummy." Madison shook her head and pushed aside the plate that still held half of her turkey club sandwich. "Ever since your sister got home, you've been so tense it's ridiculous. You say you were furious and hurt when she left."

"I was." God, the sting of that was still so fresh, the wounds inside ached.

"Well, she's *back*, and you're still furious. It makes no sense, Gracie. The two of you are *family*." Madison took a breath, shook her head and added, "And family's everything."

Just like that, she felt terrible. She looked into the other woman's green eyes, saw pain there and knew she'd inadvertently made it worse. Mad had lost both of her parents in a car accident just before she'd moved to Cache. She didn't have siblings or aunts or uncles, so of course she would look at having a sister as being a gift.

Long ago, Gracie had felt the same way. But having family didn't mean everything was sunshine and roses all the time. And pretending otherwise was ridiculous.

"I'm sorry, Mad." She took a sip of her coffee. "I really am. I know how you feel about family. But sometimes, things can't be put back together even if you want them to."

"Especially not if you don't try."

"Really?" Frustrated, Gracie sighed. "This is my fault now? Just a couple of minutes ago, I was thinking that you were always on my side and how nice it was to be able to depend on that."

"I am on your side, Gracie. But that doesn't mean I won't call you on it when I think you're wrong." She set her coffee down and reached for Gracie's hand again. Holding on, she said, "You're important to me. I want you happy. And I don't think you will be as long as this war with Emma is going on."

She pulled her hand free, crossed her arms over her chest and tried not to notice that she was acting like a child. "So I should end it? I didn't start it."

"Does that really matter?"

She thought about that for a long minute before admitting, "Yeah. It does." Gracie saw the disappointment on Mad's face, and ordinarily would have tried to wipe it away. But now, she just wanted her to understand. To see things the way Gracie did.

"My whole life, Emma was—I don't want to say a role model, because how lame does that sound—but I looked up to her. Trailed around after her." Gracie sat forward, pushed her own roast beef sandwich aside and leaned both forearms on the table. "When our mom died, I felt lost, but Emma stepped right in. She's five years older than I am and she just…became Mom, in a way. She made sure Dad and I were eating right, made sure I got to school, and she handled most of the ranch jobs alone because Dad was shattered."

"I know, you've told me," Madison whispered.

"Then she left, Mad." Gracie shook her head and glanced out the window. The diner sat alongside the river and she noticed the jewel-toned leaves were now whipping into the air as the wind kicked up. Shifting her gaze back to the woman across from her, Gracie said, "It was like Mom died all over again. One day Emma was there and the next she was gone. She'd been taking care of everything and suddenly, she wasn't. There was another empty hole on the ranch and this time there was no one to fill it."

"*You* filled it, Gracie."

A reluctant smile curved her mouth at the pride in Madison's voice. But she hadn't been in Cache back then so she didn't know how badly Gracie had stumbled. How she'd gone through the days blind and lost, trying to figure out all of the things that Emma had done so easily. "Thanks, but I didn't step up right away. I didn't know what I was doing, Mad. I messed up. A lot. I had to learn overnight how to run the ranch. How to fire men who weren't doing the work. How to stand my ground with men who looked at me and saw a kid."

"But you did it," Madison said with just a touch of impatience in her voice now. "Everyone fails at first when they do something new. You're not a failure because you messed up. You're only a failure if you quit. If you stop trying.

"That's what you're not getting," Madison said, impatience now ringing in her voice. "You're holding on to all of this old anger at your sister because you were tossed into the deep end. But, Gracie, you learned to *swim*."

She didn't want to hear that. Didn't want to believe it, and would have said so, but Mad wasn't finished.

"If Emma hadn't left, maybe that wouldn't have happened. Maybe you wouldn't have realized that you're a smart, capable woman on your own." Madison smiled and shrugged. "And maybe… Emma leaving was the best thing that ever happened to you."

Her words were quiet, but the idea behind them was earth-shattering. Gracie had never thought of it like that before and she had to admit that Madison might have a point. Yes, she'd been in over her head at first, but she was the one who had kept the ranch running the past five years.

She'd started in on her own dream of providing equine therapy by studying at the local junior college. She'd sold off some horses and bought others that would be a better fit for the clients she would start taking soon.

She'd learned how to take a stand with the foreman, with her father. She had done it all and no matter how hard things had gotten, no matter how many nights she'd lain in bed crying with frustration and fear and anger, Gracie hadn't run. She hadn't quit. She'd grown into a strong, confident woman and she had to wonder if any of that would have happened if Emma had stayed. Wouldn't she have simply stepped back and gone with the flow? Let Emma handle the big stuff and tried to find herself in bits and pieces?

A rush of pride swelled inside her and Gracie had to silently admit that it felt good. Madison had a point, she realized and wow, was that annoying. It was hard to acknowledge that maybe it was time to let go of being mad at Emma. She'd held that hurt and fury so close for five years, how would she feel without it?

"Gracie?"

She came up out of her thoughts to smile at the woman standing beside their table. Jessica Whitehead, the principal of the local high school, had grown up in Cache and gone to school with Emma. She was tall, with short black hair, sharp brown eyes and a ready grin.

"Hi, Jess," Gracie said, then nodded at Mad. "You know Madison, right?"

"Sure I do," Jessica said with a laugh. "My dogs know her much better, though."

"Nice to see you." Madison smiled. "How's Max's foot?"

Jess waved one hand. "Oh, he's fine, thanks to you. How he stepped on a bee is beyond me. My son's been taking care of him and Max is deliberately limping now to get extra treats."

Madison grinned. "Sounds right."

"So, Gracie," Jess said, "I heard Emma's back. Is it true?"

Gracie sighed a little, but nodded. "It's true."

"Is she just here on a visit?" Jess shrugged. "I ran into Stephanie Cramer in the grocery store and she said she thought Emma had moved back permanently, but I didn't know if I could believe the gossip or not."

"She says she's home to stay." And oddly, Gracie realized that she hoped Emma meant it.

Jess gave a huge sigh of relief. "Oh, good. When you see her, would you ask her to call me?"

"Sure. What's going on?"

"It's complicated," Jess hedged, "but I might have a job for her, if she's interested."

Gracie blinked at her. "A job?"

"Just ask her to call me, will you?" Lifting one hand to both of them, she said, "Good to see you guys. I've gotta run. My husband's out in the car, ready to get our date night going. We're headed to Kalispell for a movie."

"Have fun," Madison said as Jess hurried off.

"A job," Gracie muttered, shaking her head in disbelief. "She's gone five years, shows up out of nowhere, flowers, balloons, cheers from the crowd, and then presto—a job."

"Don't look now," Madison pointed out, "but you're sounding bitter again."

Still irritated, she snapped, "And why wouldn't I?"

Madison glanced out the window. "Hey, it's snowing."

Gracie's gaze went right to the window. Snowflakes were flying along with the autumn leaves now and the snow was coming in thick. October snow wasn't all that unusual in Montana, especially at their elevation. But this sudden burst of thick flying snow made Gracie think it would soon turn into a big storm. "We'd better get going."

"Right." They left money on the table for the bill and tip, then hurried out to the parking lot.

The wind was like a frozen knife, slicing right through them both and driving down to the bone. Madison tugged her hand-knit, bright red hat down low on her head and looked at Gracie.

"It's already coming down so hard, why don't you just stay at my place in town tonight?"

Gracie pulled on her own hat, then shoved her hands into her coat pockets. "No, I'd better get back to the ranch." She threw a worried glance at the sky and got a face full of snow for her trouble. Shaking her head, Gracie said, "Dad's alone there with the baby."

"Emma might be home by now."

"She might," Gracie acknowledged, "but I can't count on her. I've got to make sure everything on the ranch is okay and ready for the storm."

"Don't look now, but you're still in charge."

"Really?" Gracie shook her head. "An I-told-you-so right now?"

Madison shrugged and smiled. "Couldn't resist."

Laughing, Gracie said, "Fine. Point made. Again. I've got to go, before this gets worse."

"All right." Madison nodded, then stepped up and gave Gracie a hard, tight hug. "Just be careful, okay? And text me to let me know you got home safely."

Gracie hugged her back, then let her go. "I will. And don't worry. I've been driving these roads in all kinds of weather since I was a kid."

Helplessly, Madison shrugged. "I'll worry anyway."

Gracie grinned. "I will, too. So get home safe. I'll text you."

The ride to the ranch was harrowing and it seemed with every passing minute, the snow got thicker and the wind harder. Her windshield wipers were barely up to the task of keeping the glass clear and Gracie held the wheel in a white-knuckle grip. By the time she turned into the drive at the ranch, the snow was so thick she could barely see.

A sudden blizzard wasn't surprising, but it was a pain in the ass. She hoped the ranch hands had gotten all the horses into the stable—and she'd be checking on that herself as soon as she made sure her dad was all right. But the first thing Gracie noticed as she parked and jogged to the front porch was that Emma's car wasn't parked where it had been. Which meant she wasn't home yet. And judging by this storm, she wouldn't be turning up anytime soon.

From the porch, Gracie turned and looked out at the swirling wall of white blowing over the yard. For the first time in five years, she felt worried for her sister.

* * *

Caden walked into the kitchen and realized the room was dark. How long had they been upstairs? He hit the light switch and the hanging copper-and-glass pendant lamps over the island blinked into life.

His beer was warm, so he got a new one for both of them and then sat down beside her to grab a sandwich. For a few minutes there was an almost companionable silence between them. But Emma had never been one to appreciate quiet for long. Now was no different.

"How did you do it?" she asked.

"What?"

"Build this place." She swept one arm out as if to encompass the whole house. "I was only gone five years. How did you manage all of this so quickly?"

He could have ignored the question on the grounds that she'd given up her right to know about his life. But why shouldn't she know that he'd succeeded? That his life had marched on without her? Besides, he was damned proud of what he'd accomplished.

He shrugged. "I found gold."

She choked on a sip of beer and slapped her hand against her chest as she coughed violently. Holding up one hand when he tried to help, she fought for breath. When she finally could speak, she only said, *"Gold?"*

He nodded, satisfied at her reaction. Hell, he'd been nearly that surprised himself. "Remember how my dad used to talk about all the gold that was still up in the mountains waiting to be discovered?"

"Of course I do," she said, taking a sip of her beer. "The summer I was sixteen, we rode up to the high country a couple of times a week, looking for lost gold mines."

He smiled at the memory, then let it go. Because they hadn't spent all of their time looking for gold. Up in the mountains, they'd had picnics and sex in the sunshine and skinny-dipping in the lake, which led to more sex and then once, even sex on horseback.

Memories filled him, taunting him with images of Emma, reminding him what they'd had, what they'd lost. Finally, Caden deliberately shut his treacherous brain off.

Taking a long sip of his beer, he set the bottle down onto the granite and looked at Emma. Her hair was a wild tumble, her eyes were shining, and her delicious mouth was curved in a half smile that tugged at something deep inside him. Looking at the beautiful woman next to him, he could still see the girl that had driven him crazy.

Getting a grip, he said, "Well, when you left, I spent that spring riding the ranch." He'd needed to be by himself. To be away from every place that reminded him of the woman he'd loved and lost. The problem was, he acknowledged now, almost every square inch of the ranch was imprinted with her memory. He saw her everywhere and had felt her loss as he would have a limb. So he had lost himself in a hunt for the gold that could change his life. Build his dreams.

Caden forced a half-hearted laugh. "It got to the point where I swear my horse tried to hide from me every morning."

"Caden…"

"Not an accusation," he said, cutting her off. He didn't want another damn apology that changed nothing. "I'm just telling a story." His gaze locked with hers. "Do you want to hear it or not?"

"Really do," she said, picking up her beer for another sip.

Nodding, he kept his gaze locked on hers and said, "You'd been gone a month when I found a nugget in the river."

"A single nugget didn't do all of this," she interrupted.

One dark eyebrow lifted. "Am I telling this or not?"

"Sorry." She held up a hand. "Go ahead."

Shaking his head, he curled his fingers around the cold beer bottle and twirled it absently in the wet ring it had made on the granite. "I found the nugget, figured it had washed downstream."

"Makes sense."

Nodding still, he said, "So I followed the river, found a few more small nuggets, and finally after a few weeks I stumbled across the source." Smiling to himself, Caden remembered that flush of success when he'd spotted the thick vein of gold behind an outcropping of rock. It was a stray ray of sunlight glittering on the golden surface that had caught his eye. Without that extra splash of light, he might have ridden right past it.

"Anyway I didn't have much equipment with me, but I hacked out a bit more, took it into Kalispell and had it appraised. Came back almost eighty-four percent pure."

"Wow."

"Yeah." He laughed shortly. "That was pretty much my reaction. And the appraiser's. Said he never saw raw gold that pure. It was 20k gold and I'd found a thick vein of it on the property."

"That's amazing, Caden." She reached out to lay one hand on his forearm and he glanced down. He liked the feel of her hand on his arm and for that reason moved away from her touch.

"It was. Dad laughed his ass off when I told him about it." He chuckled a little at the memory. "You know how he loves being right."

"I do. So what happened next?"

Caden shrugged, took a drink of his beer and looked at her. "A couple months later, I went back with Jack and we took out more."

"A couple of months? Why'd you wait so long to go back—" She broke off, and looked at him suspiciously.

"I had a lot to do here," he said flatly, avoiding her gaze. "Jack and I were working on the plans for this place, helping my folks move to Texas…"

"All good reasons," Emma said, and her mouth twitched as she tried to hide a smile. "But that's not why you waited, is it?"

Caden scowled at her, but Emma's smile only got brighter and her eyes sparkled in the overhead lights.

"You couldn't find it again," she said with a laugh in her voice. "Oh, my God. You got lost coming back to the ranch the first time so you couldn't remember where the gold was!" Her laughter spilled out into the room. "You never did have a sense of direction!"

He sighed and took a moment to enjoy the sound of her laughter. Emma had always teased him about his ability to get lost on his own damn ranch. And it felt… good, to hear it again. Though he still said, "This isn't funny."

"Sure it is."

"Anyway…" He ignored the last of her chuckles and grasped hold of what dignity he could find. "We pulled in enough out of that one vein to build this place, stock it with horses and set my folks up with a smaller spread in Texas."

"That's a heck of a story," she said at last and he waited, sure there would be more. He wasn't disappointed.

"You're still the only cowboy I know who can get lost on his own ranch."

"I don't get lost," he corrected. "I get *turned around*."

"Turned around," she said, perfectly in time with him.

Irritated, he took another swig of beer. "Funny."

She laughed. "It's what you always said."

"Not anymore. That almost never happens now. Besides, I've always found my way well enough. Seems to me you're the one who's been lost."

Just like that, her smile died and her eyes went cool. "I guess you're right about that. I have felt lost for a long time."

"And now you're back," he said. "And you're having all your questions answered… Now it's my turn."

"What's that supposed to mean?"

Before he could ask his question, someone pounded on the back door just before it swung open. A blast of cold air rushed into the kitchen, followed by Jack Franklin, who swept off his hat and slapped it against his thigh, sending a tiny blizzard of snow to the floor. "Sorry, boss." He nodded. "Emma. Big storm blew in in the last half hour or so. Thought you'd want to know."

"How bad?" Caden was already up and moving.

"Most of the horses are safe inside. A couple of the guys are bringing in the mares from the south pasture."

Nodding, Caden said, "Good. Send a couple more

out to help. If the snow's too bad, they'll need it coming across the river."

"On it," Jack said, turning for the door again.

"I'll be out there in five minutes." He shot a look at
Emma. "Make that ten."

"Right." The door closed and Jack was gone. Emma
got up, went to the window and stared past the darkened
glass to the wall of white beyond. "How could we not
notice what was happening?"

He snorted. "We were busy."

"Yeah." She threw him a quick look. "I've gotta get
back."

"No way in hell, Emma." He said it flatly, brook-
ing no argument. "Not even you can navigate a road
you can't see."

"I know every bump in that road, Caden. I need to
get home. Help Gracie. Check on Molly and Dad."

"Call 'em," he ordered. "No point in you crashing or
getting stuck. That won't help your family any."

She really hated it when he was right. "Okay. I'll
stay. I'll get coffee on and make soup or something for
you and the guys." He nodded, already heading out of
the kitchen, stalking down the hall. Emma was right
behind him. "Once I've got it going, I'll come out and
help in the stable."

He whirled around, looked down at her, then yanked
her to him, planted a fast, hard kiss on her mouth, before letting her go. "All right."

Swaying a little, Emma stared after him as he took
the stairs, then she fell into step. They had to get dressed
and take care of business. Everything else would just
have to wait.

It only took a minute or two for Caden to dress and

then he was gone. Emma picked up her cell phone and walked to the windows overlooking the front of the ranch and hit speed dial. Staring out at the swirling rush of white, she shook her head. Caden was right. Nobody should be driving in this.

"Emma?" her father said when he answered. "You all right?"

"Yeah, Dad. But it looks like I'm stuck here at Caden's until the storm blows out."

"Good. I was worried you'd try the road. No need."

"But Molly…" Guilt. She'd brought the baby home with her and she should be there caring for Molly herself. She had never intended to hand off responsibility for her to the family.

"Molly's fine. We'll keep her safe and warm. You do the same for yourself." That was an order, too, not a request, and Emma realized she had a couple of men in her life who had no problem dishing out commands. And she had no problem arguing with them. When it made sense.

"I will. Is Gracie okay?"

"Got home just a while ago," her father said. "She's fine. Out in the barn helping the men bring in the horses."

"Okay, then." Emma nodded to herself. Everyone was safe. That was the important part. "I'll call again in the morning. But if you need me, call and I'll find a way there."

"We're fine," her father said again. "You just sit tight and take care of you and Caden."

When he hung up, she looked down at the ranch yard and watched Caden and another of the cowboys getting a couple of horses moving to the stable. Even in the rush of snow, she had no trouble picking Caden out of a crowd. She never would. If her eyes couldn't do it, her heart could.

And now was a hell of a time to admit to herself that she was still in love with the cowboy of her dreams.

Seven

I'm home. Everything's good. Emma's staying at Caden's till after the storm.

Gracie hit Send and waited, hoping Madison would answer right away. When she did, Gracie smiled.

Be careful. I'm fine, too. And I'm in for the night unless that cow has other ideas.

Frowning, Gracie texted back.

Let the cow handle her own problems. You're not used to driving in snow like this.

A moment later, *Don't worry so much.*

But Gracie was worried. She looked out the open

stable door at the wall of icy white outside and shivered. This kind of storm could blow out in a couple hours or settle in for days. No one knew what would happen, not even the weather guy on TV who had predicted mostly cloudy skies today.

"Gracie! Need some help over here!"

She shoved her phone into her back pocket and rushed down the wide center aisle to the stall at the back. Her latest purchase, a gelding named Herman of all things, was refusing to go inside. So she'd take care of business, help her father with the baby and hope that Emma and Madison stayed safe.

An hour later, she was in the house, looking for hot coffee, and found her dad in the kitchen with the baby.

"Where'd you find the high chair?" Gracie asked, watching Molly slap both hands on the tray in front of her.

"Up in the attic," Frank said. "Your mom never threw out anything that her girls used."

True. Somewhere in that attic was every report card, every history paper and even a few stuffed animals that Gracie and Emma had outgrown. A swell of regret filled her when she looked at Molly and realized how much Gracie's mom would have loved having a baby in the house again.

Heck, *she* was enjoying it. Molly was happy, always smiling and seeing what a miracle the baby had brought to Gracie's father was especially endearing.

"I've got her tied into the chair," Frank was saying. "She can't really sit up well on her own yet, but that'll come, won't it, Nugget?" He tapped Molly's nose with his index finger and the tiny girl laughed in delight.

Gracie poured a cup of coffee and looked around

the large, familiar kitchen. The walls were still a sunshine yellow because that was what her mom had loved.
The cabinets were white and the oak floor was scarred,
but shining clean. The old table under the window had
been the spot that she and Emma had gravitated to after
school, for cookies, milk and homework.

"You're really enjoying this, aren't you?" Gracie
dropped tiredly into a kitchen chair.

"Having my granddaughter in the house?" Frank
asked, obviously surprised at the question. "'Course I
am. About time you girls started giving me grandkids
to spoil." He winked at Gracie. "It'll be your turn soon."

She only frowned and looked down into her coffee
to avoid meeting her father's gaze. "Hard to do it on
your own," she muttered.

"Oh, you'll find someone when the time's right."

She risked a glance at him and wondered what he'd
say if she told him her secret. If she took the risk and let
him know what she'd been hiding for too long. But how
could she chance it? He was only now looking healthy
again. For so long, he'd been sliding into a depression,
and now that Emma and yes, Molly, had come home,
he was like a new man. Did she really have the right to
throw something at him that might set him back again?

"Everything all right, Gracie?" Frank sat down at
the table opposite her. "Your face is telling me something's on your mind." His soft, understanding gaze was
locked on her and she could only shift uncomfortably.

She hated lying to her father, but she wasn't ready
to take a step from which there was no coming back.

"Yeah, Dad. I'm fine." Gracie forced a smile and
made herself believe it. "I just needed some coffee,
then I'm headed back out there. We've still got a few

horses to bring in and I want to make sure they've all got fresh feed and water."

"All right." He nodded and set a few slices of banana on the baby's tray.

Instantly, Molly's little hands curled around them and smushed them completely. Then she licked the mess from her fingers, spreading it all across her face.

"You're happy, aren't you?" Gracie whispered, looking from that sweet baby to her father.

"'Course I am," Frank said, reaching out to pat his youngest daughter's hand. "I've got my girls and this little nugget. What more could a man ask for?"

Nodding again, Gracie told herself she was doing the right thing by keeping quiet. Her secrets would have to stay buried deep—at least for now. She took a long drink of her coffee, then set the cup down. "I'd better get back."

"You tell the boys I've got some beef stew going. When they need it, just come on over and get it."

"Wondered what smelled so good," she said, taking a deep breath of the wonderful, steamy air. "I'll tell them."

And the men would be expecting it. At times when the whole crew was working nonstop, the big house always provided a hot meal and hot coffee to keep everyone going.

"Tastes even better." Frank winked and gave Molly more bananas to smush. "You come in to eat, too."

"I will." She turned to leave, but paused for one more look at her father and the baby. It wasn't fair, considering how hard she'd worked the past five years to keep this ranch alive, to keep her father going—that it was Emma and her daughter that had brought everyone back from the brink.

But as that thought settled in, Gracie pushed it out again and remembered Mad telling her she was being bitter and deliberately clinging to her own anger. It didn't really matter what had turned things around, did it? Wasn't the important thing that her father was better? That the ranch had someone else now to help care for it?

Some of the anger she'd been carrying around in her heart slowly drained away and it was simply amazing how much lighter she felt. Not that she was ready to throw her big sister a party or anything, but she was willing to give her the benefit of the doubt. If Emma was here to stay, then Gracie would just try to be happy about it. And if her sister up and left again? Well then, she'd survive. As she had before.

And with any luck, her father would continue to get stronger and someday soon, she could reveal her own secrets without risking the loss of those she loved.

For hours, Emma worked side by side with Caden and it was like old times only better. When they were younger, he'd had more of an I'm-in-charge-do-what-I-tell-you-to-do attitude. Naturally, she hadn't paid any attention to *that*, so they'd butted heads more often than not. Now, though, things were more equal between them as they worked together to get the horses in and secure for the night.

The storm kept raging and in just a couple of hours almost a foot of snow covered the ground. With the wind howling, Emma felt frozen to the bone. Cowboys took turns going into the kitchen in shifts for hot soup and coffee. By the time the work was done and everyone settled in for the night, she was exhausted.

Emma was also proud. She'd stood her ground and proved that those years in Hollywood hadn't changed the ranch girl inside. Spending time with the horses, calming them, feeding and watering them, had been nearly a spiritual experience. It brought back to her exactly what she'd figured out more than a year ago—this was where she belonged.

Now if she could just convince Caden that she also belonged with *him*. But sex wasn't commitment and when he looked at her, she could still see suspicion shining in his eyes. He was waiting for her to leave again. How long would it take to prove to him that she wasn't going anywhere?

With that depressing thought circling her mind, Emma stopped on her way to the house and though she was half-frozen, she paused long enough to enjoy what was happening. The air was silent and icy. The sky was obliterated in the wall of white rushing down. Snow settled on her eyelashes, her cheeks and her hair and she laughed with the glory of it. This was something she'd missed in California. The changing of seasons. The hush of winter snow. Now she was back and it felt right.

"Are you crazy?"

She turned to look at Caden and smiled. "Maybe, but this is beautiful."

"*You're* beautiful," he murmured and her eyes widened. Before she could enjoy it, though, he added, "And frozen. Come on."

He took her hand and pulled her toward the back door. They dumped their coats and hats in the mudroom, stomped the snow off their boots and brushed it off their jeans before walking into the warm kitchen.

There was a stack of dirty bowls and utensils in the sink, melting, snowy footprints on the floor, and the scent of the beef soup still hung in the air.

Shaking his head, Caden said, "We'll worry about kitchen duty tomorrow."

"Sounds like a plan," she said, because honestly, even the thought of trying to clean up tonight made her want to lie down and weep. On the other hand, the thought of lying down with Caden, wrapping herself around him, made her feel downright perky. "You want more soup?"

"No," he said and went to the fridge for a beer. "You want one?" he asked. "Or wine?"

"Wine. Definitely." Emma sat down on one of the stools and watched him get their drinks. Working with him had been good. They'd reawakened the rhythm they used to have and made Emma think that maybe, even if they couldn't go back, they could rebuild what they'd once had.

He handed her the wine, then took a seat across from her and had a long pull of his beer. Shoving one hand through his hair, he said, "Thanks. For the help tonight and for the soup. The guys appreciated it."

"You're welcome." Well, weren't they being polite? The camaraderie she'd felt earlier was quickly draining away and she didn't know how to get it back.

A second or two of silence passed with the two of them staring at each other across the center island. He was studying her, and the look in his eyes wasn't what she'd hoped to see.

"Had plenty of time to think tonight," he said, his voice quiet, thoughtful, "while we were getting the horses tucked away."

"Yeah?" She felt as if she should be bracing for something, but how could she when she didn't have a clue what it was he'd been thinking about? Was he going to tell her he didn't want to see her again? Tell her he still loved her, but would never trust her? She had a stomach full of raucous butterflies inside her going absolutely nuts.

"We've done a lot of talking since you've been here and that's fine. But what I keep coming back to is one thing, Emma."

"What's that?"

"You left because you said you had to chase your dreams and that didn't leave room for getting married or having a family." He set his beer down on the countertop and idly twisted it in circles. "But when you come home you've got a baby. Now, what am I supposed to think about that?

"Who's Molly's father? Who were you willing to have a family with, Emma?"

"Caden—" Those butterflies in her stomach became dragons. She'd come home with a secret and he was asking her to share it. But if she wanted him to trust her again, didn't *she* have to trust in him, too?

"No stalling." He shook his head and locked his gaze on hers, making it impossible for her to look away. "I answered your questions earlier today," he reminded her. "Now answer mine. Tell me about that baby."

In a way, she wasn't surprised that he was asking about Molly. Emma had known when she came home that eventually she'd have to tell people the truth. Especially Caden. There was just no way the man she loved would calmly accept, without an explanation, that she'd left him only to have a child with someone else.

But damn it, this had been a *good* day. She and Caden were, if not back together, at least not at open war with each other anymore. She didn't want to lose that. But if she didn't talk, wasn't she risking losing him anyway?

As soon as that thought scuttled through her mind, though, something else stood up, demanding to be recognized. Emma had to protect that baby no matter what. And if she were to open the box and let the secrets out, how could she keep Molly safe?

Shaking her head, she said firmly, "I'm really sorry, Caden. Believe me, I am. But I can't talk about Molly."

He scrubbed both hands over his face, inhaled sharply and stood up. Coming around the end of the counter, he loomed over her, and Emma had to tip her head back just to meet those glittering blue eyes of his.

"Damn it, Emma. You owe me this. You left me, found yourself someone else and had *his* baby."

She could see the anger in his eyes, but beyond that, she saw hurt, and that she couldn't stand.

"Then you left him, too," he continued. "So what the hell is going on with you? Enough secrets, Emma. Tell me."

She looked up into his eyes, firing with hurt and anger and frustration. His entire body was tense and his jaw muscles twitched he was grinding his teeth so hard. Her heart ached because she'd never meant to hurt Caden. She was just trying to do the right thing.

"Stop thinking, Emma. Hell, I can almost hear your brain spinning." He grabbed her shoulders and held on. "Just say it."

"Molly's not mine."

* * *

"Well, find her." Dorian Baxter's voice was cold, sharp and impatient.

His assistant—what was his name? Ted? Tom? *Tim*— jolted.

"We're looking, sir," Tim said quickly. "We think she's gone home to Montana."

Dorian Baxter was forty-five years old, at the top of his game in Hollywood and had the biggest stars in the world on speed dial. He wasn't used to being placated and wouldn't accept it now. "You *think*?"

Another jolt from the younger man and this time the assistant took a step back, toward the door. Dorian noticed and told himself that it must be time for a different assistant. Why the hell hadn't he hired another woman? At least when a woman was giving him grief, she was better to look at.

"The investigator is on it, sir," Tim said, checking his notes briefly. "But apparently, there's a big snowstorm and he can't get out of the airport yet."

"Snow? Why the hell does anyone want to live in *snow*?"

"I don't know, sir."

"Of course you don't know. You don't know a hell of a lot." Dorian came out from behind his desk and only took a small zip of pleasure from the way Tim scooted farther out of his way.

He'd been on edge since the night before when he got the tip from a reporter he kept on his payroll. Someone had talked to another so-called "journalist" who was busy chasing down a lead that could bury Dorian if he didn't kill it first. He had to find the damn woman before this story made the papers. In

this climate, he'd be crucified by a bunch of scream-
ing women demanding his head and he wasn't going
to go down like that.

His office, sitting high above Hollywood Boulevard,
was an airy, modern place with chrome and glass being
the main decorative statement. Chrome frames on the
wall displayed posters from his award-winning movies. His desk was the most imposing piece of furniture
in the room—as it should be. Careers were made and
broken from behind that desk. And on either corner
of that desk were the two Best Picture awards that his
movies had won. Dorian had worked too hard and too
long and kissed way too many butts to get where he
was and damned if he'd give it up.

"You tell that guy to get his ass out on the road. I
don't care if he has to rent a snowplow to do it. I need
to know where that bitch went." Dorian glared at Tim
and watched the man pale. Stabbing his index finger
toward him, he said, "That article's going to run in another week and I want this sewn up before then. You
understand me?"

"Yes, sir. I'll get right on it."

Dorian turned his back on him in a clearly dismissive
gesture, then walked to the closest window. He stared
down at the ants streaming down sidewalks, driving
along the streets. He had this city by the balls and he
wasn't about to give up any of it.

"I want this taken care of. I want answers and I want
them yesterday."

"Yes, sir." Tim scuttled out of the office, leaving
Dorian alone to muse over his lifestyle, his power and
all that he'd managed to achieve.

No stupid bitch was going to ruin this for him.

* * *

Emma slapped one hand over her mouth the second she blurted out the words. But it was too late. Her secret was out now and the way Caden was looking at her in stunned surprise told Emma that there was no going back.

"What the hell does that mean?" He let her go and threw both hands in the air. "If Molly's not yours, why do you have her? Why does your dad think she's his granddaughter? And what aren't you telling me?"

Oh, God. Emma took a deep, shaky breath and still her head felt light. To either help with that or make herself pass out, she picked up her wine and took a healthy swallow. Dutch courage, as her grandfather used to call it. Whatever, she appreciated the low burn the wine left in her system, fighting the arctic cold now pouring from Caden's eyes.

"I can't believe I'm telling you this."

"You haven't told me much," he countered, then grabbed his beer and took a drink. "So why don't you just dive right in and get it all out? You said Molly's not yours. Explain."

Her throat felt tight, so she lifted one hand to the base of her neck as if she could dislodge the knot of emotion inside. "It means just what you think it means. I didn't give birth to Molly. My roommate, Terry Stone, did."

He backed up a step, shaking his head as if trying to make sense of the insensible. Rubbing one hand across the back of his neck, he demanded, "Well, where's Terry Stone and why did she give you her baby?"

"Terry's dead," Emma said and her voice broke on those two words. Because months-old memories enlarged that knot in her throat until she felt as if she was

going to really choke. Images rose up in her mind, of
Terry, curled up in a chair in their apartment. She hadn't
wanted to eat, to go anywhere, to take care of the baby.
Nothing could reach her because she'd withdrawn so
deeply inside herself.

"Emma," he said and this time, his voice was lower,
softer. "Talk to me."

Another sip of wine, another deep breath and Emma
murmured, "Terry got pregnant by a big producer who
told her if she slept with him, he'd put her in his new
movie."

Caden looked furious at that piece of news. Well,
Emma knew how he felt. She'd seen it too many times in
Hollywood. Powerful men using young, hopeful, naive
women, then tossing them aside for the next one in line.
Terry had probably been one of hundreds.

"But he didn't, of course. He used her, then hired
someone else for the movie." Battling the tears that blos-
somed in her eyes, Emma continued. Now that she'd
finally started telling the story, she didn't think she'd
have been able to stop even if she'd wanted to. "Terry
was so ashamed. So shaken. Then the bastard spread
the word in town that anyone who hired her would go
straight to his enemies list. She couldn't get a job. Her
agent dropped her. Then she discovered she was pregnant and she went back to Mr. Powerful and told him."

"He didn't help."

It wasn't a question. "No, he didn't. He gave her five
hundred dollars to 'take care of it.'"

Caden's eyes flashed and his hands fisted at his sides.

She took a deep breath and admitted, "That's what
broke her finally, I think. She didn't talk about it again
and all during her pregnancy, she just sort of drifted.

We worked at the same diner as waitresses, so I kept an eye on her as much as I could. But I couldn't *reach* her. Couldn't make her see that there was so much she could do. She could go home. Teach. She had her teacher's certificate, but she had dreamed her whole life of being a star."

"Like you," he said.

"Yes, like me," she agreed with a little disgust because she'd wanted the same thing that Terry had. Dreams were bright and shiny and appealing and when they splintered in your hands, you were blinded by the loss and couldn't see past the ruin to what could be. Hadn't she been blinded herself? Hadn't she stayed in Hollywood two years longer than she should have because leaving felt like more of a failure than staying?

Admitting you had failed was hard. For Terry, it had been *impossible*.

"What happened?" He came up close and smoothed a strand of hair back from her face. "Why do you have Terry's baby?"

She couldn't just sit there. Had to move. Being chased by her own thoughts, Emma pushed off the stool and started pacing the gigantic kitchen. She didn't see the beauty of it, she was simply grateful that it was big enough to give her plenty of room to move. Her insides were jumping, her mind was filled with images of Terry. The tiny apartment they'd shared. Of Molly.

Emma swiped tears off her cheeks with her fingertips and kept walking. Tears were useless. They couldn't change anything. Couldn't help Terry. Couldn't save her. And she'd never been the kind of woman to use tears to sway a man—or anyone for that matter. All she had to do was get through this.

She took a breath and started talking. "Once Terry had the baby I thought she'd be okay. She was totally in love with Molly—we both were. She was so tiny. So beautiful. And for a while, things were better. I was convinced that Terry had finally moved on."

She stopped, looked at Caden and said softly, "She went to see Molly's father. I don't even know what she was hoping for. Interest? Love? Whatever it was, she was disappointed. She took a picture of the baby to show him and he had her thrown out without even seeing her. Told her through his assistant that if she ever came back he'd have her arrested for extortion."

In a split second, Caden muttered, "Sounds like a bastard."

"That's a generous name for him." She breathed deeply in an attempt to steady herself. It didn't really work, but she kept going anyway. "He knows enough powerful people that he could have made sure anything Terry might have said against him went away. And she knew it."

Wrapping her arms around her middle, she continued in a rush. This last bit would be the hardest. "Molly was four months old when Terry went out for a drive. I was babysitting because she needed to get out, clear her head.

"Later I found a letter she'd left for me and she said she was sorry, but she couldn't do it. Couldn't be the kind of mother her daughter deserved. Couldn't keep going on when there was just nothing left for her. She asked me to raise Molly and keep her away from her father."

Emma looked at Caden. "Terry didn't have any family, anyone else to count on, besides me. So when the police came and told me she'd died in a one car accident—she drove over a cliff in Malibu—I didn't say anything about the baby. I let them think Molly was mine. And a month later, I came home."

"So you came back because of the baby," he said finally.

Emma shook her head and met his gaze squarely, making sure he could see the truth on her face when she said, "No. I'd told Terry that I was moving back to Montana about a week before she died." More tears fell and she didn't bother to try to fight them. "I think that's why she did it. I think she knew that when I left, she'd be alone. She wouldn't have anyone to give a damn about her or Molly.

"So she killed herself and left Molly to me."

Eight

Caden was torn between dozens of different emotions. Top of the list, though, were pity, fury, and finally, understanding. It was small of him to acknowledge, even to himself that he was damn glad Emma hadn't had a baby with some other man. That had been hard for him to accept and he didn't care if it did make him sound like a caveman or something. Knowing she'd rejected him and chosen someone else had been gnawing on him.

Now she was standing there, watching him and for the first time in her life, Emma Williams looked…vulnerable. She'd always been the strongest woman he'd ever known and seeing her unsure of herself was just wrong. Not to mention the fact that she was looking at him as if she were waiting for him to call the police and report her as a kidnapper.

"Jesus, Em. Relax. You did what you had to do. I'm not going to second-guess you on it."

She blew out a breath. "Thanks."

"Beyond that, I don't even know what to say about all this."

"That's okay. Neither do I." She took a shaky breath and straightened her shoulders, stiffened her spine. As he watched, the Emma he knew completely replaced the wounded woman she'd been only moments ago. "Weird, but I feel better after telling you all of it. It feels…good to get it out. To let someone know what I've been carrying around."

He walked over to her and dropped both hands onto her shoulders. She still felt cold from being outside, so he did what came naturally to him. He pulled her in close and wrapped his arms around her, giving them both the heat and the comfort they needed.

And while he held her, he asked the one question that was now uppermost in his mind. "Did he try to use you, too? That producer?"

"No," she said, and looked up at him. "But others did. He's not the only bastard in Hollywood."

Fury whipped through him like a lightning bolt and he held her even more tightly to him. Gritting his teeth, he asked, "Is that how you got that show you were on?"

"No!" She pushed away from him and stood there, with anger boiling in her eyes and simmering around her like a white-hot aura. "Is that what you think of me? That's I'd trade sex for a job?"

"No." Frustrated, he shoved one hand through his hair again. Of course he didn't think that, but hearing that story had made him want to go back in time and pummel that man and any other who would use a woman—especially Emma. "But—"

Clearly insulted, she said, "There shouldn't be a *but* in that sentence, Caden."

"There isn't," he said abruptly. "Not really. I was just mad at myself because I wasn't there when you needed me. Hell, if I know you, any man who tried that on you got kicked where it counts."

Her lips twitched and the fire in her eyes died to a smolder. "No, but I thought about it. Not every man in Hollywood is like that, though. There are a lot of decent people. But the reason I was a waitress for the last three years is because I refused to play the game," she snapped. Another deep breath and she held up one hand. "Sorry. It's just… It's so hard out there.

"Everyone's scrambling to make the right contacts, to be seen in the right places. You can't trust people like you do everywhere else. People in Hollywood are so insular, so worried about their own career or their next agent or the big audition. More worried about how things look than how they are. It's easy to get caught up in it all and I can see why some do.

"I got that series job on my third audition." She shook her head ruefully. "I'd only been in Hollywood for two months. I'm not even sure why they hired me. Well, maybe partly because I was so new, they didn't have to pay me much. And because I hadn't been seen at a million auditions all over Hollywood. They were looking for 'fresh faces' and I guess I qualified." She gave a short laugh and even she winced at the bitter tone of it.

"It's a pretty nice face," Caden murmured.

"Thanks." She gave him a wry smile and then continued. "Anyway, I got the job, so for one season, I was the airhead astronaut in space and then the show got canceled after twelve episodes." She shrugged and sighed. "After that, almost every agent and casting director in town looked at me and said, 'Nope, too soon. You're typecast. Come back in a year. Or two. Or three.'"

"I didn't know." He gave himself a mental kick. He should have known. Should have made it his business to know. But he'd been too wrapped up in his own anger at her leaving to realize that things might not be going great for her. Caden would always regret that. "You never said."

"What was there to say?" She laughed, but it was a short, harsh sound, scraping from her throat. "The few auditions I *did* get, didn't go well. I was too tall or too short. My boobs were too big—"

"If it helps, I like them just fine."

She laughed again. "Or my hair was too long or too dark—had I considered going blonde?"

"No," he said, shaking his head. Her hair was gorgeous, tumbling dark curls with streaks of sunlight running through it. He wanted his fingers in it again, feeling that dark silk sliding across his skin.

"I have no butt—"

"Now I know they're crazy."

She grinned. "My favorite, though, was 'Your nose has a bump in it.'"

"I don't see a bump. It's a pretty nose."

"Thanks for the vote of confidence," she said wryly. "But going on auditions for a month will reduce your self-confidence to a mere shadow of its former self."

A woman as beautiful and talented and sexy as Emma should never doubt herself. He hated what they'd tried to do to her. "And yet, according to Gracie, you always talked about how great everything was."

"How could I tell them the truth?" she argued, throwing her hands up. "Was I going to call Dad and say, 'Hey, Hollywood sucks, the dream is dead and I'm a waitress at the Loa Loa Coffee Shop off Sunset'?" Shaking her head, she said, "I couldn't do that. He'd have worried himself sick."

"He did anyway," Caden pointed out.

Guilt washed over her features and he felt bad for reminding her. But truth was truth. If things had been that bad, what had taken her so long to come home?

"Yeah. I know that now. God I feel so stupid. But no one told me what was happening here." She pushed her hair back, folded her arms across her chest and said, "If I'd known, I'd have come home sooner. Trust me, the only thing keeping me there was not wanting to admit that I'd failed."

"Bullshit."

Surprised, she said, "What?"

"I call BS." Caden reached for her again. "I admit, I was pissed when you left."

"I know but—"

"Not finished," he said. "I was furious that you left me for some pipe dream of becoming a successful actor. But I'm not going to let you say you failed. You didn't, Em. You went for it. You chased it. You were on TV for God's sake."

"One season," she reminded him. "A short one at that."

He frowned at her. "More than most aspiring actors get, isn't it?"

She sighed and nodded. "Yes, I guess so."

Looking down at her, he gave her something else when he confessed, "And I thought you were really good."

Stunned, she stared at him. "You watched the show?"

He'd never admitted this to anyone before, but now seemed like the time to spill his own secrets. Hell, she needed it and if he wanted truth from her then he had to provide a few, too. "Yeah, I watched it. How could I not? I had to see if you'd done the right thing for yourself—and I'll admit this, too, that I was hoping you would suck at it. To prove that you should have stayed here. With me.

"I watched one episode. You were damn good, Emma." He huffed out a breath and said, "Seeing you on the TV, just shining and showing up every other actor in that stupid show—"

"It wasn't stupid," she countered with a low chuckle.

He lifted one brow. "Yeah, it was. But the fact that you could be that good in a show that bad only made me madder because I figured you'd proved that you were right to leave. So I never watched it again."

Emma smiled up at him and her green eyes glimmered in the overhead lights. "You know, I find that oddly flattering."

"You should," he told her and looked into those amazing eyes so she would see that he meant every word. "I almost tossed the television."

She laughed and he enjoyed hearing it rise up around him. "You were good, Emma. You didn't fail."

After a second or two, she asked softly, "Why are you being so nice to me?"

"Well," he hedged, "that's a question, isn't it?"

"And that's not an answer."

"No, it's not," he agreed. He wouldn't tell her he loved her still. Wouldn't say that having her back in Montana made the rest of his life straighten out. Wouldn't put his heart on the line because having it crushed once in a lifetime was more than enough. "Does it really matter?"

She sighed, moved in closer, laid her head on his chest and wrapped her arms around his waist. "No, it doesn't."

He tipped her face up to his, stared down into her eyes briefly, then lowered his head to hers and took her mouth fiercely. She clung to him, her tongue tangling with his and they swayed together, lost in the heat that flashed up between them. His body was on fire, his blood sizzled in his veins. She was everything. She was all. Her hands on him, his mouth fused to hers. This was what was important. The only important thing.

When he finally broke the kiss, his arms came around her and he held her tightly because he needed to feel her, safe and warm in his arms. Thinking about her alone in Hollywood used to haunt him. Now that he'd heard her story, he knew that he'd be haunted for a lot longer.

Two days later, Emma was back at her family's ranch. The snow had stopped, the sun was out and the temperature was rising enough that the fresh snow was melting as quickly as it had fallen.

When she got home, Molly greeted her as if she'd been gone a month and Emma's heart swelled with love for the baby girl. She hadn't given birth to Molly, but she'd been there with the baby since the day she was born. Emma *was* her daughter in every way that mattered. She didn't know what would happen in the future, but she knew she would fight for that baby no matter what. And now she had Caden on her side, as well.

Caden. Just the thought of him was enough to make her melt. She shivered, remembering all those hours wrapped around his body, feeling him moving deep within her. Her belly swirled with fresh desire and Emma didn't know how she'd make it through the day without touching him. So, the only thing she could do was to force her mind away from thoughts of him.

Her father was looking downright perky and even Gracie was a little less hostile. Emma was still finding her way back into the family circle, still a little unsure where she fit now, but at least she didn't feel as though she were trying to tiptoe her way across a minefield.

"Was Molly a lot of trouble?"

Gracie glanced at her. "I'd like to say yes, so I could make you feel guilty…but no. She was great. Dad loved taking care of her and I helped out when I could."

Emma leaned on the half stall door and watched her sister using a currycomb on an older gelding. "I appreciate it, you know. If I could have gotten home from Caden's earlier, I would have."

Gracie paused, the comb resting on the horse's broad back. "Yeah. I know. And don't worry… I'll think of a way for you to pay me back."

"I'm sure." Emma was willing to take this conversation, since it was the friendliest one she'd had with her sister since coming home again. "So how long have you had this old boy?"

The horse lifted his head and gave Emma what would pass for a dirty look. She laughed.

"Hey, old is a state of mind and Herman's just getting

started, aren't you?" Gracie stroked her hand down his back with a slow, gentle touch. The big animal turned his head to give Gracie a gentle nudge. "I brought him home a few months ago."

"Okay," Emma said, stepping into the stall and closing the door behind her. She picked up a brush and absently dragged it through Herman's mane. "Why?"

"He's good with kids. Patient. And—" Gracie ducked her head, shrugged, then said, "He's going to be one of my equine therapy horses."

Emma just blinked at her. "Your what?"

Gracie smiled and looked suddenly more animated than Emma had seen her in a long time. "I want to start a business here on the ranch. Boarding horses, giving riding lessons and mostly, to work on equine therapy."

She stroked her hand along Herman's neck and the older horse leaned into her like a giant puppy looking for more love. Gracie laughed a little and obliged him.

"I totally understand boarding and riding lessons, you'd be great at it. But equine therapy? What made you think of that?"

She'd heard of it, of course. The therapy was designed to help people suffering with everything from PTSD to autism to depression. It could help with physical disabilities as well and was becoming more and more widely accepted.

The familiar scents of hay and horse and weathered wood surrounded Emma like a warm hug as she waited for her sister to speak again.

"I didn't, at first. But when we hired Tom, a year or so ago, he was...on edge a lot."

Emma knew she was talking about Tom Hatton. About forty, with short hair and sad brown eyes. He was quiet, kept to himself, but from what she'd seen, he was a hard worker.

"He's a veteran and he really needed the job. He hadn't done much ranch work, but Dad hired him anyway, because he could see Tom was in a bad way and—"

"Dad's a softy."

Gracie grinned. Sisters, sharing family truths, and it felt good to Emma.

"That he is," Gracie said. "Anyway, over the next few months, as Tom spent time around the horses, grooming and caring for them and learning to ride, he sort of…unwound, you know?"

Emma understood that completely. Horses were soothing to the soul. Just being around them could remind you to pause and enjoy the moment. "Not surprising at all."

"Exactly!"

In her obvious excitement, Gracie had evidently forgotten about any lingering anger she had for her sister and Emma was grateful for it.

"So the horses healed Tom and you figured you could do it for other people, too?"

"Basically." Gracie leaned her forearms on Herman's broad back. "I've studied up on the theories and taken classes at the community college. And Madison Peters, the local vet, is helping me get it started."

"Well, that's really nice of her."

"Yeah." Gracie stiffened a little, then went on. "She's helped me find old or abandoned horses. I've got five now, ready for riding lessons in the spring and Herman here will be the star of the therapy clients." Gracie stroked his neck again. "He was left tied to a fence in the middle of a field outside of town. No one knew where he was from or who had left him, so I went and got him.

"I think Herman and the others are so grateful to be loved and have a home again, that they're eager to be with people."

Emma could never understand how anyone could walk away from the animals who relied on them and she was glad that Herman had found a home with Gracie, who would always care for him.

"I've got two horses that we're boarding right now, too," Gracie said. "So that's good for income, but I'll want to expand and that means adding onto the stable or maybe just building another one."

"Big plans," Emma mused, happy that her sister had found something she was excited about. Something she wanted to do with her life. And Emma was grateful that Gracie wouldn't go through what she had. Working for yourself had to be better than having your life in someone else's hands.

"I know, but I think I can make it work. Dad's all for it and Madison thinks it's a great idea."

"No reason you can't," Emma said with enthusiasm. "It's perfect, Gracie. You're terrific with horses and with people. You were made for this."

"Really?" Gracie looked at her, and it was clear she wanted to believe Emma.

"Really." For the first time since returning to Montana, Emma felt as if there was a chance to win back her sister. To have the kind of relationship they used to have. "I'll support you any way I can. If you need help, just tell me and I'm there."

"Thanks, Emma."

The more she considered it, the better the idea

sounded. Gracie had always had a gift with animals. Plus, she was warm and friendly, and was great with kids, too. Which was a good thing because there would always be children wanting to learn to ride.

But as much as she was happy for her sister, Emma was able to look down the road and see a few speed bumps. "How big a stable are you thinking of building?"

"I'd like to have ten horses for lessons and the therapy sessions, and this stable can only hold five, plus the ranch's working horses." She looked at Emma and said, "So the new stable would have to be big enough for the therapy horses, and for boarders. I'd like to use this stable for the ranch animals and keep my business horses separate where I can."

She could actually see it in her mind's eye. "You're right. You'll need a new stable. A big one, with room to grow. You could build it just on the other side of the yard. Separate, but still close to the corral…"

"That's what I was thinking," her sister said, smiling.

Emma loved hearing how sure of herself Gracie sounded and wanted to do everything she could to help. Not only because this was the first time they'd actually "connected" since Emma came home, but because she loved her sister and wanted her happy.

"But it all sounds expensive, right? Have you already gone to the bank to set up a loan?"

Boom. Gracie's features went blank instantly and Emma knew that somehow she'd lost her.

"Not necessary."

"You've already got the money?" Emma asked. "How?" If she'd taken another mortgage out on the house, then Emma wanted to know about it. If she'd gotten the money somewhere else, Emma *really* wanted to know about it.

"I handled it, okay?" Gracie finished grooming Herman and set the comb down on the shelf alongside the door. "This is going to be my business, Emma, and I know what needs to be done. Just like I've handled everything else for the last five years."

Emma's heart sank a little. "Really? We're back to being enemies again?"

"I'm not your enemy, Emma," Gracie said. "But I'm not a kid anymore, either. I can take care of this by myself."

"Damn it, Gracie, stop shutting me out."

But her little sister just shook her head. "Thanks for helping with Herman. I'll see you up at the house later."

When she was alone again, Emma wondered if she'd ever feel as if she'd really come home. It was as if she was still an outsider. A stranger in the place where she'd grown up. Every time she took a step into the circle of family and friends and lovers, that circle narrowed and she found herself still shut out. She'd felt much the same in Hollywood—but here, the pain of it was much sharper because these were her people. This was her place. She needed to be a part of it all again.

Her past was here and this was where she wanted to build a future. But the present was filled with potholes and mistrust that she hadn't figured out how to conquer yet.

When Caden's truck pulled into the ranch yard late that afternoon, Emma's heart gave a solid jolt. Her skin buzzed and every one of her nerve endings bristled. She walked out of the house to meet him and her mouth went dry as he climbed out of the truck and settled his hat on his head.

He looked across at her and their gazes clashed with all the heat and need and passion they'd shared during the storm. God, she'd missed him. One day away from him had her burning to hold him, to feel his arms come around her. She wanted his kiss, his touch, and knowing that she couldn't have any of it right now was the only thing that kept her from hurrying over to him.

Instead, she leaned against a porch post and watched him. "This is a nice surprise. What's up?"

He came around the front of the truck, and everything about him screamed cowboy, badass, *dream lover*.

"Thought I'd come over to meet your…daughter."

Emma threw a quick glance behind her at the house, making sure her father wasn't overhearing the hesitation in Caden's voice. Frowning a little, she waited until he was close enough that she could keep her voice low when she spoke. "Dad doesn't know. Neither does Gracie. You're the only one I've told."

His expression clearly said her he didn't think much of that. "Why, Emma? They're your family. You don't trust them?"

"Of course I do," she whispered, still casting a worried glance at the house behind her. Yes, she felt terrible, keeping this secret from them. But sometimes, hiding the truth was the only way to protect someone you loved. In this case, both Molly and her father.

Then meeting his gaze again, she said, "But Dad's doing so well now, I don't want to throw him back into a decline when he finds out the granddaughter he loves so much isn't really his. How can I tell him?" She straightened up, and shot a look at the stables, where the vet's

van was parked. Madison and Gracie were inside, dealing with the horses and Emma hoped they stayed there.

"As for Gracie, well, we haven't exactly been chatty
since I came home," she pointed out with a sense of
grief over what she'd lost. "Except for earlier today
when we managed to actually talk without swiping at
each other for like ten minutes, she can hardly stand
to be in the same room with me. So pardon me for not
catching her arm in the hall and confessing everything."

Caden shook his head and scowled at her. "Em,
you're making this harder than it has to be."

"Am I?" she countered. Nerves rattled around in her
stomach and she slapped one hand to her belly to try to
quiet them. It didn't work. "I don't have legal custody of
Molly. All I have is a letter from her mother asking me
to take her. I can't tell my family because I don't want to
include them in what I've already done by taking Molly.

"Plus, I can't risk someone finding out she isn't
mine because what if *they* say something and then that
spreads until finally I have Sheriff Eagle dropping by to
handcuff me and hand the baby over to social services?"

His eyes widened. "I don't know whether to be impressed or horrified by how your brain works. How the
hell do you build up an entire scenario in your head?
You don't know any of that would happen."

"I don't know it wouldn't, either," she told him. "I
brought Molly here to keep her *safe*."

He yanked his hat off, stabbed his fingers through
that thick, beautiful black hair of his, then jammed his
hat back on. Narrowing his gaze on her, he said, "That
letter's not enough for you to keep her safe. You know
that, right?"

"Thank you, Mr. Obvious. Yes, I know. But it's all I have."

"All right." Caden sighed, looked into the distance for a long second or two, then shifted his gaze back to her. "Here's what we're going to do. I'll take you into Kalispell. We'll talk to my lawyer."

"A *lawyer*?" Panicked at the thought, Emma tried to sift through the dozens of thoughts that sprung into her mind. "I'm trying to hide and you want to take me to a lawyer? Doesn't he have to tell someone? I mean, officer of the court and all that?"

"Confidentiality," Caden reminded her.

Okay, her fear dropped a notch or two. "Right, right."

"I trust Max, Em. I've known him for years. He can give us an idea of what to do from here."

"Us?"

"You," he corrected and Emma was sorry to hear it. For a second there, she'd thought they were a team. "It all boils down to this. Do you trust me, Em?"

That was an easy question to answer. She looked into his eyes and saw the steady, strong man she'd always known. She saw her lover. The man who made her hunger like no one else ever had. His eyes were steady, cool and fixed on hers. Of course she trusted Caden. So she'd trust his lawyer, too. She'd accept his help and be grateful for it.

"Yes, Caden. I do trust you," she said, taking a deep breath of the crisp, cold air. "When do we go?"

"Tomorrow. No point in putting it off, is there?"

"No," Emma said, fighting a fresh tide of fear washing through her, "I guess not. So you want to come in and meet Molly?"

"In a minute." Caden climbed the steps until he was

on the porch with her, then he pulled her up close. So close, his belt buckle dug into her middle and the hard, thick proof of his passion pressed against her belly, quickening so many new fires inside her, she could hardly breathe.

Looking into her eyes, he said, "Damn it, Emma, I missed you last night. I didn't want to, but damned if I didn't."

Her heartbeat actually *fluttered*. She hadn't known it could do that. "Oh boy, I missed you, too."

One corner of his mouth lifted and his eyes burned with the heat that could scorch her in seconds. "Good to know." Then he bent his head to kiss her and everything that wasn't Caden drained right out of her mind.

For seconds, minutes, hours? Her mouth tangled with his, their tongues entwined, their breath moving from one to the other and back again. Emma felt herself melting into him and somehow, her mind woke up as she half wondered how she had ever managed to leave him. He was in her heart, her soul. He was so much a part of her that without him, she'd never really felt whole the entire time she was gone.

And Emma knew, with everything in her, that if he wasn't with her, she'd spend the rest of her life with a gaping hole inside. When he finally lifted his head and stared down at her, Emma could only stare back, lost in those cool, blue eyes.

"Well, this is fun. Hi, Caden."

Emma jolted, but he didn't let her go. Just turned his head and said, "Hi, Gracie. Madison."

Blinking hard and fighting for a few remaining brain cells to fire, Emma shifted a glance to her sister and the grinning redhead standing beside her.

"Hi, Caden," she said, then stuck out her right hand. "And you're Emma. Nice to meet you. I've heard a lot about you."

"I'll bet," Emma said, shaking her hand and sparing her sister a quick look.

Gracie shrugged. "Are you two going to stay out here and grope each other or are you coming inside? I'm putting some fresh coffee on."

"Sold," Caden said and when Emma would have moved away from him, he kept one arm around her shoulders, pinning her to his side.

All of them went into the house and while Gracie and Madison headed for the kitchen, Emma and Caden followed the sound of Molly's excited squeal to the great room.

Frank was on the floor, making mooing sounds and Molly was braced against a pile of pillows, clapping her hands in delight.

"Well, hello, Frank."

Emma laughed as her father looked up. "Hey, Caden, good to see you. Emma, our girl here about said 'cow' a minute ago."

Emma laughed. "Dad, she's not going to talk at five months."

"Can if she wants to. This baby girl is a smart one."

"Is she?" Caden walked over, crouched beside Frank and let the baby give him a thorough inspection. When she finally gave him a toothless grin and babbled a stream of sounds, Caden laughed and Emma's heart stopped.

He reached out, picked her up, and Molly patted his cheeks. "Well, you're a beauty, aren't you?"

Caden shot a look at Emma and just like that, everything in her dissolved into a puddle of goo. What was it about seeing a strong, sexy man being kind and gentle with a baby? It plucked every heartstring and tightened every nerve until her body felt like it was burning up. Her gaze met Caden's and what she saw there fired up her hormones and sent them into a wild dance of anticipation.

This was her cowboy, Emma told herself. And she would never give him up again.

Nine

"Well?" Dorian glared at his assistant— *What* was his name? "What have you got?"

The younger man swallowed hard, looked down at his notes, then spoke quickly, words tumbling over each other. "The investigator made it out of the airport last night finally."

"I didn't ask you for his travel plans, did I?" Dorian felt his temper inching higher and higher. "What did he find?"

Tim—that was his name—Tim, cleared his throat nervously, walked to the desk and timidly set down a sheet of paper. Dorian glanced at it.

"He's got her address, phone number, email. She lives in some tiny town near Kalispell."

Dorian scanned the paper, hardly listening.

But Tim kept talking. "Her family has a small ranch,

nothing special. Her father's been in a bad way for a while and her sister's been running the place—"

Finally, Dorian lifted his head and speared little Tim with an icy glare. "What makes you think I care about any of that? I only worry about backstories in my movies. All I need is the information. I've got it now, so get out."

"Yes, sir." Tim turned and scuttled across the room and out the door, shutting it quietly after him.

Dorian's temper was developing a life of its own. He heard his own thundering heartbeat in his ears and could actually *feel* his blood pressure rising. He had about five days before the shit hit the proverbial fan. So this woman…he checked again. Emma Williams. Had better do exactly what he told her to do.

"Well, I like her."

Gracie laughed shortly. "Of course you like Emma, Mad. You like everybody."

"I try to, yes." Madison shrugged and leaned against the wall by the front door. "Why live your life grumpy?"

"Is that a clever way of telling me I'm crabby?"

"I said grumpy."

Gracie nodded. "A fine distinction."

"It is," Madison said with a smile as she straightened up. "And actually, you were pretty nice to Emma tonight at dinner. Oh, and thank your dad for me. That spaghetti was terrific."

Gracie smiled, too. "His specialty." She glanced toward the great room. "Now that Caden's gone home and the baby's asleep, he's probably nodding off in his chair."

"Sounds good to me," Madison said, stifling a yawn.

"I've been up since three when the Porter's dog went into early labor."

"Lots of baby news around here," Gracie muttered.

"And speaking of babies, Molly is adorable." Madison grabbed Gracie's hand and squeezed. "I saw you with her. You're crazy about that little girl."

Sighing, Gracie thought it was just a shame sometimes how easily Madison could read her. There was simply no point in trying to hide things from the woman. "Okay, yes. She's a cutie and yes, I'm nuts about her. Happy?"

Madison laughed, then clapped one hand over her mouth to quiet the sound. "Sorry. Don't want to wake your dad. But yes, I'm not *un*happy. Now, I'm going home to give you and Emma a chance to talk."

"We already did."

"And yet," Madison pointed out, "there's still so much to say."

Gracie shook her head in amazement. "You're really pushy sometimes, did anyone ever tell you that?"

"Only you," she said, then reached out to give her a hug. "I'll call you tomorrow. Maybe you could come to my place for dinner."

"That sounds great." Gracie opened the front door for her. "Be careful, the roads can be icy."

"Yes, Mom." Madison's laughter trailed after her as she hurried out to her truck.

Gracie stood in the doorway until Madison was on her way, headed down the drive. Then she locked up, and threw a quick look at her dad, asleep in his chair with an open book on his lap and his glasses sliding down the end of his nose. A wave of love for him crashed over her along with that niggling worry she couldn't shake. What would he say if he knew her secret? What would he think of her? What would it change?

She did as she always did, buried those fears deep and tucked them away behind the secret she protected. Taking a deep breath, she walked down the hall to the kitchen because a cup of hot tea sounded perfect. When she entered the big square room, though, she stopped dead. Emma was sitting at the table, scrolling on her phone. She looked up when Gracie came in.

"Hey. I like your friend Madison."

Whether she told herself it didn't matter or not, Gracie was glad to hear that. Lips curving, she admitted, "Mad just said the same thing about you." Picking up the teakettle, she grudgingly offered, "I'm making myself some tea. You want some?"

"Thanks, Gracie. Yeah, I would." Emma sat back in her chair and watched her move around the kitchen.

Familiar tasks freed up your mind for other things, Gracie told herself. Which meant she could think about her sister. She'd really missed Emma all the time she was gone. And she'd been so busy letting her hurt feelings and anger drag her around for the past several days, she hadn't really taken the time to admit that it was good to have her home.

Muffling a groan, Gracie rolled her eyes and thought it was really *frustrating* to have to admit that Mad had been right. Again.

"Oh, my God. No."

Heart suddenly racing, Gracie spun around. Emma's voice was horrified and when she looked at her sister, Gracie could see real fear stamped on her features. "What's wrong, Em? What happened?"

She didn't speak. She just stared at her phone, eyes wide, mouth open as if waiting for a shriek to slip out. A sheen of tears glimmered in her eyes. Gracie'd never seen her big sister like this and she didn't like it.

"Emma." Gracie hurried over to her. "What is it?"

Emma looked at her. "Oh God, Gracie, I don't know what to do."

Gracie dragged a chair out and plopped down, then bracing her forearms on her thighs, she leaned toward her big sister. "You're scaring me."

"I'm scared, too." Emma pulled in a long, shuddering breath and twin tears streaked along her cheeks unheeded.

"Talk to me, Em. Tell me what's going on."

Shaking her head, she handed over her phone. "Here. Just read this. Then I'll explain."

Ms. Williams. You will return my daughter to me or you will be charged with kidnapping. I expect to hear from you immediately. Dorian Baxter

Stunned, shaken and mostly confused, Gracie looked at her sister. "His daughter? Kidnapping? What the hell, Em? Who's Dorian Baxter?"

"Molly's father," Emma blurted, snatching the phone from Gracie and turning it off, as if that could make the email disappear.

"You kidnapped Molly?" If she had said she was a notorious bank robber with a château in France as a safe house, Gracie wouldn't have been more surprised.

"No, of course not," Emma said, shaking her head. "I mean, not really. Legally maybe, but not— Oh, God. What am I going to do?"

Gracie didn't know what to think.

The fear on Emma's face was real, though, and it was contagious, because Gracie's stomach started spinning in sympathy. "Tell me what's happening and maybe we can figure it out."

Panic shining in her eyes, Emma nodded and reached for her hand. Holding on, she said, "Okay, I'll tell you, but you can't let Dad know. I couldn't bear it if this whole thing made him sick again and—"

So she wasn't the only one with secrets, Gracie thought. Nor the only one worried about upsetting their father. Strangely enough, that knowledge made her feel closer to her sister. "Agreed. Just talk."

Emma did. Gracie sat quietly—it wasn't easy because there were plenty of times she wanted to curse and a few times she wanted to apologize for giving Emma such a hard time since she came home. Her heart hurt for her sister and for Molly and for the baby's mother. But she didn't say a word, just listened. The more she heard, the worse it got. Emma's grip on her hand tightened and Gracie squeezed back in solidarity.

When Emma finally finished talking and silence dropped down on the kitchen, Gracie was as scared as Emma. "I don't even know what to say. This is all—"

"A mess?" Emma asked. "Yeah, I know." Jumping up from her chair, she stared out the window at the darkness beyond. Her reflection stared back into the room and Gracie's gaze met Emma's mirrored eyes.

"He doesn't even really want her, does he?"

"Of course not," Emma said, biting her lip. "I don't know why he's doing this. He didn't give a damn about Terry or Molly, so what's changed?" She whirled around to look at Gracie. "Nope, doesn't matter what changed. I won't do it. I don't care what happens to me, I'm not giving Molly to that man. I just won't."

"Damn straight you won't."

Emma and Gracie both jolted and turned around to face their father, standing in the doorway. Frank Williams was furious and Gracie couldn't remember the last time she'd seen him with his temper boiling. His usually placid features were a thunderstorm and his eyes were flashing. Under the overhead light, his gray hair was rumpled from his nap, but his features were set like an ancient warrior about to go into battle.

"Dad," Emma said quickly, "I never meant to hurt you. I mean, I know you thought she was your granddaughter, but I didn't know how to tell you the truth and—"

"Dad, maybe you should sit down," Gracie interrupted Emma.

"I don't need to sit down," he said, biting off every word.

Gracie blinked and threw a quick look at her sister. She looked as confused and surprised as Gracie felt.

But Frank was still talking so they both paid attention. "As for Molly, she *is* my granddaughter and I'll fight anyone who says different."

Gracie looked at Emma again and saw tears coursing down her sister's face. Her own heart turned over in sympathy. Gracie had assumed Emma's life was perfect, unlike her own. Instead, her sister had been worrying in silence, hugging her secrets close, just as Gracie was. And rather than seeing past her own anger long enough to actually talk to Emma, Gracie had kept them at odds when they might have been helping each other. If she could have kicked her own ass, she would have.

But right now, she had other worries. "Dad? Are you okay?"

He looked at Gracie. "Stop watching me like you're waiting for me to keel over. I feel fine. I'm just mad as hell is all."

"Okay…" He did have fire in his eyes and his shoulders were squared, his spine ramrod straight.

"I wanted to tell you before, Dad," Emma was saying, "I just didn't know how."

"Doesn't matter," he ground out and walked to her. Pulling her in for a hug, he kissed the top of Emma's head and said, "That baby belongs with us. I won't see her go to a father who doesn't deserve her. Especially not to a man like that one. Damned if I will."

"But she's not my daughter." Emma's voice broke. "I don't know what we can do."

Frank looked from one to the other of his daughters and said, "She may not be your daughter, but she's our family. We love her and when it all boils down, love is the only thing that matters."

Gracie's heart lifted and tears stung her eyes as she moved across the kitchen to join the group hug. This was what she'd needed to hear all along. This was what she needed to believe. She should have trusted that her father would be the man to see clearly right down to the heart of the matter.

"Caden's taking me to Kalispell tomorrow to talk to his lawyer."

"That's a good idea," Frank said.

"It is good," Gracie chimed in, looking into Emma's eyes to reassure her. "Max will know what to do."

"That's right, he will. And if he for some reason can't come up with a plan, don't you two worry," Frank said softly, holding them both. "We'll figure this out. Together."

The next morning, Emma was at Caden's ranch just after dawn. She hadn't been able to sleep and after trying most of the night, she'd given up and headed to the only man who could, hopefully, untie the knots in her stomach.

They'd be meeting with his lawyer in a few hours and Emma's nerves were strung so tight, it was a wonder her body wasn't throwing off sparks.

Caden opened the door and she only stared at him for a long minute. His chest was bare, his jeans on but unbuttoned and his hair was still damp from his shower. Instantly, her mouth went dry and heat rushed through her body.

"Emma, what're you doing here? I was going to pick you up in a couple hours."

"Couldn't sleep," she admitted and slipped past him into the house. She dropped her black shoulder bag on the entry table, then turned to face him. "I'm all tangled up inside, Caden."

He closed the door, then leaned back against it, folding his arms across his chest. He looked her up and down slowly and his gaze felt as hot as a touch. Straightening up, he moved to her, laid both hands on her shoulders and she felt the fire of him slide deep within her.

"You're smart, beautiful and brave," he said softly. "And Max is a damn good lawyer. So stop worrying."

"I can't," she said. "My mind keeps spinning and—"

He grinned. "Then let's give it something else to

think about." He kissed her and instantly, Emma's mind emptied.

His mouth claimed hers, his tongue twisting with hers, his breath sighing into her lungs. She slid her hands up and down his bare back, her fingernails scraping his skin. He dropped his hands to her butt and squeezed, pulling her in so tight, she felt his erection pressing against her.

Anticipation rolled through her. Excitement. Eagerness. She wanted him. This was why she'd had to come to him. He was the only man in the world who could turn her fears and nerves into blistering hot desire.

"Jacket off," he muttered when he tore his mouth free.

"Okay." She slid it off and let it drop to the floor.

"And the shirt," he ordered. "Take it off, but be sure to wear it a lot after today. I like it."

Emma tipped her head to one side. "You know I don't take orders, right?"

One corner of his mouth lifted. "You do today."

He wasn't wrong. There wasn't a woman alive who could stand in front of a half-naked Caden and say "no."

She smiled even as her breath came faster, harder. The red, scoop neck, long-sleeved shirt was alongside her jacket in seconds.

"Now the boots. And the slacks." He watched her strip right there in the foyer and his eyes gleamed with a dark heat that fired everything inside her.

Lastly, she stepped out of the black lace panties that had gotten a low whistle from Caden, and she was naked in moments. Then she was in his arms and while her mind was quiet, her body was burning.

He grabbed her, lifted her and swung around to plant

her back against the closed door. The wood panel was cold against her skin, but couldn't dampen the fires licking at her bones, her blood, her soul.

Emma hooked her legs around his hips and watched as he freed himself from his jeans. She reached down to curl her fingers around the thick length of him and watched his eyes glaze over. Then he growled and in an instant, he was inside her, filling her. She tipped her head back against the door and stared at the ceiling as he drove her past sanity into a world that revolved only around the two of them.

Again and again, he took her, pushing her higher, faster, than ever before. She lowered her gaze to meet his and saw an all-encompassing desire to match her own. His hunger was etched on his face and seeing it, fed hers.

Fast. So fast. She had been primed for this before she arrived and now, the payoff was almost on her. She felt a climax coming and welcomed it. Rushed to meet it. His big, strong hands cupped her butt, supporting her while he pushed into her depths with desperation. Together, they raced toward that end that was always more of a beginning for them. An orgasm didn't finish things between them, it only set them up for the next one. And Emma knew she would never have him enough. Never lose this magic that happened only when he was inside her.

"Stop thinking, Em," he ordered. "Feel me. Feel me inside you and come. Let go and come."

"I am," she said, as splintering sensations opened up deep within her. She locked her gaze with his. "Right now."

And her body exploded. She called out his name

helplessly as wave after wave of satisfaction flooded her system. His gaze held hers and she couldn't have looked away even if she'd wanted to. Instead, she watched as his body joined hers, as her name erupted from his lips. As his eyes burned into hers.

When the trembling stopped, she dropped her head to his shoulder. "Well, you did it. I'm not worried anymore."

He gave a short bark of laughter. "Then my work here is done."

She looked him in the eye. "Oh no, it's not."

"Good to know," he answered and bent his head to give her a quick kiss.

Then something occurred to her and she blurted out, "We didn't use a condom."

Caden shrugged. "If something happens, we'll deal with it then."

A tiny flicker of hope for a future flared to life in her heart. If he wasn't worried by a pregnancy scare, then he was thinking beyond the moment.

Lifting her off him, he looked down at her. "I think we could both use another shower."

Her legs were still trembling, but she nodded, because she had a vision of shower sex floating through her mind.

"You go on up. I'll get your stuff."

"You're really bossy this morning," she said, a soft smile curving her mouth.

"You complaining?"

"Not today," she said, because really, all she could think about was having him again. Then she turned and started up the stairs. Feeling his gaze on her, Emma deliberately swung her hips and paused half-way up to look over her shoulder at him.

His eyes were on fire. "You trying to tell me something, Em?"

She licked her lips, tossed her hair back and gave an order to him for a change. "You bet. Get moving, cowboy. I want that shower."

He grinned. "Yes, ma'am."

A few hours later, Caden sat next to Emma at his lawyer's office. That email from Dorian Baxter had to be handled legally and Caden knew they had to act fast. If they hadn't had to be here, he never would have left the ranch. Not after having Emma against the door, in the shower and on the bed. The woman stirred him up like no one else.

Even thinking about their morning was enough to stir his blood and make his dick cry for mercy.

Max Finley scanned the letter from Terry that Emma had handed him and when he was finished reading, he looked up and took off his glasses. "This is the only proof of custody you have?"

Emma blindly reached for Caden's hand and he took it, folding his fingers around hers.

"Yes." Emma's voice sounded breathy, vulnerable, and Caden didn't like it. "She left me that note the day she died."

Max leaned back in the burgundy leather chair. "It's not enough. You know that, don't you?"

"Yes, I do," she said softly. "But I couldn't leave Molly with that man. He didn't want her. I can't imagine why he's trying to get her now."

Caden hated hearing that uncertainty and fear in

Emma's voice. He owed this Dorian Baxter a world of hurt for causing it.

"Probably someone found out about the baby," Caden said. "Maybe they're hoping to make him look bad and he's trying to head that off at the pass."

"Could be," Max mused, then his gaze fixed on Emma again. "Do you have any evidence of what you say he did to your roommate? Any proof at all of his character?"

"Or lack thereof," Caden muttered. It would almost be worth a flight to Hollywood if he could plant his fist in the man's face.

Max nodded at him.

But Emma said, "No. No proof. But it's an open se-cret in Hollywood. People know what he's like, it's just that no one talks about it."

"Again, it's simply not enough."

"Look, Max," Caden said gruffly, "what Emma's done was to protect that baby. You have to admire that. God knows I do."

From the corner of his eye, he saw Emma's surprise. He couldn't blame her for that. Over the last week or so, they'd been closer than ever before and at the same time, as distant as the earth from the moon. Having her here again tangled Caden up in so many knots, he couldn't count them all. Hours ago, she'd been naked in his bed and God knew he still wanted her. Still loved her. But how the hell was he supposed to trust her to stay?

She'd left him to chase a dream and run home when that dream crashed down around her. But if they went forward from here, didn't that make Caden her second choice? How could he live with that? How could he spend the rest of his life wondering if she'd always be looking for more than they had together?

He didn't know where the hell they went from here, but Caden would do all he could to help her protect her friend's baby. Because Caden hated men who took advantage of women. He'd do whatever he could to keep that child away from a man who drove her mother to suicide. And because he'd do anything for Emma—anything but trust her.

"Listen, Max," he said, "Baxter doesn't know what Emma might have. For all he knows, she's got Terry's diary, spelling out everything."

"I think I see where you're going," Max said, and a slow smile spread across his face. "We send an email—followed up by a very official registered letter—telling him to back off or our evidence will go public."

"Exactly," Caden said, nodding. "In the current atmosphere—especially in Hollywood—his career would be over."

"You really think it'll work?" Emma asked.

He looked her in the eye. "I do. Baxter won't want to test us. He has too much to lose." Then he turned to face his lawyer again. "But on the off chance he won't let this go, I want you to do something for me."

Max smiled again. This is why he was Caden's lawyer. They'd been friends for years and were usually on the same page about most things.

"Let me guess," Max mused. "You want me to hire an investigator in LA. Do some quick digging."

"Always said you were a smart guy," Caden said. "Hire as many investigators as you think we need. Offer bonuses if they come up with something fast that we can use against this guy."

"Caden... I can't pay for that," Emma protested.

"I didn't ask you to." Caden caught her gaze and held it. "You can be hardheaded about something else, okay? Let this one go."

She thought about it for a minute and he knew her pride had to be dented. But finally, she nodded. "Okay. For Molly. And thanks."

"I know some people in LA," Max said. "I'll make some calls and get this moving."

"Thanks, Max. Knew I could count on you."

Emma was grateful for Caden's help. Without him doing all of this, she didn't know what she would have done. The thought of giving the baby over to Dorian Baxter was enough to give a statue cold chills. The only other thing she could have done was take the baby and run—and God knew how that would have ended.

At Tucker's, a steak house just outside Kalispell, Emma looked across the table at him. He was dressed all in black but for the crisp white dress shirt beneath his jacket. His black hat and gleaming black boots only added to the picture of professional, gorgeous and just that delicious touch of wicked that she loved.

She'd seen that wicked side of him a few hours ago. And just remembering what they'd done sent a thrill up her spine and settled an ache between her thighs. How could she want him so much? And what would she do if he pulled back from her? If he never believed that she was home to stay?

"Thank you, Caden," she said when the waiter left after taking their order.

"For lunch? Not a problem."

"Not for lunch. For what you're doing for me and Molly."

He sipped at his beer, then set it down on the white-cloth-covered table. He was quiet, thoughtful and for a few seconds, Emma held her breath.

"I don't like men who use power against people," he said. "And I really don't like them using it against *you*."

A flush of warmth raced through her and her heart filled with hope again. Hope that there was a future for them.

Coming here, to Tucker's was a good sign, too. This used to be "their" place. The restaurant had been in the same spot for fifty years. There was a stone hearth, with a roaring fire sending waves of heat across the room. Dozens of heavy wooden tables, draped with midnight blue cloths were crowded with laughing, talking people and the restaurant served the best steaks in Montana.

"Do you think it'll work? Bluffing Dorian?"

"I think so." He shrugged and didn't look the least bit worried. "If it doesn't, Max will get a backup plan in place."

Something suddenly occurred to her and Emma said softly, "Speaking of plans, Gracie told me what she's going to build at the ranch."

"Did she? Well, good."

"She said she already had the money for the project," Emma added. "You loaned it to her, didn't you?"

His eyes flashed and his lips twisted into a frown. "Yeah, I did. It's a good idea and Gracie will be great at it. She's smart and steady and she works hard. So if you're thinking of giving me grief over it—"

"Thank you."

He stopped midsentence and stared at her. "You surprise me, Emma. I expected anger from you over this. You haven't been real happy with what close friends Gracie and I are. I wasn't expecting gratitude."

"Well," she said, "I am grateful. For this. For all the help you gave my dad while I was gone. For looking out for my family while I was gone."

"You don't have to thank me," he said tightly.

"I am anyway, so just deal with it."

He laughed shortly. "That's more like the Emma I know."

"Emma?"

She turned in her chair and grinned as Jess Whitehead hurried over to the table. The woman shot Caden a quick smile. "Hi, Caden, good to see you."

"You, too, Jess."

"I'm not going to interrupt—well, not for long anyway," she said with a laugh. "Did Gracie give you my message?"

"What? No," Emma said, curious now. "But with the storm and everything, she probably forgot." At least she hoped that was the reason Gracie hadn't said anything.

"Well, I'll make this quick. Gracie said you're back to stay?"

"I am." She looked at Caden and saw in his eyes that he still didn't believe her on that score.

"That's great. Since you're staying, I've got a job for you."

Curious, she asked, "What kind of job?"

"You know I'm the principal of Cache High, right?"

"I do now. Imagine that. The ditching queen is now the principal." Emma laughed, remembering all the times she and Jess had cut school to go to a movie or shopping, or pretty much for any reason at all.

"Hmm," Jess said, with a wry smile. "Ironic, huh? Anyway, I need a drama teacher and I've already spoken to the superintendent and he said that with your education and real-world experience, you qualify for a provisional teaching certificate…"

"Me? A teacher?" Emma thought the idea was crazy, and yet, something about it really appealed to her. What was the old saying? "Those who can't, teach."

"You'd be great, Emma. Tell you what, come to the school tomorrow, I'll introduce you around and you can think about it." She glanced over her shoulder and waved at her husband at a far table. "I've gotta go. Bill's waiting. I'll see you tomorrow?"

"Um, sure," Emma said hesitantly. "I guess so."

"Great. Good to see you, Caden!" Then she was gone.

He was watching her and she could see questions in his eyes. "What do you think?"

Caden picked up his beer, studied the label for a long minute, then said softly, "I think if you were really planning on staying, you'd have jumped at that job."

She flushed and felt the heat of it rising inside. Would he ever believe her? Trust her? He wanted her. Might even still love her, but he didn't trust her and she had no one to blame for that but herself. "I am staying, Caden."

His gaze fixed on hers. "Then take the job, Emma."

"There's other things to consider, you know," Emma argued, wondering if he would ever stop looking at her with suspicion, mistrust. "There's Molly to look after, and the ranch. Dad and Gracie."

"The ranch and your family survived you being gone for five years. I think they could make it through you having a day job." He set his beer down and leaned in toward her, keeping his voice low enough that no one would overhear him. His gaze held hers as he said flatly, "I think you didn't take it because you weren't sure you'd be here long enough to make it worthwhile. I think you've kept one foot out the door this whole time, Emma."

"You're wrong. I am staying, Caden." Frustrated now, she clamped her mouth shut when the waiter delivered their meals. But once he was gone again, Emma leaned toward Caden and lowered her voice. "After how we spent our morning, how can you not know what you mean to me?"

He leaned in, too. "That was sex, Em. Great sex, but that's all."

"Liar," she countered. "It was more than that and you know it."

He took another sip of his beer. His eyes were cool. Distant. And she wanted the fire back.

"How can I make you believe me?"

"You can't, Emma." He said it offhandedly, but his gaze never wavered. "You walked away once. Why shouldn't I expect you to do it again?"

Then he dismissed the conversation completely, sat back and sliced into his filet mignon. Hurt, frustrated and yes, angry again, Emma looked down at her strip steak and pushed it aside. Her throat was so tight now, she wouldn't have been able to swallow.

Caden suddenly felt further away from her than ever.

Ten

The next day, Emma was back in high school. It still smelled the same. Hormones, hair spray and desperation. What was amazing to her was how much *smaller* everything seemed.

"We've got a growing drama department," Jess was saying and ushered Emma back to the costume and props area behind the stage in the gym. "A big donor in Kalispell gave us a ton of money because his grandson went here and loved being in the plays."

Emma stood in the center of the room and did a slow turn, admiring everything. There were racks and racks of costumes, glass-fronted shelves holding wigs and hats and along one wall were stacks of props and plywood ready to be built into whatever backdrop was needed.

When Emma herself took drama at the high school, they'd had donated old clothes from local families and whatever furniture they could scrounge from local charity shops. Things change, she told herself.

"This is amazing…"

"I know, right?" Jess grinned, grabbed Emma's hand and tugged her along behind her. "The former drama teacher took a job in Miami, so we really need you, Emma. The kids are great and they're so excited to meet you."

She laughed a little. "Why?"

"You've been on TV," Jess said. "You're from Cache and you succeeded in Hollywood!"

Success, she knew, could look like different things to different people. And Emma had to admit that if she'd had a teacher who'd actually worked in television, she'd have been impressed, too. It wasn't until actually *going* to Hollywood herself that she'd found out the truth of the shiny, unreachable goal.

"Come on, I want you to meet a few of the kids."

Nerves rippled inside Emma. If she took this job, it might prove to Caden that she was staying. But should she have to prove herself? Couldn't he take her at her word? Was she going to have to pay penance for years for taking a chance on her dream? In spite of the help he'd offered yesterday, she couldn't help but remember how the day had ended. With mistrust. Suspicion.

But this wasn't only about what was between her and Caden, Emma told herself. Taking this job, she'd be walking a fine line between encouraging the kids to go for what they wanted while at the same time cautioning them about a hard reality. Would they want to hear it?

It had been a while since she'd had to relate to a teenager. But when she stepped out onto the stage where two girls and a boy were waiting for her, Emma immediately felt at home. This school, this very stage, had first awakened her dreams of stardom. Seeing the expression on the faces of these kids, she knew they were feeling the same thing she had so long ago.

"Ms. Williams!" One of the girls, a short brunette, hurried forward. "Mrs. Whitehead says you're the new drama teacher."

"Well—"

"I *loved* you in *Space Port*," the boy said. "The way they wrote you as stupid but you played her as more mysterious than that."

"Thanks," she said, glad someone had noticed that she'd tried to give her airhead character on that series a little more depth.

"And what was it like working with Jacob Hall?" the last girl asked, eyes shining with excitement.

Jacob Hall, the gorgeous star of their short-lived series, was as empty as he was pretty, but Emma doubted that they wanted to hear *that*.

"He's a very good actor," she said instead, and at least it was the truth.

"You know what?" Jess smiled at Emma. "I'll just leave you here to talk to the kids about drama class and about the play they want to put on next spring."

"Oklahoma!" One of the girls said. "I love the music and we were just talking about set decorations…"

Emma laughed a little as she looked from one animated face to the other. Their enthusiasm was contagious. She remembered when her class had done *Oklahoma!* and Emma had played Ado Annie and except for the fact that she wasn't much of a singer, had had a great time.

The boy said, "My dad said he'd help build whatever we need."

"And my dad said he could provide haystacks and stuff…"

Emma's head was spinning, but she hardly noticed when Jess left. Instead, she was drawn into the stardom dreams again. This time through these kids who had stars in their eyes and hope in their hearts. A part of her wanted to warn them to not give up everything in pursuit of something else. But she also realized that they wouldn't believe her—that was a lesson you had to learn yourself. As she had—chasing a dream had cost her Caden.

She also acknowledged that the chances that any of them would have the kind of career they wanted were tiny. But was that any reason to stop dreaming? To stop reaching for what you wanted?

And maybe, Emma told herself, if she could give them real-world tips and warnings and teach them what they needed to make a real try at it…none of them would be as crushed as she had been.

With the kids talking, planning, peppering her with questions about agents and producers and scripts, Emma smiled and took another step toward being a part of Cache again. And soon, Caden would have to admit that she was here to stay. Then he'd have to deal with what was between them. Because she wouldn't let him ignore it much longer.

"I took the job." Emma stood in the kitchen looking at her father and sister. Molly was sitting in her high chair while Gracie fed her spoonfuls of baby food.

"That's great news," her father said, and stood up to

give her one of his famous bear hugs. "And don't you worry about Molly. Gracie and I can watch her during the day while you're at school…"

"We can?" Gracie fed Molly another bite of applesauce.

Emma knew what her sister was thinking and she didn't want to risk the tentative moves they'd made toward fixing their relationship. So she said quickly, "You don't have to. I'll get a babysitter and—"

Her father shot that idea down. "We're not going to have strangers watching our girl, are we, Grace?"

"Oh no," Gracie blurted, standing up. "If Emma needs something, let's just rush to accommodate her! How high would you like me to jump, Emma? Any specific direction you'd like to see?"

"Gracie…" Their father sounded disappointed.

And Emma's heart sank. She and her sister had started coming together and now, it seemed they were back to square one again.

"No, Dad. Emma shows up and the whole world falls at her feet. She's even got her hooks back into Caden!" Shaking her head, Gracie held up both hands and said, "I've got to go check on the horses."

Emma could have let her leave, let the fury between them keep simmering, but she'd finally reached maximum tolerance. She'd tried patience. Tried to be understanding and apologetic and it had gotten her exactly nowhere. They were going to get everything out and settle this, whether Gracie liked it or not.

"Don't worry about your sister—"

Emma looked up at her father. "Would you watch Molly for me?"

"Sure, but—"

"Thanks, Dad." Emma raced out of the house and toward the stable. The air was cold, but Emma's anger kept her warm as she hurried across the yard. She found Gracie outside Herman's stall.

Gracie heard her run into the stable, but she didn't turn to look at her. "I don't want to talk to you," she said.

"Fabulous. Then just listen instead," Emma countered, then led with, "Why are you so bugged that Caden and I are together again? Have your eye on him?"

Gracie whirled around, more surprised than angry. "You're nuts."

"Is that right?"

"Yeah." Gracie slapped her hands onto her hips and faced Emma down. "Caden's my *friend*. He was there for me when you abandoned us. I was twenty when you took off, Emma. What the hell did I know about running this ranch?" She threw her hands up. "What did I know about *anything*? Now you're back and you pick up your life like you were never gone. You've got Caden and Molly and a job and I'm still running in place living a lie!"

Gracie clapped one hand over her mouth, horrified that she'd slipped and hoping that Emma would just let it go. Or maybe, she wouldn't care what she'd meant. Her heart pounding, she turned away from her sister and took a deep breath to ease the wild jitters in her belly.

"Gracie, tell me what's going on. What're you talking about?"

Shaking her head, she looked back at Emma and let out a long sigh. "Nothing. And I'm sorry I got mad. I wasn't even really mad at you, Emma." Looking at the older sister she'd always admired, Gracie could admit to herself at last, that it was because Emma had always gone after what she wanted that she'd looked up to her. Emma fought for what she wanted. While Gracie kept quiet and pretended everything was fine.

"Then why all the venom?" Emma asked. "If it's not my fault, why yell at me?"

"Because it's just not as satisfying to yell at myself," Gracie muttered thickly. "I'm mad at *me*, Em. God, I never thought of myself as a coward, but I so am."

"No, you're not." Emma grabbed her arm and squeezed. "Sweetie, you're one of the strongest women I know."

Gracie choked out a laugh and shook her head. "I wish that was true."

Frustrated, Emma threw both hands in the air. "For heaven's sake, Gracie, just *tell* me what's going on. Maybe I can help."

She couldn't help and Gracie knew it. But the need to talk to her big sister was huge. Ever since Emma had come home, Gracie had wanted to confide in her, but anger and resentment had clouded everything to the point where she felt as if she were wandering around the ranch blindfolded.

Looking at Emma now, seeing the confusion and sympathy in her eyes, helped Gracie decide to just take the plunge. To get everything out in the open. It would be a relief to say it out loud, even if nothing came of it. Even if Emma looked at her differently afterward.

"Okay," she said, steeling herself for whatever might happen next. "I'm not interested in Caden, because I'm already in love." She stuffed her hands into her coat pockets. "I haven't told anyone but Caden..."

There was a long pause, then Emma said, "I'm glad

you had him to talk to. But it's great news, Gracie. Why wouldn't you want everyone to know?"

The stable was cold and watery sunlight pouring through the open doors was the only light. They were alone but for the horses in their stalls, and the air was so quiet it seemed made for revelations of secrets. She looked at Emma. "Because I'm afraid how Dad will take it."

"He'd be happy for you," Emma said and Gracie so wished she could believe that.

"I don't know if he would be or not," Gracie admitted. "All I know is it's killing me and it's hurting Mad."

"Madison?" Emma whispered. "The vet?"

"Yes!" She blew out a breath and felt relief course through her like a cool rain on a hot day. God, it was freeing to admit the truth. To feel the freedom of saying that she was in love with a wonderful, talented, kind, funny woman. "I'm in love with Mad. Have been almost from the moment I met her."

Emma just watched her. Didn't say anything, and Gracie's fears rose up inside to grab hold of her throat and squeeze. She was laying everything out and if she lost her sister, she didn't know what she'd do.

A single tear tracked down her cheek before Gracie swiped it away angrily. Lifting her chin, squaring her shoulders, she said, "There. My big secret life. I'm a lesbian, and I didn't know how to tell you or Dad because I was terrified of how you guys would take it."

A couple of seconds ticked past before her sister spoke.

"You idiot." Emma's voice was quiet.

That she hadn't expected. "What?"

Her big sister stepped up to her and wrapped Gracie up in a tight hug. "I called you an idiot. How could you think I would care? Gracie, you're my baby sister. Whoever you love is okay by me. I'll love her, too. As long as she treats you right and doesn't make you cry, because then she'd be in big trouble with me—"

Fresh tears sprung to her eyes and these she didn't bother wiping away. They felt cleansing somehow. She couldn't believe this. Ever since Emma got home, Gracie had worried about what her sister would think. What she might say if she found out the truth. It was a shock to find out she hadn't had to worry at all.

Gracie's throat tightened as Emma stepped back and looked her dead in the eye. "As for Dad? He'd be furious if he knew that you were anxious about this. Dad's not going to care who you love, Gracie. For God's sake, it's the twenty-first century, sweetie."

Her big revelation had fallen flat.

Gracie felt both relieved and a little embarrassed that she'd made this into such a huge deal in her mind. "God, I do feel like an idiot."

"Good, you should." Emma squeezed her hard again, then let her go. "I love you, Gracie, and I want you happy. If Mad does that for you, then I'm really glad you found her."

More tears built up in her eyes, but this time, it was liberation. Happiness. The unbelievable sensation of finally being true to herself. She let out a breath that she felt as though she'd been holding since Madison first moved to town. Longer. It seemed as if all her life, Gracie had been hiding the truth of who she was.

"It's not fair to Madison you know," Emma was saying. "Keeping her a secret."

Guilt pinged inside Gracie as she nodded. All the

nights she'd sneaked over to Madison's house for a few stolen hours. The days they spent together, but unable to touch, or hold hands or even give each other a kiss goodbye for fear someone would notice. "I know that. I do. But I was just so scared to say anything—"

"No buts, Gracie," Emma told her. "Didn't Dad just say the other night that *love* is the only thing that really matters? That's all he'll care about. That you're loved."

Was it really that simple? Had she been putting herself and Mad through misery all this time for nothing?

"If you want me to, I'll be there when you tell Dad," Emma said softly.

Gracie looked at her and nodded. "I'd like that. Thanks, Em."

Emma grinned, hugged her again, then said, "Okay, now that you and I are good again, I'm going to tell Caden I've got a job. Maybe then he'll believe that I'm really staying."

"You still love him, don't you?"

"More than anything," Emma answered.

Gracie smiled. "Then *make* him believe."

Caden was saddling up for a ride when Emma strode into the stable, looking like a woman on a mission. She simply took his breath away. That long, curly hair flying out behind her. Tight black jeans, cream-colored sweater and a forest green jacket and scuffed brown boots. Heat pumped through him in a rush. She walked with confidence, always had. She was strong, hardheaded, and if he allowed it, she could bring him to his knees.

But he'd done that once. Given her everything, offered her all he was, all he'd hoped to be, and she'd left him broken. He wouldn't let that happen again no matter how much he loved her and wanted her.

She was smiling when she came to a stop just in front of him and God, what that smile did to her eyes. What it did to *him*. His whole body went tight with tension. His blood simmered in a slow boil and it felt like his skin was electrified. This wasn't going to be easy, he told himself, stepping back from the only woman he'd ever loved. But he refused to risk the kind of pain he'd already survived again.

"Gracie told me her secret."

He nodded, glad for that. Whatever happened—or didn't—between the two of them, Emma and Gracie were sisters and he was pleased they'd finally talked. "Happy to hear it. Worrying over it has been tearing at her for a long time."

"You've been a good friend to her," Emma said. "Thank you for that. Seems you're pretty important to both of the Williams girls."

He tightened the saddle cinch on his horse and forced a short laugh. "You know, I wouldn't have slept with Gracie even if she wasn't a lesbian."

"Is that right?"

He shot her a look and his heart thumped hard in his chest. "It is. Because you're the one I always wanted."

"I'm right here," she said softly.

And the scent of her was filling him. The urge to take her, hold her, was almost overwhelming, and still, he fought it.

"For how long, Emma?" That was at the bottom of all of this. The one thing he couldn't forget. She'd left once. Why wouldn't she again?

"For good, Caden." She moved in closer, laid one

hand on his arm and said, "I took the job at Cache High. I'm teaching drama."

That sounded like a good thing, but jobs could be walked out on if she found something better. He couldn't forget that she'd turned away from the plans they'd made together to find something for herself somewhere else.

"That's good, Em," he said, turning to face her, to meet her eyes. Everything about her called out to him, but he ignored it. "You'll be great at it. But you taking a job's not proof that you're staying. You walked out on your life—me—before."

She sighed and he could read the disappointment in her eyes. "That was different, Caden," she said. "I was a kid. I'd never been out of Montana and suddenly we were talking about getting married and having babies and—"

"And you ran," he finished for her, feeling the fresh sting of that betrayal all over again. She'd crushed him once. He wouldn't allow it to happen again.

"I had to go," she argued. "But I came back, too."

"Because California didn't work out. If it had, you'd still be there, wouldn't you?"

"No," she said, shaking her head. "California wasn't my place. I didn't belong, Caden. Everything about it felt wrong to me. I belong here. With you."

God, he wished he could believe her.

She must have read his features accurately because she asked, "How do I convince you?"

"Hell if I know," he said.

"I love you, Caden."

He closed his eyes briefly and savored those words. He'd never thought to hear her say it again and it was like having fresh air breathed into starving lungs. But he couldn't bring himself to trust it. Maybe it was something inside him that couldn't bend. If that were true, then he didn't know how to change it—or even if he should try.

"I love you, too, Em," he said and her eyes brightened before he qualified that statement with, "But I don't trust you."

She winced and he hated to see it. Hated to know that he'd caused it. But she had to know. Love wasn't always enough.

"I don't know how to fix that," she admitted. "How to convince you."

"I don't think you can. You already told me yourself that if you had to, you'd take Molly and run."

She spun around, took two steps away from him, then came right back. "*You* changed that. You have your lawyer working on it for me."

He nodded. Caden had had a lot of time to think since that trip into Kalispell. And he'd come to one solid conclusion. Loving, wanting, even needing wasn't enough. He had to know that he could believe in Emma. Trust that she'd be there, not going off looking for some other "dream" that looked better than real life.

"And if Max can't solve this? Then what?"

"I—don't know," she admitted. "I'll have to find another way to fight Dorian Baxter. And I will fight."

"And if you lose, you grab Molly and disappear?"

She didn't say anything and Caden knew she didn't have to. Shaking his head, he said quietly, "See? Emma, I admire you for your determination to save that baby. And I'll do whatever I can to help you. But I won't risk believing in you again only to watch you disappear."

"Caden—"

He kissed her deeply, savoring the moment, relishing the feel of her body leaning into his, then lifted his head, her taste swimming through his mind. "I'll help, Em. Any way I can. And I'll always love you. But I won't be with you."

She took a step back and looked so shocked and hurt that it tore at him. "Just like that? It's done?"

"Has to be," he said and it cost him. Caden wanted nothing more than to hold on to her, to skim his hands up and down her body, to slide into her heat and lose himself in her.

But it wouldn't change anything. Fix anything. He had to get used to living without her.

"Caden, are you really going to walk away from me?"

"I'm going to make a hell of a good attempt at it." He grabbed his hat off his head, shoved one hand through his hair and said, "Damn it, Emma, when I asked what you'd do if Max couldn't help, you should have said you'd come to me. That you'd trust *me* enough to help you stand against that bastard.

"But your first instinct is still to leave. To go somewhere else. On your own."

When she would have argued, Caden shook his head firmly. "You don't see it. The dreams we'd build together are bigger than anything we could do alone."

"I *am* trusting you, Caden," she argued and he could see in her eyes she believed that.

"Until you can't," he said tightly. "I'm not going to watch you leave again, Em, looking for something else. Something different. Or better. I need you to believe in *us*, not just yourself."

"I've been on my own for five years, Caden," she reminded him. "That's a hard habit to break."

"Maybe it is. But it was your choice, Em. You left. You stayed away even when you yourself said you should have come home sooner."

"Caden—"

Shaking his head, Caden looked at the woman he loved and tried to take a hard step back. "Home was your second choice, Em. If you had a shot at stardom again, you'd be gone again. Until you're really *here*, there's nothing for us."

Without another word, he shoved his foot in the stirrup, swung aboard his horse and rode out of the stable, leaving her alone in the shadows.

Eleven

A few hours later, Emma was back home, watching Gracie and Madison laughing together. Gracie's "secret" hadn't been as secret as she'd thought. When her little sister had finally taken the plunge and talked to their father, Frank had said only, "Hell, I know that."

After Gracie's surprise wore off, Frank had kissed his youngest daughter and sent her off to bring Madison home for dinner.

Now, Emma had to wonder how she could have missed how her sister and Madison looked at each other. She saw the same gleam of love in Gracie's eyes that shone for Caden in her own.

Now that their secret was out, they were holding hands, finishing each other's sentences and looking so damn happy, they were both beaming.

They talked about their plans for the new stable and

Gracie's business, and Madison had some great ideas. The two of them were going to make a terrific team. And, Emma felt like a ghost at a wedding. Happiness bubbled all around her, but she couldn't catch any of it for herself. She kept remembering Caden riding away, leaving her alone. And she was forced to realize that was how he must have felt when she'd turned away from him.

God, she hadn't known. Hadn't realized what she was sacrificing for the chance at a nebulous dream. Yes, if she hadn't tried, she might have regretted it all her life. But trying and failing had cost her both the dream and Caden.

Losing that dream was hard, but losing Caden was unbearable. Emma simply could not imagine a life without him in it.

"You know," Frank said idly, "Madison, there's no reason you can't move in here with us."

"What?" She looked from Frank to Gracie and back again. "Really?"

"Sure. No reason for you to be driving in and out of here at all hours. Winter's coming and the road to town is going to get bad. Besides, we've got plenty of room. And," he added, "you know there's something else, as well. Since Buck quit, his house has just been standing empty." Frank shrugged. "It's behind the barn there and you could make it into your office. See your clients in there and be right on-site to help Gracie out with this new business you're planning."

"That's a great idea, Dad," Emma said, and plucked Molly out of her high chair. Settling the baby on her hip, she looked at Gracie. "If you want, I'll give you two my bedroom, it's bigger."

"Seriously?" Gracie grinned at her sister.

"It sounds perfect," Madison said, looking at Gracie. "What do you think?"

"I think I love you and how soon can we pull this off?"

Madison laughed, jumped up and ran to the end of the table to hug Frank and kiss his cheek. "Thank you, Frank. This means so much."

Gracie was right behind her. "Thank you, Dad."

He patted both of them. "You girls are going to give me lots of fun and keep this old house from being too quiet. It's a win-win for me."

"And me," Gracie said, looking at Madison. Stepping right up to her, she cupped Madison's face in her palms and kissed her with all the love she'd been hiding for too long.

Seeing the two women share in the joy of loving each other only made Emma realize just how much Caden meant to her and just how much she'd lost.

Over the next few days, Emma concentrated on her new job. Though Caden was continually on her mind, she forced herself to focus on the kids. Teaching them reminded her of what she'd loved about acting. The purity of stepping into a new role, becoming someone else for a while and understanding what drove that character.

And when she did that, she found herself imagining Caden and what was driving him. She knew that man better than anyone else in her life. They'd been together for years and always, until she left, they'd shared a view of what their lives would be like. Then when he began to talk about getting married, Emma had done a 180 on him.

Even as much as she'd loved him, the thought of *forever* had scared the hell out of her. Especially when she'd never been outside Montana. Never tried to do anything with the dreams that danced at the edge of her mind. So she'd walked away from the man who meant everything.

And when she did that, she'd destroyed something beautiful. Those years in California, Emma had been lonely and the longing for Caden was a physical ache that she carried with her every day. But now it was so much worse. She was home. She'd been with him again, reminded herself of what she'd once had and now she'd lost him again.

But she wasn't going to quit. She wouldn't leave and give him the satisfaction of saying, *See? I knew she wouldn't stay.* No. She'd be right here. Day in. Day out. Until he believed again. Trusted again. And if someone tried to take Molly from her, then she would run, straight to Caden, and ask him to stand with her. To fight with her.

He'd called her hardheaded? Well, he had no idea just how stubborn she could be.

The email arrived first thing Saturday morning.

When Emma saw the name of the sender, her heart gave a hard jolt. Mouth suddenly dry, palms damp, she clicked on it, read the two short sentences and knew she was in trouble.

Arriving this afternoon at three o'clock to retrieve my daughter. Be there.
Dorian Baxter

"The bluff didn't work," she murmured and swallowed back a wave of nausea. She was scared, but not surprised. She'd known this would happen. Dorian Baxter wasn't the kind of man to give up easily. With his money and power behind him, he steamrollered people who tried to stand against him.

She glanced over at the baby, lying on a quilt in the great room, kicking both legs and waving her arms in a golden slice of sunlight as if she were a cheerleader. Molly was *her* daughter now and nothing was going to change that.

"Don't you worry, sweetie. I won't let him have you. Ever."

"What happened?" Gracie came into the room, a worried frown carved into her features.

"Molly's father's coming today to take her."

"Well, screw that," Gracie blurted and Emma smiled, thankful for the support.

"Screw what?" Madison came in behind her.

Madison had moved most of her things into the house a few days ago. They were still working things out and settling in, but it was amazing how happy Gracie was now that she was free to be in love.

"That Hollywood bastard is coming to take Molly," Gracie said, then turned to Emma. "I told her all about it."

"Well, he can't have her," Madison said, instantly going to the baby and scooping her up off the floor. Holding her close, she looked at Emma. "Right?"

"Absolutely right," she agreed. "But we need a plan."

"You're not going to run, are you?" Gracie asked quietly.

Emma looked at her sister. When would it stop? she

wondered. When would the people she loved stop expecting her to leave? She hadn't *run away* five years ago. She'd run *to* something. And a little more than a week ago, she'd done the same thing.

She'd run to Montana. To home. To family. To *Caden*.

"I'm not going anywhere," she said firmly, meeting Gracie's eyes to drive home the message.

"Of course she's not leaving," Madison said, gently swaying Molly from side to side. Looking at Emma, she asked, "What do we do?"

Emma smiled at her and felt a rush of affection for the newest member of the family. She was turning into a great sister. "Thanks, Mad. What we're going to do is fight back. I have to call Caden. Tell him what's happening."

More nerves. She hadn't spoken to him since that awful day in his stables. When he'd told her he couldn't trust her. When he told her that what they had was over because he couldn't risk a relationship with her again.

But he'd also said that he would help her fight for Molly. Now, she told herself as she hit speed dial, she'd find out if he'd meant it or not.

At three o'clock on the nose, Dorian Baxter walked into Emma's house. And it felt like storm clouds sailed in with him. Tall and handsome, he was dressed in a perfectly tailored three-piece suit, and looked just what he was—rich, powerful, sure of himself.

Caden wasn't there. He'd told her he would be, but he hadn't arrived yet. Emma was facing the man down, and her family was there to support her. Frank, Molly and Madison ranged themselves behind her in sort of a defensive line. Madison was holding Gracie and giving Dorian a look that should have set fire to his hair.

"Is that her?" he asked abruptly.

"You don't know?" Emma countered, feeling her fury begin to rise to match the panic clawing at her insides. Molly's black hair and blue eyes were so much like Dorian's it's a wonder he had to ask.

He gave her a dismissive glance. "Why would I know? If that's her, get her ready to go. I assume you have a car seat for her? I'll need that for the drive to the airport."

"You can't have her," Frank said.

One dark, expertly shaped eyebrow lifted. "And you are?"

"Frank Williams. This is my place and that baby's not going anywhere."

Dorian merely shifted his gaze back to Emma. "I don't have time for this. You will hand over my daughter or I will have the sheriff out here to arrest you for kidnapping."

"Then that's what you'll have to do," Emma said, and hoped she sounded braver than she felt at the moment. She didn't want to go to jail. She didn't have the money to fight Dorian in court. But there was simply not a chance in the world that she would give Molly to the man who had driven her mother to suicide.

The great room was big, comfortable and right now had sunlight filtering through the big window. Dorian looked as out of place in her home as she had in Hollywood.

Molly began to fuss as if she knew what was going on and Madison jiggled her to keep her quiet.

Dorian never took his eyes off Emma. "If you don't

hand her over, I'll tell the police you threatened me with untrue, salacious stories. Attempted extortion."

"You don't want to do that," Emma said. "If that got into the news—and it would—you'd have to spend all of your time defending your reputation."

"I can kill the story."

"Before it damages you?" Because she knew as well as he did that his name would still be splashed across websites and headlines across the country. Even if he could prove later that she had been bluffing, he would have been ruined.

He shot his cuffs, tugged at his lapels and said, "Very well. We'll try this another way."

Worry jittered through Emma and she wondered where the hell Caden was. Why wasn't he here, standing beside her? Had he completely written her off now?

"What is it?" she asked, not really interested in his plan, but she did need to stall, to give Caden more time to arrive.

"All right. The truth is," he acknowledged with a slight tip of his head, "there are rumors flying around Hollywood and I've received a tip from a reporter friend—"

Translation, Emma thought, *a reporter on his payroll...*

"There's going to be a story coming out soon that the baby's mother committed suicide and that someone is hiding the kid."

Emma's stomach tightened.

"So here's my final offer," Dorian said, ignoring everyone in the room but Emma. "I will put you in my next movie—a modern take on the classic Western—" He looked around and sniffed. "Seems you'd be uniquely qualified for the role. You would be the second lead. A jumping-off point for your career that most actresses would kill to be offered."

Emma took a breath and held it. "In exchange for?"

He smiled and gave the impression of a snake, opening its mouth to envelop its prey. "You sign a paper saying that I've been paying you to care for the kid and that I visited and blah, blah, blah…" He paused for effect. "You do that, and you're a star. Turn it down, and I'll destroy you."

The whole house got quiet as if everyone in the room had taken a collective breath in anticipation of how Emma would handle this.

But for Emma, she was suddenly calm. She was being offered everything she used to dream about—and she didn't care. Whatever happened next, she knew Dorian had nothing she wanted. She wasn't interested in Hollywood. Didn't trust Dorian. And she wouldn't let him anywhere near Molly.

"No thanks," she said.

He shook his head as if he hadn't heard her correctly. "I'm sorry?"

"I said no," she said firmly, so there'd be no mistake.

"I'll let you keep the kid," he tossed in as an added temptation.

"Why you—" Frank took a step toward him, but Emma held up one hand to keep her father back.

"You don't have anything I need or want," Emma said. "I have everything, right here. This place holds my dreams. My home. My family. My *daughter*. Caden."

"Caden?" Dorian repeated. "Who the hell is that?"

"I'm Caden," he announced as he walked into the room. Tall, gorgeous, wearing black jeans and boots with a dark green shirt and his heavy brown jacket.

He took off his hat as he marched across the floor and tossed it onto the nearest table.

Emma's heart leaped up into her throat and tears welled in her eyes. She shouldn't have doubted him. Caden would always keep his word. He would always be there for her. When he walked up to her side and faced Dorian with her, Emma had never been happier.

"Ah, the cowboy hero," Dorian mused. "There's nothing you can do here. I've come for the kid and since Emma here won't make a deal, we're done."

"Not quite," Caden said, and reached into his jacket for a sheaf of papers. In an aside to Emma, he said, "Sorry I'm late. I had to go see Max first."

"What's this about?" Dorian demanded.

"This is about the investigators my attorney hired," Caden told him. "Seems we found several women ready and willing to come forward and testify against you for assault and harassment. And guess what? One of those women was underage when you went after her. In California, that's statutory rape."

"You rotten no good—" Frank muttered it, but Gracie gave him an elbow nudge to quiet him.

"You're bluffing again," Dorian said, but he looked a bit less confident than he had a few minutes ago.

"Read it for yourself," Caden said and handed over the papers.

Emma looked up at him and Caden nodded, dropping one arm around her shoulder in support. She drew on his strength, curbed her curiosity and waited. For the first time since opening that email a few hours ago, she felt…hopeful.

Dorian scanned them, one after the other and Emma

watched him pale. Lifting his gaze to Caden, ignoring Emma completely, he said only, "What do you want?"

Caden dipped into his pocket again and drew out a single sheet of paper. "I want you to sign this."

Eyes narrowed suspiciously, he demanded, "What is it?"

"Simple." Caden's lake-blue eyes were winter cold as he stared at the man. "You sign away all interest in the baby, releasing her to be adopted by Emma...or I give these statements to the press and you can kiss your freedom and your lifestyle goodbye."

Clearly furious, Dorian folded up the statements and tucked them into his suit jacket. Then he snatched the single sheet of paper from Caden, took a pen from his pocket and leaned over a table, scrawling his name across the bottom. When he was finished, he threw the paper back at Caden. "There. Our business is done?"

"Yes," Emma said, forcing him to look at her. To recognize her. "We're finished. You can leave, Mr. Baxter."

"With pleasure." He turned and stormed out of the house, slamming the front door behind him.

"Well, now," Frank said with admiration as he grinned at Caden. "I have an urge to open some windows and let the stink out. But that was the smoothest thing I've seen in years."

Caden smiled back. "I get the feeling that man's not used to losing. But he'll have to adapt soon enough."

"What? Why?" Emma asked. "He signed, it's over. But, Caden, would you really have released those statements?"

"Hell yes," he assured her. "To keep that baby away from a predator? You bet. But as it turns out, I won't have to. Instead, Max is faxing those statements to the

LA police. I suspect they're going to have questions for Mr. Hollywood when he gets home."

Gracie laughed out loud, swept the baby out of Madison's arms and danced with her around the room. Mad kissed Caden's cheek and said, "Our hero."

"All right now, everybody into the kitchen. We'll feed our baby and have a beer to celebrate!" Frank led the way and Gracie, Molly and Madison were right behind him.

"Thank you," Emma said when they were alone. She could hardly believe it was over. Molly was safe. And Caden was here, with her. All she had to do now was find a way to convince him to stay with her.

"I told you I'd be here for you and Molly, Em."

She looked up at him and thought Madison was right—he was a hero. But he hadn't done it for her. He'd done it for Molly. To keep that baby safe and in a loving family.

"And I told you, I wouldn't run. Not from you." Emma took a breath and said, "I'll never leave you again, Caden. I wish I could make you believe—"

"I do believe you," he said.

Shaken, Emma staggered a little. "You do? Why? Since when?"

"Because I heard you, Emma. Yeah, going to see Max slowed me down, but when I got here, I was in the foyer when that oily bastard offered you everything you left me for five years ago. I waited to see what you would say to stardom. A big movie. The dream." He lifted one hand to stroke his fingertips along her cheek. "And you said no. You chose me. You chose *us*."

"I'll always choose you, Caden," Emma said and blinked furiously to keep her tears at bay. She wanted to see him and didn't want a blur distracting from the sight of him looking down at her with love in his eyes.

"This is my home. My place. My dreams are here now." She smiled at him and said, "I love that job at the school. I'm going to be helping Mad and Gracie. Molly's going to grow up here knowing she's loved. And I'm not going anywhere. Why would I when everything I've ever wanted is right here?"

His mouth curved and that smile lit up his eyes. "I really do believe you, Emma. I trust you. And I love you more than I thought it was possible to love anyone."

Her heart swelled until she was sure it would simply burst out of her chest. "Then I've got something else to say to you, Caden Hale."

"Yeah?" Still smiling. Still loving her.

Slowly, Emma went down on one knee in front of him and he tried to pull her to her feet.

"Come on, Emma, get up."

"No." She looked up at him and saw everything she'd ever wanted in her life, shining in his eyes. "I know this isn't the usual way, and maybe I'm swallowing a little pride here, but I can do that. For you. For us. Caden, I'm asking you to marry me."

His eyes flashed and his jaw went tight.

"It's only fair that I be the one to propose because it was me who made such a mess out of things to begin with." She blinked back tears and hurried on. "I'm not sorry I went to California. But not for the reasons you might think. It's because being there, away from you, made me realize just how much you mean to me. You're everything, Caden. There are no dreams without you."

"Damn it, Emma, stand up now…"

"Not until I finish." She took another breath and kept

her gaze fixed on his. "I want you to marry me. And love me. And adopt Molly with me and then make more babies with me. I want to live with you in that beautiful house and hunt for more gold with you, if you can find that vein again—"

He gave her wry smile. "Ha ha."

She grinned. "I want to help build that ranch of yours into the best in the state. Maybe in the country," she said and then added, "I love you, Caden, more than anything and now I want to know when you're going to say something!"

"Where's my ring?" he asked, smiling.

"Your ring?"

"Who proposes without a ring?"

Emma glared at him. "Are you kidding?"

"Yes." Grinning, Caden reached down and pulled her to her feet. "I was just waiting for you to run out of words." He took her face in his palms, looked into her eyes and said, "Yes, I'll marry you. I love you, Emma, now and forever. And if you ever need to run again, all you have to do is speak up and we'll run together."

Emma covered his hands with hers and felt as if she'd finally, completely, come home.

"I won't have to run, Caden. My world is right here. My dreams are here. With you." She went up on her toes and kissed him, then said, "Who knows, maybe one of my students at the school will go off and take the world by storm. But as for me, the only storm I'm interested in is the one that happens between us whenever we touch."

"Then get ready, honey," he whispered, leaning down to kiss her. "There's a hell of a storm headed our way."

* * * * *

COMING SOON!

We really hope you enjoyed reading this book. If you're looking for more romance, be sure to head to the shops when new books are available on

Thursday 11th July

To see which titles are coming soon, please visit

millsandboon.co.uk/nextmonth

LET'S TALK
Romance

For exclusive extracts, competitions
and special offers, find us online:

Get in touch on 01413 063232